Praise for David Handler and His Previous Novels

"One of my all-time favorite series! . . . David Handler is so good at writing one smart, funny page-turner after another that he makes it look easy."

—Harlan Coben

"Hoagy and Lulu tickle your funny bone and touch your heart."

—Carolyn Hart

"David Handler is the master of the sly, comedic mystery."

—Adriana Trigiani

"If not for David Handler, I wouldn't be a writer. He's one of my very favorites: a novelist whose champagne-fizzy mysteries—as winning as the madcap adventures of Carl Hiaasen, as hilarious as Janet Evanovich's Stephanie Plum series—tickle the brain, heart, and funny bone in equal measure. (Same goes for his ghostwriter-sleuth hero, Stewart Hoag: think Sherlock Holmes meets *Castle*.) Love stylish, deftly plotted whodunits? Read David Handler. Love warm, witty, snort-out-loud comedy? Read David Handler. Love basset hounds? You know what to do."

—A. J. Finn

"Kept me turning the pages. . . . The plot is influenced by a range of mystery masters, from Ross Macdonald to Agatha Christie. . . . *The Girl with Kaleidoscope Eyes* will help you remember the sun-crazed Hollywood excess of what now seems like an innocent time."

—*Seattle Times*

THE MAN
IN THE
WHITE LINEN
SUIT

THE MAN
IN THE
WHITE LINEN
SUIT

A STEWART HOAG MYSTERY

DAVID HANDLER

wm

WILLIAM MORROW
An Imprint of HarperCollins*Publishers*

P.S.™ is a trademark of HarperCollins Publishers.

HarperCollins books may be purchased for educational, business, or sales promotional use. For information, please email the Special Markets Department at SPsales@harpercollins.com.

FIRST EDITION

Designed by Diahann Sturge

Library of Congress Cataloging-in-Publication Data has been applied for.

ISBN 978-0-06-286330-0
ISBN 978-0-06-293001-9 (hardcover library edition)

19 20 21 22 23   LSC   10 9 8 7 6 5 4 3 2 1

*For Gretchen Salisbury Weir, and all the amazing
Fire Island sunsets we shared a million or two years ago*

Chapter One

I was standing in the lobby of the Algonquin Hotel looking around for my agent, Alberta Pryce, popularly known as the Silver Fox, and Sylvia James, popularly known as the single most reviled woman in all of publishing. We were supposed to be meeting there for a drink at five-thirty. You've heard of the Algonquin. It's famous for being the onetime home of the Round Table, where such razor-tongued wits as Robert Benchley, Dorothy Parker and Alexander Woollcott jousted and traded barbs for the sheer vicious delight of it. But that was back in the 1920s. It was 1993 now. No one makes a witty remark unless they're getting paid to, preferably on their own nationally syndicated TV talk show. And nine times out of ten, they're not even witty.

These days, the Algonquin was hardly a hipster's paradise. It was sedate, bordering on musty, and you'd seldom find anyone under the age of forty there. But the lobby remained popular with the publishing crowd. As I stood there looking around, I spotted Gloria Steinem, looking tanned and fabulous in a white sleeveless dress—and to hell with the Labor Day Fashion

Police—catching up with Clay Felker, the very first editor who was willing to give her meaty writing assignments way back in the early sixties when he was features editor at *Esquire*. After he started *New York* magazine in 1968, he gave her a home there.

I found the Silver Fox and Sylvia seated at a table over by the wall underneath a framed Thurber cartoon. Alberta was smoking a Newport and drinking straight bourbon. Sylvia was drinking what appeared to be a Shirley Temple. It definitely had a maraschino cherry in it. As Lulu and I made our way over to them, the Fox spotted me and rang the bell on their table. Gaylord scurried over at once to take my order. A Macallan for me and a small plate of pickled herring for Lulu, who has very strange eating habits for a basset hound—and the breath to prove it.

It was the first Tuesday after Labor Day weekend, which marked the official kickoff of the fall literary and theatrical season despite the fact that the calendar said summer wouldn't end for two more weeks. In fact, it had been 92 degrees that day in Central Park and at least 100 degrees in my crummy, sweltering fifth-floor walk-up on West 93rd Street, where I'd spent the day in my boxer shorts pounding away on my solid steel 1958 Olympia portable while the Ramones blasted from the stereo as a box fan blew hot, humid air across me and Lulu panted glumly at my feet. Right now I was dressed in the featherweight glen plaid worsted suit from Strickland & Sons, a lavender shirt, royal blue bow tie and spectator balmorals.

I'd been spared the worst of the summer heat by accepting my celebrated ex-wife Merilee Nash's generous invitation to live in the guest cottage on her eighteen-acre farm in Lyme, Connecticut, where I'd devoted body, mind and soul to working on my long-awaited second novel, *The Sweet Season of Madness*, an ode to the gritty, grimy crime- and punk-rock-infested New York of the seventies, when I'd arrived there to seek fame and fortune. *My* New York. It was the first good thing I'd written in the ten long years since I'd published my spectacularly successful first novel, *Our Family Enterprise*, lost my voice, lost Merilee and then proceeded to crash and burn. I could not have been more excited. I'd shown the first three chapters to Alberta, who'd told me she found them "thrilling."

Once Labor Day weekend arrived, I decided it was time to return to the city. Merilee had remained on the farm to putter in her garden and sort through several film offers, not to mention her feelings toward me. The summer had brought the two of us closer than we'd been in many, many years. Years that I'd spent scratching out a living ghosting celebrity memoirs. I'm not terrible at it. Have three No. 1 bestsellers to my non-credit. But, trust me, it's a humbling step down for a writer who *The New York Times Sunday Book Review* once proclaimed as "the first major new literary voice of the 1980s."

I'd been taken aback when Alberta phoned me that morning to say that Sylvia James, editor in chief of Guilford House, was desperate to meet with me.

"Why on earth would I want to meet with Sylvia James?"

"Trust me, dear boy. It will be worth your while."

The Silver Fox, who was called that because of her helmet of silver hair and because she was the savviest, toughest literary agent in New York, had no seasonal wardrobe issues. She was dressed in a standard-issue Harmon Wright Agency black Armani suit and white silk blouse. The oversize pair of round glasses that she wore made her look like a devious owl. She was a tiny woman, barely five feet tall, who had just turned seventy-three. Had run her own boutique agency for years. Represented such giants as Cheever and Styron. But she'd surrendered to the changing times a few years ago and sold out to Harmon Wright, the former Heshie Roth of Bed-Stuy, Brooklyn, whose behemoth multimedia agency had offices in New York, Los Angeles, London, Paris and Tokyo.

The dreaded Sylvia wore a plain white cotton blouse that was beginning to fray at the collar and a shapeless gray jacket and skirt that did nothing to help her lumpy figure. Her jacket had a number of greasy food stains on it, and she kept shifting around in her chair and tugging at her skirt. Her stockings had runs in them and her low heels were scuffed. Sylvia James was famous for being the messiest editorial executive in town. And it wasn't just her clothing. Her mouse-colored hair, which she seemed to comb in three different directions, flew this way and that—and wasn't helped in the least by her nervous habit of picking at her scalp with her fingernails. She always seemed to have pencil smudges on her hands and face, too. Sylvia was in her midforties. Had good cheekbones and a nicely sculpted nose. But her brown eyes were remote and cold and she had a nasty jagged inch-long scar just underneath her left one. She also had the unfortunate habit of curling her lip as if she'd just stepped in a puddle of fresh vomit.

Not once had I ever seen her smile.

The three of us murmured politely to one another as I sat. Lulu circled around three times under the table before she curled up at my feet to wait for her herring.

I did mention that Sylvia was the single most reviled woman in all of publishing, didn't I? Chiefly, this was due to the pride that she took in her viciousness. I can still remember the rejection letter she sent Alberta for my first novel: *I loathe this manuscript. Its author does not possess one original thought. Perhaps he should consider a different career. House painting might suit him.* If you've ever wondered whether authors remember rejection letters word for word twelve years later, the answer is hell yeah. But Sylvia wasn't merely vicious. She was also dishonest, unscrupulous and appallingly unprofessional. Didn't return her authors' phone calls. Failed to show up for lunch dates with them. Made them wait an hour or more outside of her office before she'd usher them in to eviscerate their works in progress. The woman was so devoid of common courtesy that during the course of her twenty-year publishing career she'd driven away four future Pulitzer Prize winners, two National Book Award winners, and a dozen other writers who'd gone on to become No. 1 bestselling authors for other publishing houses.

Any other editor in chief possessing Sylvia's spectacularly awful personality, track record and personal hygiene would have been fired long ago. Not Sylvia, who was the chosen editor of Addison James, the seventy-eight-year-old literary giant who'd been the single most successful author of mainstream American fiction for the past forty years. And who also happened to be her father. Addison James had been reliably cranking out spicy, well-researched No. 1 bestselling historical sagas for so long that the movie and TV miniseries adaptations of his 800-page epics spanned the generations from Clark Gable to Rock Hudson to Tom Selleck. He was acknowledged to be the wealthiest author in America, owner of a fifteen-room penthouse on Riverside Drive, a shorefront summer mansion on Lily Pond Lane in East Hampton and an array of sprawling vacation retreats in Aspen,

Jackson Hole, Montecito, Maui, Provence, Tuscany and somewhere in Switzerland. He also had a thirty-two-year-old blond trophy wife, Yvette, a would-be actress who'd been making ends meet by typing Addison's manuscripts for him until she managed to wriggle her way into the septuagenarian widower's bed a few years back.

You may pause here to shudder if you wish to. I just did.

As for Sylvia, she would remain editor in chief for as long as her father's bestsellers paid the salaries of everyone who worked at Guilford House—no matter how detested she was.

Gaylord arrived with my drink and Lulu's herring. I sipped my Macallan and waited Sylvia out. Somehow I felt certain that this so-called desperate meeting had something to do with her father. It was *Life* magazine that had famously dubbed Addison James "The Man in the White Linen Suit" way back in 1953. His first two novels, *Moscow* and *Berlin*, which drew on his experiences as a member of the OSS during World War II, had received critical praise but failed to find many readers. When his decidedly sexier third novel, *New Orleans*, went straight to the top of the bestseller list, *Life* decided to feature him in a cover story standing on Bourbon Street looking like a rakish adventurer in the white linen suit he was sporting along with his black eye patch and Malacca walking stick. He'd lost his left eye during the war when he was working with the French Resistance. Nearly lost his left leg as well. Was shipped home and ended up marrying the U.S. Army nurse who'd helped him through his lengthy rehab at a Veterans Administration hospital in North Carolina. They'd had one child together, Sylvia. After Sylvia graduated from Bryn Mawr, Addison persuaded his publisher, Guilford House, to take her on as an editor. *His* editor.

She rose rapidly through the ranks to become editor in chief despite antagonizing nearly everyone with whom she came in contact. She'd never married. In fact, no one in the publishing world could recall her ever having had an intimate companion, male or female. She was friendly with no one. Attended no book launch parties. Avoided the literary scene entirely. Avoided the city as well. Lived alone in a mansion in Willoughby, which was out past Scarsdale on Metro-North's commuter rail line.

Sylvia continued to shift around uncomfortably in her chair, tugging at her bra strap, sipping nervously at her Shirley Temple or whatever the hell it was. "Before we go any further, Stewart," she said finally, her eyes fastening on my bow tie. An inability to make eye contact was another of her non-virtues. "I have done business with Alberta for years and have come to know her as someone whom I can trust completely. But you I have never done business with. Therefore I must have your word that what is said at this table will never, ever be repeated to anyone. And if I find out you've gone back on your word, I'll break you."

"Too late, I'm already broken. I did that all by myself. Sylvia, I wouldn't be the top ghost in New York if I didn't know how to keep my mouth shut. But if you lack confidence in me, then feel free to confide in someone else. It makes no difference to me. I'm strictly here as a personal favor to Alberta. I'd rather be home working on my novel."

Sylvia made eye contact with me just long enough to glare at me disapprovingly before her eyes returned to my bow tie. "Fair enough." She lowered her voice discreetly. "I am about to tell you something that absolutely no one else in publishing knows. Addison's longtime research assistant, Tommy O'Brien, who I understand is a friend of yours, was the real author of Addison's last two bestsellers, *San Francisco* and *Havana*, not Addison."

I sat there thinking how odd it was that she referred to her father by his name, as if they weren't related. "And . . . ?"

She cleared her throat, choosing her next words carefully. "The unfortunate truth is that Addison isn't up to the job anymore. He's a senile old man. Forgetful, cranky, quite crude. He also doesn't see very well anymore out of his only eye. He needs a magnifying glass in order to read. I've managed to shield his deteriorating condition from the public. He no longer appears on *Good Morning America* or any other shows to promote his newest title. He no longer gives print interviews or does bookstore signings. And no one at Guilford House is aware that Tommy has taken over the writing of his novels. Tommy knows his style so well that the handoff has been virtually undetectable. He's just completed the manuscript for Addison's latest, *Tulsa.*"

"Just to be clear, my dear," Alberta interjected. "Are you absolutely sure no one knows that Tommy has been writing Addison's books?"

"No one," Sylvia replied with total certainty.

Which prompted Alberta to ring Gaylord for another bourbon for herself, a Macallan for me and a plate of pickled herring for Lulu. Sylvia was still nursing her Shirley Temple, or whatever the hell it was.

I should say a few words here about Tommy O'Brien, a proud native of Jackson Heights, Queens, who began his career as a beat reporter for the New York *Daily News*. Tommy's dream in life was to follow in the footsteps of his New York tabloid idols,

Jimmy Breslin and Pete Hamill, and become a star columnist and bestselling novelist who wrote gritty tales about the "real" New York of cops, firemen and cabdrivers. Tommy enrolled in a series of lectures on short-story writing that I gave at NYU way back when I was a young hotshot who'd sold a couple of my own stories to *The New Yorker.* We hit it off and became buddies. Drank together. Went to Knick games together. Talked writing endlessly. I thought that he had genuine promise. He just needed to find his voice. I didn't think that he'd find it when he quit the *Daily News* eight years ago to become Addison James's research assistant. But Tommy was convinced that working alongside a bestselling novelist would be a valuable learning experience. Addison also offered him twice what he was earning at the *Daily News,* which meant a lot to a man with a wife and two young daughters who was scraping by in a two-bedroom apartment in Stuyvesant Town.

"How much more money did you offer Tommy to take over writing Addison's books?"

Sylvia frowned at me. "I have no idea what you mean. Tommy's already a well-paid, salaried employee who's simply doing what's asked of him."

"Okay, allow me to rephrase that. What does he *think* you offered him?"

"Ah, now I see where you're going. Tommy does seem to be under the mistaken impression that I promised to give him coauthor credit as well as a percentage of the royalties."

"And however did he get that mistaken impression?"

She curled her lip at me. "I don't know what you mean, Stewart."

"It's possible that you aren't aware of this, but in the world of publishing what you just told me is popularly known as 'Sylvia being Sylvia.' You promised him coauthor credit and a percentage of the royalties, but you never intended to keep either promise. You committed nothing to paper. It was strictly a verbal commitment. And Tommy, a good guy who has no agent looking out for him, got himself royally hosed, didn't he?"

"I resent that," she snapped at me.

"Go ahead and resent it. I don't care."

The Fox sipped her bourbon. I sipped my Macallan. Lulu polished off her second plate of herring and fell asleep with her head on my foot, snoring softly.

Sylvia heaved an exasperated sigh. "As it happens, Tommy *has* become convinced that I've royally hosed him, as you so inelegantly put it. And has grown so increasingly bitter that the unspeakable has happened." She fell silent, scratching at her scalp. Stayed silent for so long that I was beginning to wonder if it truly was unspeakable. Finally, in a quavering voice, she said, "Tommy has absconded with the completed first draft of *Tulsa*."

The Silver Fox leaned forward eagerly. "Absconded with it how?"

"Last Friday, after he'd stopped by Addison's penthouse to review the final two chapters with him, Tommy took the entire 783-page manuscript to a copier shop on Broadway to have a Xerox made for me, since there was only one copy of the first draft. Tommy's an old-fashioned newspaperman. He works at home on a manual typewriter, not a computer. And Addison refuses to have a Xerox machine in his apartment. Don't ask me why."

"No need to," I said. "I don't want one either. Or a fax machine. I'd rather not have a phone machine either, but you pretty much have to these days."

"We're not here to talk about *your* peculiarities, Stewart," she said to me in a voice that was stern enough to rouse Lulu, who let out a low growl.

Sylvia arched an eyebrow at her. "Why is she doing that?"

"She doesn't like it when people are mean to me."

"Please continue," the Silver Fox urged Sylvia.

"Tommy told Addison he'd be right back with the copy of the manuscript. Except he didn't come right back. Didn't come back at all. Or messenger the manuscript to me. Or phone me. No one has seen him. No one has heard from him. I've called him dozens of times to no avail. I've even called the copier shop, where they know Tommy well. They confirmed that he had indeed been in there Friday evening, made a copy of a 783-page manuscript, paid them and left. Nothing unusual occurred while he was there. And yet Tommy O'Brien, and *Tulsa*, have disappeared."

"I see . . ." I said, tugging at my ear.

"Any thoughts or impressions, Stewart?" Sylvia asked.

"Have you tried contacting his wife, Kathleen?"

"Tommy left her two weeks ago. Moved out and rented himself a furnished studio apartment in Hell's Kitchen." She peered at me suspiciously. "You didn't know that?"

"I've been away for the summer. Just got back into town. I haven't spoken to Tommy in months."

"He hasn't phoned you since he disappeared on Friday night?"

"No, he hasn't."

"Are you telling me the truth?"

"Of course I am."

"Then why don't I believe you?" she demanded accusingly.

"If you don't believe me, then I'm going to leave this table and walk out the door. Is that what you want, Sylvia?"

"What I believe," she went on, totally ignoring what I'd just said, "is that he intends to hold the manuscript hostage until I agree to give him, in writing, the coauthorship and royalty participation that he claims I promised him three books ago. Which has to be the sneakiest, most low-down tactic I've witnessed in my entire career."

"Very sneaky and low-down," I agreed. "Almost as sneaky and low-down as promising him coauthorship and royalty participation that you never had any intention of giving him. Did you call the police?"

"And tell them what? I don't even know what's happened."

"Which is why you're here, dear boy," Alberta put in helpfully. "You and Tommy are chums, after all."

"And you do seem to specialize in these sorts of . . . awkward situations," Sylvia conceded. "I'd like to enlist your services as a kind of go-between. You know Tommy's haunts. Find him. Convince him to come to his senses and deliver the *Tulsa* manuscript. If he refuses, then I *will* be forced to call the police and report it stolen."

"You'd actually have him arrested?"

"Without hesitation. *Tulsa* is our big moneymaker for next summer. We must have it. Well, what do you say?"

I looked down at Lulu. Lulu was looking up at me—with keen-eyed disapproval. "Sorry, I can't help you. I'm working on a novel of my own."

Sylvia nodded. "Yes, I know. Alberta told me she's read the first three chapters and that they're fascinating."

"I believe the word I used was *thrilling*," Alberta said dryly, lighting a Newport.

"Guilford House will make you a very lucrative offer for it if you're able to defuse this situation. As a good-faith gesture, I'm prepared to cut you a check for $25,000 against the generous advance we'd be expecting to give you."

"Good-faith gestures go for $75,000 this season," the Silver Fox countered.

"Let's not quibble, Alberta. This is much too important. We'll make it $50,000."

"We'll make it $75,000," Alberta insisted as I sipped my Macallan, calmly waiting for Sylvia to cave. The woman had zero leverage. None. But she had to behave as if she did. That was how the game was played.

Sylvia let out a weary sigh. "Very well. What do you say, Stewart?"

"I'll want to talk to your father."

"He knows nothing. I can assure you it's not necessary."

"It's necessary if I say it is. I won't do this unless I have a free hand."

Sylvia hesitated. "Fine. But I want to be present when you speak to him."

"As you wish. Where does your stepmother, Yvette, fit into all of this?"

"You mean Princess Lemon Jell-O?" Sylvia curled her lip again. "You should see the way she jiggles and wiggles in those tight little dresses of hers. Doesn't know the meaning of the word *bra*. She's so obvious that only teenaged boys and dirty old men could possibly find her the least bit enticing. You can guess which group Addison falls into. And if you wish to remain on cordial terms with me you will never, ever refer to that bimbo as my stepmother again. She doesn't fit into this, in answer to your question. Or I don't see how she could. Between shoe shopping, facials, manicures, pedicures and getting her hair done, the poor dear hasn't a minute to spare."

"Is she out at their place in the Hamptons or here in the city?"

"She's here. Why?"

"Just trying to get the lay of the land, as it were. I take it you're not particularly fond of her."

"She's a greedy bitch who played Addison for a fool. She's also a tramp."

"Meaning she has a man friend on the side?"

Sylvia let out a harsh laugh. "As in one specific one?"

"I believe that's what I asked."

"Yes, a Long Island attorney named Mel Klein. There's a money angle to it. With her there always is. She's persuaded Klein to try to renegotiate the prenuptial agreement she signed when she married Addison."

"Can he do that?"

"Not a chance. I will never let that happen. Nor will Addison's attorney, Mark Kaplan." She studied me—or I should say my bow tie—sternly from across the table. "Well, what's your answer, Stewart? Will you help us?"

Before I could reply, Gaylord arrived with a rotary phone, plugged it in to the floor jack under our table and handed it to me. "For you, Mr. Hoag," he said as he whisked Lulu's empty plate away.

"Stewart Hoag speaking," I said into the phone.

"Liver and onions?" Merilee said from the other end of the line.

"Only if it comes with multiple rashers of thick-cut bacon," I said as Lulu sat right up and whimpered. She can always tell when I'm talking to her mommy.

"Blue Mill Tavern, seven o'clock?" her mommy said.

"I'll see you then. Shall I take this to mean that you're back in town?"

"Can't put anything over on Mrs. Hoag's boy Stewie, can I? I've been calling your apartment every half hour, darling. Don't you ever check your messages? I had to find you through Alberta's office."

"What brings you back here, Merilee?"

"Something wonderful. I'll tell you about it at dinner."

"It's a date," I said, hanging up the phone.

Sylvia glanced at her watch impatiently. "I'd really like to catch the 6:57. What's your answer, Stewart? Will you do it?"

"I'm in the middle of something very exciting, but I can take a few days off and ask around." After all, Tommy was a good guy and was clearly in deep trouble. So was my bank account, which could use that $75,000 cash infusion. And it certainly wouldn't hurt to have Guilford House make an offer on my novel. Alberta would then be able to show it to a select group of editors at other houses and start a bidding war. "But let's be clear about something, Sylvia. I'm not doing it for you. I'm doing it for Tommy. I hate to see him get buried because of the way you lied to him. This sort of thing never used to happen in publishing. It was an honorable business. Am I right, Alberta?"

"I hate to disillusion you, dear boy, but I've been in publishing since 1948 and it has never been the gentlemanly profession that people made it out to be—particularly the Hollywood crowd, who were totally taken in by anyone who had an Ivy League degree and didn't spit when he talked. I've known quite a few publishers in my time who were outright thieves. And believe me, some of the finest fiction ever produced was a J. P. Lippincott royalty statement."

"When can I see your father, Sylvia?"

"I still say it's not necessary."

"And I still say it is."

"Very well. I'll meet you at his penthouse tomorrow at noon. The address is 110 Riverside Drive." Sylvia reached for a tote bag at her feet that bulged with manuscripts and stood up. "And *please* be discreet about this."

"Not to worry. Discretion is my middle name."

Actually, I lied. It's Stafford. But there was no need for her to know that.

LULU AND I caught a cab from the Algonquin to the Blue Mill, which happened to be where Merilee Gilbert Nash and I first met, for those of you who've ever wondered. A college chum and I were heading toward our booth when we happened to stroll by the one where Merilee was having dinner with a playwright whom I knew. Introductions were made, pleasantries exchanged, and as I got lost in those green eyes of hers, I realized she was staring right back at me. Within a week we were an item in Liz Smith's column.

God, that was a lifetime ago.

The Blue Mill was down in the Village, where it occupied

a quirky little crook in Commerce Street near Barrow, a few doors down from the Cherry Lane, which has the distinction of being the city's oldest continuously running Off-Broadway theater. Sam Shepard's *True West* had its New York premiere at the Cherry Lane in 1982 with John Malkovich and Gary Sinise. Right now a one-man drag show called *Lypsinka!* was playing there.

The Blue Mill opened in the early 1940s, and whenever I walked in the door its vintage decor gave me an inkling of what it must have felt like to live in New York City back in those days. The menus were hand-scrawled on individual chalkboards parked beside each wooden booth. The waiters were career professionals, not struggling actors. Most of them had worked there for at least twenty years. They knew their regular customers by name. Always, they fussed over Lulu and made sure she got a nice fresh piece of Dover sole.

Merilee was already seated there, sipping a martini. She drank martinis whenever we went to the Blue Mill. Never drank them anywhere else. I kissed her on the cheek, sat down across from her and ordered one myself. I never drank them anywhere else either. It was a tradition.

Lulu was so excited to see her mommy she whooped and whimpered and crawled up into her lap.

"Yes, sweetness," Merilee cooed at her. "Yes, I've missed you, too."

Merilee looked bright-eyed and excited. Her waist-length blond hair was tied back in a ponytail. She was wearing a faded Western-style denim work shirt with snaps instead of buttons, khaki slacks and Arche sandals. No makeup. She never needed any. Merilee was still strikingly beautiful at forty, and my heart never failed to race a bit whenever I caught sight of her. Not that she'd ever been conventionally pretty. Her jaw was too strong, her nose too long, her forehead too high. Plus she was broad shouldered and nearly six feet tall in her bare feet. But the camera loved the planes of her face and those green eyes. And whenever she walked out onto a stage, she owned it.

Lulu gave Merilee's face a good, thorough licking before she finally settled next to her with her head in her lap and made contented argle-bargle noises.

Stavros brought me my martini. I clinked Merilee's glass with mine and took a careful sip. Martinis transform me into a blithering, flannel-tongued idiot.

"So what were you and Alberta doing at the Algonquin?" Merilee asked, tilting her head at me curiously.

"Can't tell you."

Her eyes widened with girlish delight. "It's a *secret*?"

"That's correct."

"Whose memoir is it? God, it must be huge. Let me guess. Is it Ol' Blue Eyes?"

"We were not discussing Frank Sinatra."

She furrowed her brow. "I can't imagine anyone else's memoir being so top secret unless . . . it's not Jackie O, is it?"

"It's not a memoir at all. I've been asked to help a certain publisher find a certain something that's gone missing."

"What's gone missing? Is it animal, vegetable or mineral?"

"It's a manuscript," I replied, wondering if she was already on her second martini. "If I'm successful, Alberta will be able to get an auction going on my novel when I finish it. And if I'm not, I'll still get $75,000, which will allow me to keep working on it without wondering how I'm going to pay my rent and keep Lulu in 9Lives canned mackerel."

"Darling, I have plenty of money. If you want to stay focused on your novel, just let me write you a check."

"Merilee, I'm not taking money from you. I carry my own weight."

"Oh, pooh. You are so quaint and old-fashioned. Mind you, that *is* one of the things I find most attractive about you. That and your tush."

Possibly her third martini.

"I promise I'll tell you all about it when it's over," I said. "But enough about me. What's this wonderful news of yours?"

She waited to tell me while Stavros arrived with Lulu's Dover sole and our plates of the best calves' liver, onions and bacon in New York City, along with our family-style side dishes of green beans and mashed potatoes. You must, must have mashed potatoes when you order calves' liver, onions and bacon at the Blue Mill to sop up any morsels of sautéed onions that are left on your plate. I ordered a bottle of Côtes du Rhône as Merilee spooned green beans and mashed potatoes onto our plates and Lulu vanished under the table to enjoy her sole.

"My wonderful news," Merilee informed me, cutting into her liver, "is that I'm leaving on an early morning flight tomorrow to spend the next five weeks in Budapest. Our financing for *The Sun Also Rises* has finally come through." Last winter she'd been cast in the prized role of Brett and had flown over there to launch production, only to have the financing fall apart. "And this time it's rock solid. Paramount has gotten involved."

Stavros returned with our wine, showed me the label, uncorked it and poured a taste in my glass. I sampled it and pronounced it excellent. He filled our glasses and retreated.

"That's terrific, Merilee. Truly. Is Nick Nolte still in as Jake Barnes?"

Her face fell ever so slightly. "Nick has a conflict now. He's out."

"Who's in?"

"Mel Gibson."

"Oh, him."

"He's a very gifted actor and I'm looking forward to working with him."

"Does this give you an inside shot at a featured role in *Lethal Weapon 4*?"

She didn't dignify that with a response. Just ate with great appetite before she paused to sip her wine, letting out a sigh of regret. "I'm going to miss the farm. It's so lovely there in the fall. The apples and pears are ripening. The leaves on the maple trees are turning gorgeous colors. The air is so crisp and clean. I just love to curl up in front of a big fire in the fireplace with a good book. You should feel free to go out there and write any time you want. You can take long walks in the woods with your hands buried in the pockets of your Norfolk jacket and Lulu trotting along beside you, thinking deep thoughts."

"Just to be clear, is it Lulu who'll be thinking these deep thoughts or me?"

"I'm serious, darling. Mr. MacGowan will be keeping an eye on the place. I'll let him know you may come out and stay for a while."

"Thank you, Merilee. That's very kind of you."

"Which brings me to what I actually wanted to talk to you about. Should we order another bottle of wine?"

"That's what you wanted to talk to me about?"

"No, that was an awkward non sequitur."

"You say that as if there's such a thing as a seamless non sequitur."

"Are you being a writerly pickle puss, mister?"

"Little bit."

I caught Stavros's eye and raised the bottle into the air. He nodded and returned with a fresh one and clean glasses. We replayed the entire ritual of his showing me the label and uncorking it and pouring me a taste, my sampling it and pronouncing it excellent. Then he filled the fresh glasses and retreated.

"What I wanted to say is that it's still summer and it's going to be miserably hot and sticky for at least two or three more weeks, maybe even four."

"All very true," I said as I ate. Lulu was already done and had climbed back up next to Merilee with her head in her lap.

"It must be horribly hot in that starving writer's garret of yours."

"It's a tad subequatorial, but I'm taking my salt tablets."

"Why don't you two stay in my place while I'm away?" Meaning her prewar eight-room apartment on the sixteenth floor of a luxury doorman building on Central Park West that enjoyed magnificent park views from nearly every window, most of which were equipped with whisper-quiet air conditioning units. Meaning the apartment I'd once called home. "You'll be much more comfortable there. I've just refurnished the office, as it happens. I think you'll find it to your liking. And Lulu suffers terribly in the heat. She's covered in hair, you know."

"So I've noticed."

"Use the Jag, too, if you want." Meaning the red 1958 XK150 that we'd bought when we were married. She got it in the divorce settlement, same as she got the apartment. "It'll just be sitting in the garage on Columbus gathering dust."

"Things don't gather dust in New York, Merilee. They gather soot." I cleaned my plate and took a sip of my wine, gazing at her over the rim of my glass. "Tell me, what's brought all of this on? You've gone away numerous times for months at a stretch and never offered me the use of your apartment."

"You make a good point," she conceded, turning serious on me. As in hugely serious. Actresses don't possess small emotions. "Okay, here it is. I feel as if our relationship changed this summer. You writing every day in the guest cottage and puttering in the garden. Me directing my play. The two of us eating dinner together out on the porch looking out at Whalebone Cove and talking about everything and nothing. It felt like it used to back when we were . . . God, please say something before I stab myself in the eye with this steak knife."

"Merilee, you know how I feel."

"No, mister. I don't know how you feel."

"We belong together. We always have. We always will. I put you through hell, I know that. I've spent the last ten years trying to make up for it. We can't ever go back to our sunshine days. I'm not the same person. Neither are you. We've been battered, bruised and humbled. And we're not kids anymore. But for me there's you and there's only you."

She reached across the table and gripped my hand. "Thank you for that, darling. I did try, you know. Seeing other men.

But I still haven't met anyone who's half as fascinating or good-looking as you are."

"Why, Merilee Gilbert Nash, are you flirting with me?"

"Trying to. I've never been good at it. I want you to feel as if the apartment is yours. It *was* yours, after all, before everything turned to poo. What do you say?"

"On behalf of Lulu, who is rather fond of her creature comforts, I accept your generous invitation."

"Good. Then it's settled."

After I'd paid the check we strolled arm in arm over to Hudson, Lulu ambling happily along ahead of us, and caught a cab. As we sped our way uptown, Hudson became Eighth Avenue, and when it hit 42nd Street, blazed its way through the middle of the Great White Way. The fall season's new shows would be opening soon, but most of the Broadway theaters were still showcasing the same splashy, stupid tourist musicals that they'd been showcasing for the past several seasons. *Phantom of the Opera* anchored the Majestic, *Miss Saigon* the Broadway. And the stupidest of them all, *Cats*, was still selling out at the Winter Garden same as it had been since Merilee and I attended the gala opening-night performance way back in 1982. I had found it so boring that I fell asleep ten minutes into Act 1. Merilee had to elbow me awake. I managed to rally during intermission only to sleep my way through most of Act 2. As the curtain mercifully came down, I can still recall betting her a shiny quarter that *Cats* would be posting its closing notice by the time we walked in the door of our apartment. And yet here it was, still packing 'em in eleven years later.

It's a good thing I never became a drama critic.

"Tell me, Merilee," I said as we rode along. "After you've done your location shooting in Budapest, will you film the interiors in London or L.A. or—?"

She kissed me. It had always been that way with her. She would just suddenly kiss me right in the middle of a sentence. It was a tender kiss at first, but turned into something quite a bit more than that by the time our cab pulled up in front of her building on Central Park West and West 82nd Street.

"I've installed a new washer-dryer combo in the kitchen," she said softly, her eyes glittering at me.

"Is this some arcane form of Miss Porter's School dirty talk?"

"No, silly man, it's for real. I ought to show you how to use it. The washer's a special low-flow model made in Sweden and the controls are hard to understand. It took me weeks to figure them out."

"You're inviting me up, in other words."

Lulu let out a low moan of protest.

"Both of us up."

"You don't mind, do you?"

"No, we don't mind."

The night doorman, Frank, who'd always hated me, gave me the evil eye after he greeted Merilee with a great big smile. I'd never understood what his problem was. Patrick, the day doorman, loved me. Lulu scampered across the lobby, pawed at the elevator and whooped excitedly. The elevator doors opened and up we went to the sixteenth floor to inspect Merilee's new Swedish washer-dryer.

She'd furnished the place in mission oak after she'd given me the boot, but not just any mission oak—signed Gustav Stickley Craftsman originals, each piece spare, elegant and flawlessly proportioned. There was an umbrella stand and a tall-case clock in the marble-floored entry hall. Also a pair of Il Bisonte suitcases and a matching carry-on bag, all packed and ready for her early morning flight.

I started for the kitchen to examine her new laundry appliances.

"Darling, where are you going?"

"The kitchen."

"Whatever for?"

"You wanted me to look at your new washer-dryer, remember?"

She tore open all of the snaps on her denim shirt with a flourish, whipped it off and tossed it aside. She wore nothing underneath it. "Please don't take this the wrong way, but for an incredibly smart man, you can be awfully stupid sometimes."

And that was how we ended up in bed together having crazy monkey sex for the first time in so long that I'd forgotten how many years it was.

I'd also forgotten how much I enjoyed being a crazy monkey.

WHEN I AWOKE, it was a few minutes after six o'clock in the morning and she was gone. It had been the sound of the front door closing behind her that awakened me.

That and Lulu whimpering mournfully from the entry hall.

She'd left a scrawled note on her indented pillow next to mine: *Mad about the Boy*, which was Norma Desmond's inscription in the gold cigarette case that she gave Joe Gillis in *Sunset Boulevard*. There was no gold cigarette case for me. Just the note and the hollow feeling that I always got when I knew she was going to be out of the country for a long time.

I felt a tremendous need for orange juice and coffee. Padded toward the kitchen in my boxer shorts, pausing to gaze out the living room windows at Central Park sixteen floors below, and discovered that a tropical summer rain was falling in torrents. As I stood there gazing down at the street in air-conditioned, dehumidifed comfort, I recalled how easy it is to get used to the sweet life.

I went into the black-and-white-tiled kitchen—which genuinely did feature a brand-new bright red Swedish washer-dryer—and filled Merilee's schmancy espresso machine. Poured myself some orange juice and drank it down, examining the contents of the refrigerator. I wouldn't starve. She'd brought two dozen fresh eggs home from the farm, vine-ripened to-matoes galore and plastic bags filled with three different kinds of lettuce, fresh basil and Italian parsley. She'd also picked up a ball of fresh mozzarella and a loaf of crusty bread at the Italian market on Columbus. As Lulu began following me closely now, her nails clacking on the tile floor, I poked around in the walk-in pantry closet for the reserves of 9Lives mackerel for cats and very weird dogs that Merilee kept there in case she was called upon for babysitting duties. I found three cans. Opened one, dumped it into a cereal bowl and put it down for her next to the water bowl I'd put down last night. Lulu, that noted Nose Bowl champ, went right to work.

When the espresso was ready, I poured myself a cup and took a grateful gulp, then wandered down the hall to check out what she'd done to the office. She hadn't gone to very much trouble. Merely parked a breathtaking Stickley library table and leather-backed swivel desk chair in front of the windows overlooking Central Park, installed floor-to-ceiling book-cases, a leather Morris armchair and a stereo outfitted with a

Dual turntable for the vintage vinyl Ramones albums that I'd been listening to all summer long at the farm while I wrote. An amazing depiction of the rugged Maine coastline by my favorite painter, Edward Hopper, was hanging in a frame on the wall over the armchair. Not a print—the actual oil painting. I couldn't even imagine how much it had set her back. But that was Merilee. When she was in, she was all in, I reflected, running a hand over my face. I needed a shower and a shave, but I didn't have my razor or a change of clothes. I decided to dash home in the rumpled clothes I'd been wearing last night, pack a few essentials, and come right back. I would make a more thorough wardrobe run in a day or two.

I'd flung my lavender shirt and featherweight glen plaid suit onto the bedroom floor last night when I'd followed Merilee in there. Likewise my shoes and socks. My bow tie was nowhere to be found. No matter. After I got dressed, I grabbed an oversize Channel 13 umbrella from the Stickley umbrella stand and locked the front door. Lulu and I rode the elevator down to the lobby. Patrick was delighted to see me and implored me to stay good and dry under the awning while he whistled me a cab.

Like I said, it's really easy to get used to the sweet life.

It's also really not a good thing for Lulu to get wet, because nothing smells quite as nasty as a soaked basset hound's oily coat. If Lulu gets caught in the rain you do not, repeat not, want her on any of your furniture. For damned sure, not anywhere near your bed.

The cab delivered us directly to the front door of my crummy fifth-floor walk-up on West 93rd. We darted inside and climbed the five flights to my door, feeling it get warmer and stickier as we reached each landing. It was a steamy 90 degrees in my nonspacious living room as the rain pelted hard against the big glass skylight over the kitchen. I turned on the box fans in the bedroom and living room, stripped off my suit and put on a pair of gym shorts and a T-shirt. Made sure Lulu was good and dry by rubbing her from head to tail with her designated wet dog towel, which I kept stored inside of a sealed plastic bag in the narrow entry closet. She was of the opinion that this indignity qualified her for a second breakfast. I'm not that big a softy, though she did get an anchovy fresh out of the fridge. Anchovies are her favorite treat. She likes them cold because the oil clings better.

Then I got busy. Packed Lulu's travel bag, an old black leather doctor's bag in which I stowed her cans of 9Lives and her bowls. I fastened my solid steel 1958 Olympia manual portable tightly shut inside its carrying case. Grabbed my battered Ghurka bag from the top shelf of my bedroom closet and fetched the one and only copy of the manuscript of my novel from the vegetable bin of my refrigerator. I always store it there. You would, too, if you ever got an up close and personal view of the ancient wiring and furnace in my building. I tucked my Ramones albums in the Ghurka bag along with the manuscript and a collection of Irwin Shaw short stories that I reread every few years just to remind myself what good writing is. Added a small supply of socks, underwear, neckties and pressed shirts. Also the water-resistant Gore-Tex street bluchers that I'd had custom made for me by a stooped little Greek man who'd been making shoes on West 32nd Street since the early 1950s. Those I tucked in their chamois travel bags. My navy blue blazer and two pairs of cream-colored pleated gabardine slacks went in a plastic weekend garment bag.

I was just about to fill my shaving kit when I suddenly heard the sound that no one who lives on the top floor of a New York City brownstone *ever* wants to hear: footsteps on the roof over my head.

I tensed immediately. Lulu let out a low growl.

"HOAGY . . . ?" A voice called to me through the skylight. "IT'S ME, TOMMY! LET ME IN, WILL YA?"

I opened my door, climbed the stairs to the steel door to the roof, unlatched it and let him in as the rain continued to pelt down. I slammed it shut behind us, latching it, and took a look at him. He was ashen-faced, exhausted and soaked to the skin. "Jesus, Tommy, what are you doing on my roof?"

"Hiding out, whattaya think?" he answered in that Jackson Heights accent of his. "I been up there all night waiting for you to come home. Nobody in your building would buzz me in but a kid delivering a pizza a few buildings down let me in there so I made it from their roof to yours."

Tommy was in his late forties, short and stocky, with pale blue eyes, thinning sandy hair and graying stubble. His nose was red and rough. A drinker's nose. He wore a drenched polyester double-knit suit in a murky brown color that I couldn't imagine looked good wet or dry, a blue button-down shirt and a pair of heavy, steel-toed work shoes. He was a tabloid reporter through and through. None of them dressed well. It was a point of working-class pride. A way of setting themselves apart from the high-toned *New York Times* crowd.

I ushered him in, gave him a bath towel, another pair of my

gym shorts and a T-shirt. When he came padding barefoot out of the bathroom a few minutes later, he was still toweling his hair dry. The shorts fit him okay. The T-shirt was so big on him he looked like a little kid wearing his big brother's clothes.

"Hiding out from whom, Tommy?"

He slumped onto my loveseat with a weary sigh as Lulu nosed at him, sniffing and snuffling. He was so wiped out he didn't even notice her there. "I'm in a real jam, man. The worst kind."

"So I've heard."

His pale blue eyes studied me warily. "What have you heard?"

I told him about the drink I'd had yesterday with Sylvia. How she'd revealed to me that he'd secretly authored Addison James's last two bestsellers and had just finished his third. How he'd taken the only copy of *Tulsa* to a copier shop on Broadway last Friday. How both he and *Tulsa* had vanished without a trace and that she'd hired me on the quiet to find him. "She thinks you're trying to leverage a better deal out of her," I said. "That you figure you've got the upper hand because there's no way Guilford House wants the world to know that Addison James can't write his own books anymore."

"Don't trust Sylvia," Tommy warned me, his voice rising.

"Not to worry, I don't. Neither does the Silver Fox."

He puffed out his cheeks. "God, I wish I'd had an agent like her looking out for me. I wouldn't have gotten suckered the way I did. Sylvia *lied* to me, Hoagy. Looked me right in the eye and *lied*. She promised me if I wrote the books I'd get my name on the cover as Addison's coauthor *and* a one-third share of the royalties, which is huge. That crazy old bastard sells in, like, thirty-eight different countries. But she never meant a word of it. Not one. Me, I'm just a guy from the old neighborhood, you know?" Every New Yorker I'd ever met who grew up in Brooklyn or Queens called himself "just a guy from the old neighborhood." "If someone makes you a promise, their word is gold. Not Sylvia. She's a lying bitch."

"No offense, Tommy, but it was pretty naive for a streetwise guy like you to believe her. No one in the publishing business trusts Sylvia."

He scratched his stubbly chin ruefully. "She played me for a fool, that's for damned sure. But I found out too late."

"Is that why you took the *Tulsa* manuscript?"

"I *didn't* take it, Hoagy, I swear. *That's* why they want to kill me!" His eyes had suddenly taken on the look of a wild, desperate animal.

"Wait, who wants to kill you? Slow down and lay it out for me, okay? Everything that's happened since you left Addison James's apartment on Friday."

Tommy took a deep breath and let it out raggedly. "Okay, sure. I went over to Broadway and had that Xerox of *Tulsa* made, like you said. Put the original and the copy in my briefcase, paid them and left. When I was two, three doors down from the copier shop, two black guys mugged me. They were young, in their late teens, early twenties, but so slick they've probably been snatching purses since they were twelve. One was a big dude, the other small. They came walking toward me on the sidewalk, rapping, cool as can be. As they got closer to me, they eased away from each other to create a space for me to walk in between them. As soon as the big one went by me he grabbed me from behind and threw his arm around my throat. The little one yanked the briefcase out of my hand, and bam, they took off with it. I let out a yell but it was no use. They sprinted down the block and tossed the briefcase into the open window of a cab that was idling at the curb maybe a hundred yards away. Whoever was sitting in the back seat passed the little one some money and they kept right on running. Me, I started toward the cab when suddenly this voice on the sidewalk next me says, 'I wouldn't do that if I were you, Tommy. We know where you live.' I turned and there's this huge, flabby guy, maybe fifty, with curly red hair turning to gray, standing there acting real calm. He was wearing a dark blue Ban-Lon shirt, tan slacks, and a light blue windbreaker, which he unzipped to show me he was packing heat," Tommy recalled. "I was a police beat reporter for five years. I can smell an ex-cop from a mile away."

"Did he say anything else to you?"

"He said, 'We'll be watching you. Say one word about this and you're a dead man.'"

"Which you took to be a threat."

"Hell, yeah. Wouldn't you? Then he sauntered down the block to the cab, got in next to the other passenger, and they took off."

"Did you get a look at the other passenger?"

Tommy shook his head.

"Could you at least tell whether it was a man or a woman?"

Tommy shook his head.

"How about the cab? Did you get a license or medallion number?"

"No, it all happened so fast. I was in a state of shock."

I mulled it over. "So they hired a couple of street kids to mug you. Probably paid them a hundred bucks apiece. Probably paid the cabbie another hundred to forget he ever saw a thing. He dropped them somewhere and then they took off for wherever." I studied him as he sat there, forlorn and miserable. "Did you call the police?"

Tommy shook his head. "I didn't do shit. Didn't call the police. Didn't go back to Addison's apartment to tell him what had happened. I just started walking. Must have walked for three hours."

"Stupid question. Was there anything else of value in your briefcase?"

"Not a thing. Just my old tape recorder, some notepads and pens. They were strictly after *Tulsa*. Didn't even bother with my wallet or wristwatch. I was afraid to go back to my apartment. 'We know where you live,' the guy said. So I used an ATM machine to get some cash and spent Labor Day weekend in a cheap hotel over by the Port Authority Bus Terminal. Hardly ever came out of my room."

"Sylvia told me that you've left Kathleen."

He nodded glumly. "We're not together anymore."

"What happened?"

"I met someone else, is what happened." He puffed out his cheeks again. "You don't have something to eat, do you? I haven't had anything that didn't come out of a vending machine for two days."

I made us some scrambled eggs, toast and coffee as the rain continued to pelt down on the skylight, my mind racing.

"I took a chance and rode the subway up here last night," Tommy told me as he wolfed down his eggs, Lulu dozing on the loveseat next to him. "I figured you were the one person I could trust. You weren't home, but your mailbox was empty so I figured you were in town and that I'd just wait around for you. Except you didn't come home. And then it started to rain."

"Real deal, Tommy. Who would want to steal *Tulsa*?"

"Hoagy, I've been asking myself that question over and over again for the past five days. You want my best guess?"

"That would be a help."

"Addison's greedy little sexpot wife, Yvette. She has herself a boyfriend who she met in the Hamptons this summer, okay? A lawyer who's hooked up with a small firm on the South Shore." Long Island's South Shore is famously unsavory when it comes to its lawyers and its political leaders, much like the entire state of Rhode Island. "I figure he hired that flabby ex-cop to steal the manuscript for Yvette."

"What would she be hoping to get out of it? Is this about the prenup she signed when she married Addison?"

"Sylvia told you about that?"

"A bit. Tell me more."

"The old guy's worth two, maybe three hundred million bucks. Yvette gets chump change when he kicks off. Don't ask me how much because I don't know. But none of his fortune. None of the vacation getaways that he has scattered all over the damned place. None of the royalties from his backlist, which pay off like a slot machine, year after year. All of that goes to Sylvia. Take it from me, if you want that manuscript back, go have yourself a chat with Yvette. Just don't be fooled by those big, innocent blue eyes of hers. She's a treacherous little kitty cat. And she has even fewer scruples than Sylvia, if such a thing is possible. Never drop your guard around Yvette."

"Understood. Meanwhile, we have to figure out what to do

with you. I take it you don't want to stay with the new woman in your life or you'd already be doing that."

"Right. I don't want her mixed up in this."

"In that case, why don't you hang out here for now? I'm bunking at Merilee's while she's on location. I just came home to fetch a few things. I'm scheduled to see Addison and Sylvia at noon."

"Don't expect too much out of him," Tommy warned me. "He's not all there anymore. He's also a total prick."

I went into the bathroom to fill my shaving kit, then went in my bedroom and finished packing before I put on an old pink Izod shirt, jeans and flip-flops. I parked my typewriter, Ghurka bag, garment bag and Lulu's doctor's bag by the front door. Tommy was busy washing our dishes. "If that flabby, curly-haired ex-cop is now a flabby, curly-haired PI, which wouldn't surprise me one bit, then he'll have figured out that you and I are old friends," I said. "It was smart of you to hide out on the roof. Stay smart. Don't leave. And don't use the phone. He may have a tap on it. There's enough food and liquor here to last you for a couple of days. I'll be back as soon as I have some news. Can you sit tight?"

"Do I have a choice?" Tommy asked me miserably.

"Do you want me to call your lady friend for you?"

He shook his head. "Like I said, I don't want her mixed up in this."

"Are you going to tell me who she is?"

"A young editor at Deep River named Norma."

"Norma Fives?"

His eyes widened in surprise. "You know her?"

"By reputation. She's supposed to be a real up-and-comer."

"She's twenty-eight and whip smart. Went to Bryn Mawr. I met her at a pub party and we hit it off right away. I sure don't know what she sees in me. All I know is that she makes me feel like a kid again. Kathleen and me . . . what can I say? The sizzle's gone."

"Are you planning to ask her for a divorce?"

Tommy fell silent for a moment. "I don't know."

"Your life is a real mess right now, isn't it?"

"You noticed, huh? I thought I had it made, too. A real sweet deal with Addison. Good salary and health benefits. I've traveled all over the world to research his books—Barcelona, Havana, Maui. This last one, *Tulsa*, wasn't a super exotic locale, but I dug up a ton of juicy material. Found a history professor at Oklahoma State who had all sorts of great background stories about the founding families. Also amazing stuff about the 1921 race riot. Did you know that a white mob went on a rampage, killed three hundred black people and burned down an entire neighborhood of more than eight hundred homes? And not one person was ever prosecuted? I didn't. Somehow that story never ended up in the history books. *Tulsa* is a hell of a good yarn, man. It really is. I'm super proud of it but . . ." He trailed off, shaking his head. "It's amazing what can happen. One minute everything's going great. The next minute you walk out the door of a copier shop and your whole life turns to complete shit."

"Not to worry. We'll straighten it out."

He looked at me imploringly. "You really think you can?"

"Absolutely. Sylvia hired me to find *Tulsa*. I'll find it."

Lulu snuffled at me indignantly from the sofa.

"*We'll* find it. But like I said, don't go anywhere and don't make any calls. If the phone rings, don't answer it. It won't be me calling. Understand?"

"I understand. And thanks, Hoagster. I don't know what I'd do without you."

"Relax. Get some sleep. I guarantee you that one week from now we'll be sitting at the bar of the White Horse drinking beer and having a huge laugh about this whole stupid thing."

Chapter Two

America's most famous living author owned a fifteen-room penthouse apartment that consumed the top two floors of a twenty-five-story prewar luxury high-rise on the corner of Riverside Drive and West 83rd Street that was, according to an old-time sportswriter I know, the same building that Babe Ruth lived in until his death in 1948. The Bambino's widow, Claire, continued to live there until she died in 1976.

I made certain to arrive there precisely one hour early so as to get in some private time with Addison before Sylvia showed up. Since it was still pouring rain, I wore my oyster-gray summer-weight belted trench, Worth and Worth fedora and Gore-Tex street bluchers.

The doorman rang the apartment for me, spoke discreetly to someone up there, and directed me to the penthouse's express elevator, which whisked Lulu and me nonstop to the twenty-fourth floor before it opened into a small entry hall that had two doors. One was for Addison, Yvette, and their privileged guests. The other was for servicepeople. I shot for the moon and rang the bell for privileged guests.

It was Yvette who answered the door. She was thirty-two but looked younger, possibly because she was so little. Not more than an inch or two over five feet tall in her tiny, pedicured bare feet. Her toenails were painted a shade of grape that was popular that season. She wore a lightweight, gauzy summer sheath with a deep V neck that clung to her so tightly that I could tell that her belly button was an innie. Also that she wasn't wearing a bra. It took an act of sheer willpower to not stare at Yvette's nipples poking through the thin material. She was abundantly curvy, bordering on but not quite zaftig. If she weren't careful she'd blimp into the likes of Lainie Kazan by the time she hit forty. Right now she was still outrageously sexy and she knew it. And wanted to make good and sure that you did, too.

She gazed up, up, up at me, her rosebud mouth half-open as I stood there in my fedora and trench, dripping on the entry hall floor. Yvette had huge eyes that were an unusual shade of royal blue and were her strongest feature—speaking above the neck, that is. She had a round face, a weak chin, and an unremarkable nose. Her honey-blond hair had been artfully highlighted and layered.

"Oh. My. God," she gasped in a voice that was thirty-two going on seventeen, as in gag-me-with-a-spoon seventeen. She wavered there on her bare feet, her eyelids fluttering.

"Are you okay?" I asked.

She blinked at me with those big blue eyes. "I'm fine, but don't keep me in suspense. Are *you* Stewart Hoag?"

"I am," I replied, tipping my fedora. "My friends call me Hoagy. I'm here to see Mr. James. Are you Mrs. James?"

"Call me Yvette, please." She offered me her small hand. It

was smooth, soft and warm. Her manicured nails were painted that same shade of grape. "Sylvia said to expect you at noon."

"I'm a bit early," I acknowledged. "I'll wait down in the lobby."

"Like hell you will," she said. "Sylvia said you were a writer. What she didn't say was that you'd make me go weak in the knees."

"Well, she wouldn't. Not exactly Sylvia's style, is it? You can feel free to let go of my hand anytime, by the way."

"Oh, jeez, I'm sorry. You even smell good. What are you wearing?"

"Floris. I get it in London."

Yvette smelled of fruity perfume, the kind that I associated with the old ladies at Essex Meadows, the assisted living home where my parents were not enjoying their golden years. The scent was entirely wrong for her, but I didn't feel it was my place to tell her. Besides, maybe Addison got off on it.

She crinkled her nose at me. "I'd swear you also smell like the Bronx Zoo."

"That would be my short-legged partner."

Yvette looked down. "Aww, you have a beagle. How cute."

Lulu let out an indignant moan.

"Lulu's a basset hound, actually. Her coat can get a bit fragrant when it's damp."

Yvette shook her little finger at me. "I used to read all about you. You were married to Merilee Nash. And you're, like, this immortal novelist."

"That was the old me. The new me is quite mortal."

"And you're here to help Addy find his missing manuscript?"

"I'm certainly going to try."

"Well, come on in."

She led me inside, taking short, mincing little steps in that tight, tight dress. She definitely had an ogle-worthy jiggle when she walked. "Addy is in his office. I'll take you up to him."

I took off my hat and trench, leaving them on a bench by the door. It hadn't occurred to her to offer to hang them up for me. A practiced hostess she was not.

The Jameses' penthouse was formal and grand—but not so much a home as an interior decorator's idea of what a formal and grand home ought to look like. It had a vast living room with two seating areas that were set before windows that over-looked the Hudson and the New Jersey Palisades beyond. The sofas and armchairs were pure white satin, and it didn't look as if anyone had ever sat on any of them. There was a smaller parlor with a television set and wet bar that looked as if no one had ever watched TV or had a drink in there. A dining room with a table that would seat at least twenty-four yet prob-ably never had. There were no books, magazines or newspapers on the coffee tables. No paintings or photographs hanging from the walls. No artifacts that Addison had collected in his world travels over the years researching his blockbuster bestsellers. Just bare walls and surfaces. The whole place seemed incredibly unlived in—which may not have been that far from the truth. They did have six or eight other homes scattered hither and yon, not to mention their beach house in East Hampton. It was entirely possible that they were here for only a few weeks out of the year. But I couldn't help wonder if all of their other homes looked uninhabited, too.

A grand curving staircase went up to the second floor. Yvette led me up there, wiggling and jiggling. Princess Lemon Jell-O indeed. I followed her, detecting no visible panty line. Either she was wearing a thong or no underwear at all. I didn't think it would be gentlemanly to inquire. Being a gentleman can really suck sometimes.

Lulu grumbled sullenly as we climbed the stairs. She disliked any woman who showed the slightest interest in me, especially one who'd mistaken her for a beagle and passed a remark that had contained the words *Bronx* and *Zoo*.

"Addy's probably still doing his morning exercises in his room," Yvette informed me over her shoulder. "Want to check out my digs?"

"Love to."

She led me down an incredibly long parquet-floored hallway. "I have my own private suite in all of our homes. In Maui I have my own cottage and pool so I can swim in the nude. Do you like to swim in the nude?"

"Depends on with whom I'm swimming."

"You're a *bad* boy. I like you," she said, beaming at me as she stopped to open her door. "Here we are."

Yvette had a complete apartment of her own. A sitting room with a matching cocoa-brown velvet loveseat and easy chair set before a big Sony TV. A Pullman kitchen. A great big bedroom that had a great big bed buried under an avalanche of pillows, cushions and stuffed animals. Another room—her spa, she called it—that had a treadmill, an exercise bike, a Jacuzzi and a sauna. Again, there were no photographs, no mementos, no personal touches at all. Not unless you count the "music" that was blaring from the sound system in her spa—"Blame It on the Rain" by Milli Vanilli.

"I'm sorry, would you mind turning that off?"

"How come?"

"My ears bleed easily."

She frowned at me, puzzled, but obliged me as Lulu roamed from room to room, nose to the floor, sniffing and snorting.

"Why's she doing that?" Yvette wondered, watching her curiously.

"She's a scent hound. It's how she gets acclimated."

"She's not going to pee-pee on the carpet, is she?"

"Wouldn't think of it."

"Can I get you a cold drink?"

"I'm fine, thanks."

"Well then, sit, sit."

I sat, sat on the loveseat. Yvette joined me, tucking her bare feet under her, and turned to face me, studying me intently.

"Do you have live-in staff, Yvette? With a huge place like this, you must."

She shook her honey-blond head. "Addy can't stand to have strangers around. Two sisters from Haiti come in three times a week to clean. They're here for maybe four hours, then they take off."

"Were they here that day?"

"What day?"

"The day that Tommy and *Tulsa* disappeared."

Yvette furrowed her brow. "No, Friday isn't one of their days."

"Was anyone else here?"

"Like who?"

"A plumber, electrician . . . ?"

"Not a soul."

"Do you do all of the cooking yourself?"

She let out a girlish shriek of a laugh. "Me? I can barely fry an egg without setting the kitchen on fire. A chef comes in to make us dinner. A different one every night, if you know what I mean."

"Afraid not."

"Breakfast and lunch we each go our own way. I nibble on rice cakes, nuts and carrot sticks. Addy has cheese, crackers and about ten gallons of water. Dinner's prepared for us in the kitchen downstairs by a chef from Daniel, Sistina or Peter Luger, depending on whether Addy's in the mood for French, Italian or a steak. He likes to eat well, but he doesn't like to go out, so he has them bring the restaurant to us. It's kind of amazing what famous chefs will do for you if you're willing to pay them enough money."

"And he has it."

"Sweetie, you have no idea how many books in how many different languages he's sold over the past forty years. I doubt that anyone does—except for Sylvia, that is. She knows every royalty payment down to the last penny. And she shares that information with *no one*." Yvette's huge blue eyes narrowed shrewdly as she sat there studying me. Tommy was right. There was nothing bimbonic about her. "What else would you like to know?"

"I understand you started out here as his typist."

"Ten years ago. He got me from Joe Heller, who was in between books and had nothing for me. Joe's the guy who wrote *Catch-22*."

"Yes, I know."

"I was trying to be an actress in those days. Mostly they had me auditioning for roles in TV commercials as 'Silly Teenaged Mall Girl No. 3' because I looked like a high school girl."

"You still do."

She swatted at my arm playfully. "Now you're flirting with me."

"Am not," I assured her, my eyes carefully avoiding her nipples.

"I can't say it was love at first sight, but the more I got to know Addy, the more attached I got to him. He was just so incredibly sweet and considerate. We surprised everyone when we eloped to Atlantic City and got married—especially Sylvia, who thinks I'm nothing more than a conniving little fortune hunter. She's felt that way ever since I first walked in the door."

"And you're originally from . . . ?"

"Larchmont. I was a Theatre Arts major at Long Island University. People had been telling me how cute I was since I was five years old so I thought maybe I could make it as an actress. But I'm practical, too, so I also learned how to type eighty words a minute without a single typo. I made good money at it. And trust me, typing manuscripts sure beats the hell out of slinging drinks and getting groped by gorillas."

"What's your maiden name, Yvette?"

She peered at me guardedly. "Why do you want to know that?"

"Just curious. I like to know things about people."

"It's Rittenaur. I shortened it to Ritt as my professional name. And Yvette's actually my middle name. My first name is Phyllis. Ugh. I mean, all it makes you think of is Phyllis Diller."

"How did the auditions go? Did you get work?"

"I got cast in one local commercial for a furniture moving company that never ran. I don't think the owner ever intended to run it. He just wanted to screw me, like he had a prayer. The soaps didn't want me. Off-Broadway didn't want me. Let me tell you, Hoagy, there's a big difference between being the cutest girl in your high school in Larchmont and competing against the cutest girls from every high school in America, not to mention places like Sweden and Brazil. Plus, being honest, I was no Merilee Nash in the acting department. I could be a ditsy airhead, period, so it was a darned good thing I learned how to type. Addy wrote on an old Underwood. Still does. He began using me a few hours a week, and then it became more like twenty or thirty. I hear that a lot of writers are using personal computers now, so they don't need typists anymore."

"Does Tommy use one?"

"Nah, he still uses an Underwood, same as Addy."

"Does he do his writing here?"

She shook her head. "At home. Then he brings his pages over here and he and Addy go over them together. You should hear the two of them yelling. They disagree a lot. Addy has strong opinions. I love a man who has strong opinions. I love Addy. Nobody has ever believed that, you know, what with him being in his late sixties when we met. But he was still all man, if you hear me."

"Loud and clear."

"After I'd been typing here for a few weeks, he asked me if I'd like to stay for a glass of sherry. It was a Friday evening. Longest glass of sherry *ever*. I didn't go limping home to Park Slope until Sunday night. When I came in on Monday, he'd left a note on my typewriter asking me if I'd like to move into one of the half-dozen guest bedrooms here. So I did, although I ended up in his bed almost every night. Next thing I knew he'd proposed to me and I'd said yes." She giggled gleefully, recalling it. "God, was Sylvia pissed off. She's never once shown me an ounce of human kindness. I don't think she even knows what kindness is."

"And what do you think of Tommy?"

"Why are you asking?"

"We've known each other for years. We're old friends."

She eyed me shrewdly again. "Is that right?"

"That's why I find it so hard to believe that he stole the manuscript. He's not that kind of guy."

"You telling me someone else took it?"

"Not necessarily. People do change. Even old friends."

"They sure do. I can barely recognize some of the girls I went to high school with. What do I think of Tommy? Okay, sure. He's Jackson Heights to the bone. Bad haircut. Bad suit. Married his high school sweetheart. But he's always been super polite to me. Never tries to hit on me. Strictly cares about his work and his family." She moved a bit closer to me on the loveseat, reached over and neatened the collar of my navy blue blazer, not that it needed neatening. "And his girlfriend, of course. They all have girlfriends."

"By *they*, you mean . . . ?"

"All of those poor slobs who married their high school sweethearts. After twenty years they want a taste of something different. I overheard him talking to her on the phone one day. Tommy's okay, but he's got no sizzle. Not like *you*." She inched even closer, reached over and neatened my shirt collar now, not that it needed neatening. Her fingers strayed north, stroking my neck delicately as I recalled Tommy's words of warning: *Never drop your guard around Yvette.*

I glanced at Grandfather's Benrus. It was twenty minutes after eleven. "Sylvia ought to be here soon, unless she has trouble getting a cab in this rain. I hope I'm not keeping you from anything."

"Are you kidding? I'm thrilled to have you all to myself. What's your deal? You involved with anyone?"

"My ex-wife."

"*Still?* I thought you and Merilee split up years ago."

"We're working at getting back together. She is, however, in Budapest for the next five weeks."

Yvette brightened considerably. "In that case, you want a little company some evening? Addy won't mind. He lets me go my own way." She tilted her head at me curiously. "Why are you looking at me that way?"

"I'm just a bit confused. I thought you were involved with someone."

"Where'd you hear that?"

"Word gets around."

"Sylvia, am I right? That nasty bitch means Mel Klein, my lawyer. She hates him because he thinks the prenup that Addy's lawyer, Mark Kaplan, made me sign is a total rip-off. What did I know? I was a naive kid. But I don't get a penny of the hundreds of millions that Addy's got socked away when he kicks off. Or any of our vacation retreats. Sylvia gets them all."

"Where will you live?"

"Here," she said, gazing around at her sitting room. "I get our penthouse, which is, like, a sick joke. I won't even be able to make the monthly maintenance payments on it with what he's leaving me, which is a measly income of two thou a month. Mel figures, worst-case scenario, I can sell this place, buy myself a nice little two-bedroom on West End and invest the proceeds. But he honestly thinks he can get me a better deal. And he's the only lawyer I've ever met who talks to me in a way that makes sense, which most lawyers don't."

"You're not wrong there."

"Plus he's working on a contingency basis, which means he's not charging me. He's also not trying to get in my panties."

"So you do wear panties."

She swatted at me playfully. "He's just a nebbish with dandruff. We met in Sag Harbor over the summer. His law firm— Klein, Walker and Pignatano—is on the South Shore. Mel handles wills and estates, Phil Walker's a bankruptcy specialist and Joe Pignatano's a divorce lawyer."

"It's just the three of them?"

"And Jocko Conlon, who takes photos of cheating spouses doing the big naughty in motel rooms."

"He's a private investigator?"

"I guess."

"Have you met him?"

"Yeah, one time when I went to the office. He's a big fat slob. Really gave me the creeps."

"Is he bald?"

"Why are you asking me that?"

"Because I think I may know him."

"No, he has curly red hair that's turning gray."

"Oh, then I guess I'm thinking of someone else. Is that the only time you ever met him?"

"Met who?"

"Jocko, who really gave you the creeps."

"Well, yeah." She furrowed her brow. "Why do you keep asking me about him?"

"It's what I do. Ask questions."

"And, what, people pay you for that?"

"Sylvia is. Quite handsomely, in fact."

"You must be some kind of con artist. Because that woman is cheap, let me tell ya." Yvette looked at me curiously. "You have a funny way of asking them. And I don't mean funny ha-ha. I mean funny like you think maybe I'm not being straight with you."

"Are you? Being straight with me, I mean."

"Of course I am, silly. What a thing to say." She swatted at me playfully again. "I only met him that one time at Mel's office. And for real, there's *nothing* going on between Mel and me. That's not to say he isn't hot for me. But he hasn't got a chance. Not like *you*." Yvette swiveled around sideways on the loveseat and plopped her small, pampered bare foot in my lap, wiggling her painted toes. "You can suck on them if you'd like to."

I gazed at them for a moment before I said, "Not right now, thanks."

Yvette stuck out her lower lip. "Why not? Don't you like me?"

"I assure you that's not the issue," I said marveling at Merilee's uncanny territorial instincts. It was as if she'd *known* that some form of temptation would come along the instant she left town. "I'm old school, that's all. Once I start something, I like to finish it."

"Oh, I see . . ." She grinned at me devilishly, tucking her foot back underneath her. "Can I be totally honest?"

"That would be nice."

"I can't remember the last time I had such an instant case of the hots for a guy. I mean, I'm even feeling light-headed."

"That's not me, actually. That's Lulu's breath."

Yvette got up and padded over to a writing table. "Listen,

here's my private line," she said, scribbling it on a piece of note-paper. "Call me any time, day or night. I can meet you wher-ever you want in a half hour. I make house calls. And I promise you won't be disappointed." She held the notepaper out to me with a sly grin. "Okay?"

I treated Yvette to my most winning smile. "More than okay," I said, pocketing it. After all, she might prove to be very useful. Her South Shore lawyer, Mel, employed a PI who just happened to match the ID of the guy who'd threatened Tommy on the sidewalk after the muggers snatched his briefcase. That meant Yvette gave me a potential way to penetrate this scheme, as it were.

I glanced at Grandfather's Benrus again. It was eleven-thirty. I wanted a half hour alone with the great Addison James. "Sylvia must be running late. Would you mind introducing me to your husband?"

"No prob, hon. Let's go knock on his door."

I followed her jiggly tush down the long hall, wondering why she'd hit on me with such an utter absence of subtlety. Admit-tedly, I'm attractive in a devil-may-care way that's reminiscent of a vintage Hollywood leading man. Don't take my word for it. *Cosmopolitan* said so in its July '83 issue. But what was the real reason? Had her lawyer, Mel Klein, put her up to it? Or was she pursuing her own agenda? Whatever it was, my eyes were wide open. When you've been around the block enough times with the people who are close to rich, famous celebrities you learn two valuable kernels of truth:

One, every single one of them is yearning for a big payday of their own.

Two, every single one of them is a natural-born liar.

The great author's suite was at the end of the hall behind a set of oak pocket doors. Behind the doors I could hear a steady rhythmic thumping.

Yvette knocked on one of them.

"Enter!" a booming voice called out.

She slid it open to reveal a huge, high-ceilinged office. Tall windows looked out over the Hudson River. The summer rain was pattering hard against them. The office was not air-conditioned. It was so steamy in there that the windows were fogging up. Addison James was over by them at a giant walnut partners desk wearing a black eye patch, a jockstrap, a pair of black combat boots and absolutely nothing else as he ran in place, his knees high, shoulders thrown back, chin up—the very portrait of manic seventy-eight-year-old determination.

Lulu and I entered, Lulu with her nose to the floor. Yvette remained behind in the doorway.

A kitchen timer was ticking away on the desk. When Addison noticed me there, he held up a hand, warning me not to speak as he continued to run in place.

So I looked around at the floor-to-ceiling bookcases surrounding us that were filled with the domestic and foreign editions of what appeared to be every one of his forty-two best-selling epics. Hundreds of books. Hell, thousands. There was a seating area of two well-worn leather sofas and matching armchairs that were arranged around a coffee table that consisted of a pair of battered U.S. Army olive drab footlockers set end to end. There was a refrigerator next to an open door that led to a bathroom. Through another open doorway I could see a bedroom with a white cast-iron bed.

I looked back at Addison, watching the sweat pour off him

onto the parquet floor and puddle there as he ran in place in his heavy combat boots, gasping. Opened on the desk before him was a dog-eared paperback copy of the Royal Canadian Air Force exercise regimen, which had been devised back in the 1950s so that airmen who were stationed in remote, frigid locales could remain fit. Aside from it, a rotary phone and a folded towel, the huge desk was bare. His old Underwood, a fine office machine, was parked on a stand facing the windows.

The kitchen timer rang. Addison came slowly to a stop, breathing heavily, and reached for the towel to mop the sweat from his face and neck.

"I haven't seen that book since I was in junior high school," I said to him. "A gym teacher gave each of us a copy."

"I've been keeping to the regimen seven days a week for thirty years," he panted, wiping his shoulders and chest with the towel. "It's a total body workout in just eleven minutes. One minute each of push-ups, sit-ups and leg lifts. Two minutes of bending and stretching. Six minutes of running in place." He slapped his flat stomach proudly. He was remarkably lean and muscled and stood rigidly erect for a man of seventy-eight. Still an honest six feet tall. He was also remarkably hairless. He shaved his head and eyebrows as well as whatever wisps of white hair he had on his chest and shoulders. Truly, he was an amazing physical specimen aside from the deep puckered scars on the outside of his left thigh and calf.

"Almost lost that leg to a grenade when I was working with the French Resistance," he said, noticing me notice it. "It was a near thing. The docs were lopping off limbs left and right. They did manage to save it. Couldn't do the same for my peeper, though," he said, tapping his eye patch. He opened the refrigerator, which was filled with liter bottles of Perrier water, opened one and gulped half of it down, paused a moment and then gulped the remaining half, studying me with his one not-so-good eye. Or so Sylvia had told me. He went in the bathroom and returned wearing a white terry cloth robe. "It took me over a year of punishing recuperation at a VA hospital before I could walk again."

"This is Stewart Hoag, Addy," said Yvette, who'd remained in the open pocket doorway. "He has an appointment to see you."

"I'm well aware of that, Yvette," he responded testily.

"Can I get you boys anything?"

"Yes, you can get the fuck out!" he roared, hurling the empty Perrier liter bottle across the room at her with great velocity.

She let out a scream as it smashed against the wall next to her, the glass shattering into a million pieces. Then she yanked the door shut hard and I heard her scamper away. Lulu ran under the desk and hid.

Addison James approached me now in the steamy heat of his immense office and stuck out his hand.

I shook it, his moist hand gripping mine tightly. "It's an honor to meet you, Mr. James."

"Will you tell me something, Mr. Hoag?" He had a deep, strong voice. The voice of a fearless hard charger, which was exactly what he'd been during the war when Wild Bill Donovan plucked him out of Yale for the OSS. Rumor had it that he'd stayed on with the CIA after the war doing clandestine work while he was overseas researching his first two novels, which just happened to take place in Moscow and Berlin.

"Most people call me Hoagy."

He peered at me with his one not-so-good eye. "As in Car-michael?"

"As in the cheesesteak. I can try."

"You can try what?"

"To tell you something."

"Why did I marry that stupid little piece of tail? Why didn't I just keep on fucking her senseless and leave it at that?"

"Maybe you love her."

"I have never loved anyone," he stated categorically. "Stop. Backspace. Erase. I loved Sylvia's mother, Aline, who I lost to breast cancer much too young. Aline was my nurse at the VA hospital in Asheville. I wouldn't have made it if it hadn't been for her."

"So you don't love Yvette?"

"Who could love that?" he demanded scornfully. "She's a complete idiot."

"Seems pretty shrewd to me."

"In that case I was misinformed about you. You're obviously a complete idiot, too."

Addison James pulled no punches. I suppose I wouldn't either if I'd been the bestselling author in the world for the past forty years.

He peered under his partners desk, noticing Lulu for the first time. "Who let that dog in here?"

"Good question."

"Is it *your* dog?"

"Never saw her before. I assumed she was yours."

"Oh, I get it. You're a comedian. You may as well know from the outset that I have no use for comedians. Tommy liked to crack wise when he first came to me. A regular newsroom wit. I quickly broke him of the habit." He fetched another bottle of Perrier from the refrigerator, not bothering to offer me one, twisted off the top and drank from it.

My shirt was beginning to stick to me from the muggy heat of his office. I took off my blazer, laying it over a sofa.

"I hope you don't mind the warmth," he said. "I detest air conditioning."

"Not a problem. My fifth-floor walk-up hasn't got any. I'm accustomed to it."

"Did you do them?"

"Do what, Mr. James?"

"The Royal Canadian Air Force exercises."

"Briefly. I lost interest."

"At my age I can't afford to." He settled into his oak desk chair, which tilted and rolled. "Stamina and muscle tone are vital when you become ancient. So is proper hydration. I drink eight of these bottles per day. Have a seat, why don't you?"

I sat in the oak chair across the partners desk from him, which neither rolled nor swiveled. Evidently, it was the junior partner's chair.

We faced each other across the expanse of walnut for a moment before he said, "So how are the last two chapters of *Tulsa* coming?"

I looked down at Lulu. Lulu was looking up at me. "Excuse me?"

"Last time you were here you said you just had two more to go."

"I'm not Tommy O'Brien, Mr. James."

He peered at me with his one not-so-good eye. "No, of course not. *Who* are you again?"

"Hoagy, as in the cheesesteak, remember?"

"Hoagy . . ." He ran a hand over his bald pink head, his face a total blank. "Afraid I have no idea what you're doing here."

"Sylvia asked me to stop by. She should be here momentarily."

"Whatever for?"

"To talk about *Tulsa*. Someone took off with the only two copies of it Friday night. You do remember that, don't you?"

Addison sat there in befuddled silence. Sylvia hadn't exaggerated. He wasn't all there anymore. "Why . . . would they want to do that?"

"Don't know yet. Possibly to hold it for ransom, although there hasn't been a ransom demand yet as far as I know."

He shook a long, bony finger at me across the desk. "I guarantee you Tommy has it. Wants me to give him a raise. He's got two daughters in college and complains constantly about how expensive it is. God, how I hate ordinary people and their ordinary lives."

"Tommy hasn't got *Tulsa*."

"So you've spoken to him?"

"I have."

"Total hack, but he has his uses. Or he did until now. Where is he?"

"Flying under the radar."

"As in hiding out?"

"Tommy's genuinely frightened. He was mugged outside of the copier shop on Broadway. His briefcase containing the only two copies of *Tulsa* was snatched by a pair of young black street kids. They handed it off to someone who was waiting in a cab. When Tommy started running toward the cab, a guy standing there next to him showed him a gun and said, 'We know where you live.'"

Addison gazed out the fogged window at the summer rain. "Stewart Hoag . . . I just realized why I know your name. I plowed through your highly overrated debut novel. Total drivel. Just another spoiled, angry boy lashing out at Dada. Are you still?"

"No, I'm over that. He's in an assisted living facility now."

"Sylvia will never get *me* in one of those places. I'll blow my brains out first. Thinks I'm senile. Wants some fancy-pants doctor to run tests on me—which I assure you will never happen—to determine if I suffer from something called dementia, whatever the hell that is."

"I wouldn't know. I'm not a doctor."

"Correct. You're a one-and-done novelist who lives in a fifth-floor walk-up without air conditioning, ghostwrites memoirs and gets your name in the paper a lot because you used to be married to Meryl Streep."

"Merilee Nash."

"I'm quite sure it was Meryl Streep."

"And *I'm* quite sure it was Merilee Nash. Tell me about your arrangement with Tommy, Mr. James."

He shrugged his shoulders in the terry cloth robe. "It was Sylvia's idea to take him on. This was, let's see, eight years ago, I believe. An Addison James tale requires a tremendous amount of legwork. I have to travel to the locale. Do thorough historical research, collect anecdotes, folklore, legends—all of the authentic flavor that I'm known for. It's time-consuming work. I was accustomed to doing every bit of it myself, but I'm on a strict deadline. I'm expected to deliver a big fat juicy bestseller every twenty-four months, then go on tour all over the world for an entire month to flog the hell out of it. I couldn't keep up the pace anymore, much as I hated to admit it, so Sylvia suggested I take on a shoe-leather reporter like Tommy who could work one book ahead of me researching my next one. He's a damned good reporter. Assembles an immense, detailed file for me. Takes loads of photographs so I can picture what I'm writing about. Has it all ready and waiting for me when I'm set to go."

"Does he also do some of the writing?"

"Never," Addison said indignantly. "Do I look like a fraud to you?"

"No, sir."

"We do kick things around together. Rough out the bones of a story based on what he's been able to collect from his sources. But then I sit down at this same Underwood right here that I've been typing on since you were in diapers and I write every single fucking word."

"Except lately, you mean."

He glowered at me. "Don't know what you mean by that."

"Sylvia told me that it was Tommy who wrote your last two books, *San Francisco* and *Havana*. And *Tulsa* will make three."

"That's bullshit. Stop. Backspace. Erase. *Total* bullshit."

"So she lied to me? Tommy didn't write them?"

Addison stared at me coldly with that eye of his for a long moment. Got up out of his chair, went over to the window and studied the rain falling on Riverside Park and the West 79th

Street Boat Basin. Or at least stared down in that general direction. I'm not sure how well he could make out any of it. "How do I know I can trust you?"

"Sylvia asked me the very same question."

"And you answered . . . ?"

"That my business is secrets. If I blabbed those secrets, then I would no longer be in business. Furthermore, Tommy told me himself that he wrote *Tulsa*. He said he came up here Friday night to show you the final two chapters. You gave them your okay. Then he went out to make a copy of the finished manuscript for Sylvia and got mugged. *Someone* has the only two copies of *Tulsa* in existence. Maybe they intend to hold them for ransom. Maybe there's something else going on."

"Such as what?"

"I was hoping you'd tell me that, Mr. James."

"Do you do a lot of that?"

"A lot of what?"

"Go around hoping for things."

"Yes, I do. All writers do. Hope is our oxygen. Hope is what keeps us alive. Hope and fear."

"Of failure, you mean." He nodded approvingly. "You're not as dumb as you look. Do you like Perry Mason?"

"The novels by Erle Stanley Gardner or the old TV series with Raymond Burr?"

"The TV series. It's on every day at noon on one of my cable stations. I never miss it. Care to watch it with me?"

"I'd be delighted to."

The same went for Lulu, who's a huge Della Street fan.

Addison went over to a built-in wall unit and flicked on the TV with the remote. The oh-so-familiar brassy, jazzy *Perry*

Mason theme song filled the big room. Until, that is, someone started knocking urgently on the office door.

It was Sylvia, who slid open one of the pocket doors, looking wet and bedraggled from the rain, not to mention extremely ill at ease. Her shoulders were hunched, her eyes fastened to the floor. It was immediately apparent to me that in the presence of her famous father she was not the fire-breathing dragon lady whom we'd all come to know and loathe. She stepped carefully around the shards of the shattered Perrier bottle as she came in, sliding the door shut behind her.

Addison glared at her. "Damn, it, Pudge, why'd you have to show up right now? We want to watch *Perry Mason*."

Pudge?

"I-I said I'd be here at noon to meet you w-with Mr. Hoag," she stammered.

"But I want to watch my show."

"Why don't you tape it, Mr. James?" I suggested.

"Why don't I *what*?"

"Don't you have a VCR?"

"Speak English, man!"

"A videocassette recorder. You can record the telecast and then watch it later. Or better yet, you can buy boxed sets of entire seasons. I'm sure someone in Sylvia's office could order them for you. That way you can watch any episode you want any time you want."

He gaped at me in disbelief. "Just pop it in a machine and watch it?"

"Precisely."

He glared at Sylvia again. "Why didn't I know about this?"

She turned off the TV with the remote, which prompted

Lulu to let out a sour grunt of displeasure. "Father, I-I don't have time f-for this. Can we talk business, please?"

"As you wish. Just give me a minute . . ." He went into his bathroom and proceeded to take a fire hose of a piss with the door wide open.

Sylvia didn't seem the least bit fazed. She was used to his crude behavior, evidently. Besides, she was much more interested in shooting a Vulcan death stare at me. "Our agreement was to meet here at noon, Stewart."

"And it is noon."

"Yvette just told me you've been here for almost an hour."

"A slight exaggeration. I always arrive a few minutes early for important meetings in case I get stuck in traffic."

"That's a load of crap. You wanted to talk to him without me."

"What if I did?"

"I don't approve of the way you operate."

"You say that as if I give a damn about your approval."

Addison let out a cackle from the bathroom. There was nothing wrong with the old man's ears. "I'm going to like this fellow," he exclaimed, returning to us after he'd flushed the toilet and washed his hands. "We'll get along just fine now that Tommy's out of the picture."

"I'm not here to replace Tommy, Mr. James."

Addison ignored me, peering down at Lulu curiously. "What's his name?"

"Her name is Lulu."

"Ugly little mutt."

"She's not a mutt. Lulu's a purebred basset, extremely comely, and she's not little—just short. If you don't believe me, try to pick her up," I said, quite certain that a man possessing his ego would be unable to resist the challenge.

"What on earth for?"

"You accused her of being little. Go ahead, pick her up."

"I'm starting to think you're as crazy as I am." As the old man bent over to gather Lulu into his arms, she treated him to a huge yawn, the better to mouth-breathe on him. He drew back, aghast. "Good God, man, what do you feed her—desiccated seal carcasses?"

"Excellent guess, but no."

He bent over again, and just as he was about to lift her up off of the floor, she transformed herself into a dead weight. Despite straining with all of his might, he couldn't get her more than an inch off of the floor. It's impossible to pick up a basset hound that doesn't want to be picked up, just as it's impossible to make one keep walking if it doesn't want to walk anymore. It'll just lie down and refuse to budge. "Jesus H. Christ," he groaned. "How much does she weigh?"

"She got a lot of exercise on the farm this summer. No more than fifty pounds, I'd say."

"That's nothing. I should be able to pick her up."

"You should, except she doesn't want you to."

"Why not?"

"Because you called her an ugly little mutt."

"You make it sound as if she understands what people say. You *are* as crazy as I am." He sniffed at his hands. "And why do I smell like castor oil?"

"It's the rain. Her coat is imbued with an oil to repel water."

He went in the bathroom again to wash his hands and came

out drying them on a towel. "You're acquainted with Hoagy, aren't you, Pudge?"

Sylvia's mouth tightened. "Must you humiliate me in front of m-my colleagues by using that h-horrible childhood nickname?"

"Can't help it. You still look like the same fat little girl. If you'd do your Royal Canadian Air Force exercises every day like I do, then you wouldn't resemble a Hubbard squash and men wouldn't flee at the sight of you."

"C-Can we please talk business?" she stammered miserably. "We're here to t-talk business."

"If you'll stop that damned stammering!" he hollered at her. "Stand up straight! Stop picking at your scalp! And *when* was the last time I saw you in a dress that didn't make you look like a Jewish grandmother?"

Sylvia stood there fighting back tears, utterly mortified. I doubted that very many people had ever witnessed how abusively her father treated her. I found myself feeling sorry for Sylvia James, which was something I'd never imagined happening.

Addison let out a disgusted sigh. "Fine. We'll talk business. You've fired Tommy and this fellow's taking over, right?"

"Wrong," I said. "I was talking to you about the theft of the *Tulsa* manuscript, remember? Did Tommy talk to anyone on the phone before he left to get it copied?"

Addison nodded. "His girlfriend."

"You heard him say her name?"

"No, but just before he hung up he said, and I quote, 'Have I told you how much I love you?' Trust me, the man wasn't talking to his wife."

I considered this, my wheels turning. Could Norma Fives, a rising star at a rival publishing house, be involved in this? Could the entire mugging story be a fabrication? Was Tommy complicit in it? I looked over at Sylvia. "What do you know about her?"

"Who, Norma?" She curled her lip. "I know she has no scruples. We've gotten in several bidding wars. Each time I've been assured by the author's agent that the book is mine. Each time I get a call back an hour later, and somehow it's Norma's."

I turned back to Addison. "Tommy arrived here with the last two chapters of *Tulsa* at what time?"

"Maybe four o'clock," Addison replied. "He brought me the final fifty pages of material that we'd roughed out together. Ran them through his typewriter at home during the week. He's happier working there than here. Can't imagine why."

"And did you read them?"

"Didn't need to. I already knew what was there."

"Was that how you collaborated on the rest of the book?"

"What do you mean?"

"I mean, did you ever actually *read* the damned thing?"

"I *wrote* the damned thing," he fired back angrily. "Dictated it, scene by scene. Tommy put it down on paper, that's all."

"But you never read what he put down on paper, did you?"

"What for? I've just told you, I knew what it said. Are you dense or something?"

"And then off he went to make a copy of the completed manuscript. What time was that?"

"Six or so. And that was the last I've heard from him." He turned to glower at Sylvia. "Why haven't you told me that I could buy whole seasons of *Perry Mason* on videocassette?"

"I-I assumed that you knew."

"Unacceptable. Not credible. Bullshit. You purposely didn't tell me."

"Father, w-why would I d-do that?"

"What was supposed to happen next?" I broke in.

"They were supposed to give one of the finished copies to me so that I could read it," Sylvia answered.

"How much of it had you already read?"

"None. Father never lets me see a book until it's completed."

"I make many, many changes along the way," Addison explained airily. "Throw out characters, add new ones, jettison entire sequences. I don't believe in showing a work in progress to anyone. Not Sylvia. Not Yvette. Not Bingo."

"And Bingo is . . . ?"

"Fellow at the garage around the corner who wipes down my GT Hawk."

"You have a Gran Turismo Hawk?"

Addison nodded proudly. "A '62, gun-metal gray. I bought her new. She's a honey. Nobody built better cars than Studebaker." He tilted his head at me appraisingly. "What do *you* drive?"

"A '58 XK150 roadster—when Merilee lets me borrow it, that is. She got it in the divorce."

"Lovely machine," Addison said approvingly.

"What about a typist, Mr. James? Was *Tulsa* being professionally typed as you and Tommy went along?"

"We don't bother with that," Sylvia answered for him. "Just wait until Father turns it in. Then a girl in my office puts it into a word processor. Much faster that way."

I tugged at my ear. "Just so I'm absolutely clear about this, what you're telling me is that neither one of you has actually read a word of the *Tulsa* manuscript, correct?"

I didn't get a response out of either of them. They just looked at me, waiting for me to keep talking. So I did. "How do you know that there even *is* a *Tulsa* manuscript?"

"Because Tommy's been working on it like a demon for more than a year," Addison answered. "And before that he spent months in Oklahoma researching it."

"And you trust Tommy," I said to him. "He's a top-notch guy. Completely reliable."

"Completely," Addison agreed emphatically.

I glanced over at Sylvia. "Yet *you* think he's a liar and a thief. You told me so at the Algonquin."

"What I told you is that I think he's playing hardball," she said. "I'll bet you Norma put him up to this—whatever *this* is."

"It happened on the Friday evening before Labor Day weekend. Why weren't you out at your place in the Hamptons, Mr. James?"

"Because I abhor holiday crowds. And Tommy had phoned to tell me that he had the pages ready."

"Do *you* believe that he was mugged?"

Addison sighed impatiently. "What I believe is that this is about money."

"Why do you say that?"

"Because when you're as rich as I am, *everything* is about money. Sylvia, why don't you just find out how much he wants and give it to him?"

"I-I can't. He's disappeared."

"Mr. James, what are you prepared to offer him to make things right?"

"Who says things are wrong?" he demanded.

"Tommy does."

"So you've been in touch with him," Sylvia said to me accusingly.

"He claims that Sylvia promised him coauthor credit and a one-third share of the royalties on your previous two books—*Tulsa* would make three—and then reneged on it."

"Preposterous!" Addison erupted. "I would *never* share cover credit with anyone else. I'm Addison fucking James! Besides, I just told you, Tommy doesn't write the books. *I* do!"

"F-Father . . . ?"

"W-What?" Addison responded mockingly.

"You h-haven't written a first draft in over five years."

"Of course I have. See this right here? It's called a typewriter. I write on it each and every day. Plan to do so as soon as you let me watch what's left of *Perry Mason* so I can get back to work."

"On what?" I asked him.

"On my next book."

"What's the title of your next book?"

He looked at me blankly.

"Is it *San Antonio*?" I asked.

He nodded. "*San Antonio*, right."

"Wrong. You published *San Antonio* in 1973."

He glared at me. "You're starting to get on my nerves, young man."

"I hear that a lot. Can't imagine why."

"Are we done here?" he demanded abruptly. "Because I need for both of you to leave right now. And that smelly dog, too. We're finished. GET OUT!"

We stepped our way around the shards of the broken Perrier bottle. I slid a pocket door open and we went out into the hallway. As I slid the door shut behind us, I could hear Raymond Burr's voice blaring from the TV.

Sylvia started down the hallway and then stopped, biting down hard on her lower lip. Her father had just totally humiliated her in front of me. I felt certain that it was taking every ounce of self-control she possessed to not break down and start sobbing.

"When I was a little boy I had a habit of humming while I ate."

"You . . . you what?"

"True story. I used to hum tunelessly under my breath. Don't ask me why. I wasn't even aware that I was doing it. I was only four years old. To break me of the habit, my father would reach across the table and flick me incredibly hard in the face with his index finger. The fingernail would leave a scratch, sometimes even make my face bleed."

"Did it work?" Sylvia asked me.

"Sure did. I stopped humming. Developed a facial twitch instead that I had until I was fifteen. I still get it to this day if I'm really tired or upset."

"I try *so* hard not to let him get to me . . ."

"He's your father. He always will. There's no way around it."

Sylvia resumed walking. As we headed down the hall we passed Yvette's suite. She was curled up on her loveseat reading a fashion magazine. "He threw a Perrier bottle at me really hard," she informed Sylvia. "If it had hit me, I'd be in the emergency room right now."

"What did you do to provoke him?" Sylvia's voice was devoid of warmth.

"She didn't do a thing," I said. "He just wanted her to leave."

"He's getting angrier," Yvette said. "And violent."

"Has he struck you?" Sylvia asked her.

"Not yet, but he's really starting to scare me. Can't you do anything?"

"Such as what?"

"Talk to his doctor maybe?"

Sylvia let out a pained sigh. "I don't know what good it'll do, since he refuses to undergo any kind of testing. But I can try."

"Thank you, Sylvia."

As we left Yvette's doorway, she waggled her little fingers at me and mouthed the words *Call me.*

We resumed walking toward the grand staircase. "Your father mentioned he has a Studebaker GT Hawk garaged near here. He doesn't actually drive the thing, does he?"

"As a matter of fact he does, even though his doctor has forbidden it."

"Where does he drive it?"

"Out to the Hamptons."

"In that case, please let me know the next time he's going, will you?"

"Why?"

"Because I want to make sure I'm not on the road at the time. I can't believe he has a driver's license."

"He doesn't. He doesn't have insurance either, but he never lets such petty concerns bother him. He's Addison James."

My trench coat and fedora were where I'd left them. I put them back on and then helped Sylvia on with her raincoat, one of those cheap black plastic ones that fold up into little travel pouches.

We rode the elevator down to the lobby in silence. The rain was still coming down hard. We waited under the awning out front while the doorman hailed a cab for us.

"I'm heading downtown. Can I drop you somewhere?"

Sylvia nodded. "My office."

The cab pulled up smartly at the awning. The doorman got the door. We hopped in and off we sped.

"Our first stop will be Sixth Avenue and 52nd Street," she informed him, crinkling her nose. Lulu had gotten damp again.

"Are you willing to pay Tommy off if that'll get *Tulsa* back?" I asked her.

"I detest the idea of rewarding such behavior," she fumed, falling silent for a moment before she said, "Do you think fifty thou would satisfy him?"

"It might. Trouble is, I'm not convinced that he has the thing. He's always been a straight-arrow newspaperman. Going on the lam with *Tulsa* isn't exactly his style. And it's not as if he's made a ransom demand."

"Where is he hiding? What does he have to say for himself?"

"Don't crowd me, Sylvia. Let me do my job."

She rode in brittle silence as the cab worked its way slowly down Broadway in the sluggish rainy day traffic. "Tell him I'll pay him whatever he wants to buy his silence," she said finally. "The media must never find out that Tommy has written Addison's last three books. If they do, then Addison will be painted as a world-class literary fraud. His name will be ruined, his life's work trashed. Nothing that he's accomplished over the past forty years will ever be seen in the same light again."

"I understand."

"Do you?" She glared down her nose at me. "I don't think so. For you, this is nothing more than a payday. For me, this is Addison's legacy. I can't imagine that means anything to a man such as you."

Lulu let out a low growl from the floor of the cab. I told her to let me handle it.

"*A man such as me?* What's that supposed to mean?"

"It means that you don't care about a single damned thing."

"Sylvia, if it makes you feel better to believe that, then go right ahead. But I'm not who you think I am. And I'm not the bad guy here."

"Who is?"

"I don't know yet. But I will before long. There's something clumsy about the way this went down. We're not dealing with a polished professional."

"Whom are we dealing with?"

"Someone who's greedy and frightened."

"Everyone I know is greedy and frightened."

"Then you need to start hanging around with a better class of people."

"I don't 'hang around' with any class of people. I have better things to do with my time."

After that Sylvia James didn't say another word to me. Just sat there silently picking at her scalp as we worked our way toward Midtown. When the cab dropped her outside of the offices of Guilford House she didn't offer to split the fare. Didn't say goodbye. Just got out, slammed the cab door shut behind her, schlumped across the sidewalk in the rain and passed through one of her building's revolving doors, disappearing inside.

She never looked back.

Chapter Three

Stuyvesant Town, also known as StuyTown and the White People's Projects, was a vast eighty-acre complex of identical charm-free brick apartment towers that had been built east of First Avenue between East 14th and East 20th Streets back in 1947 by Metropolitan Life to serve as middle-class housing for returning World War II servicemen and their families. Along with its slightly more upscale companion, Peter Cooper Village, which filled another chunk of acreage between East 20th and East 23rd, StuyTown made for an immense slice of lower Manhattan that was not to be found on any must-see tourist guides. When starry-eyed young performers made their way to the Big Apple in search of fame and fortune, their dream destination was Greenwich Village, not StuyTown. In fact, many of them lived in the city for years without discovering that it even existed. Artsy it was not. Quite the opposite. In fact, if you happened to wander in there, you didn't feel as if you were in New York City at all—more like in a Bethesda, Maryland, enclave for federal government workers, or a minimum security prison.

The apartment buildings were situated around a central oval with a fountain. Oval was the theme of the entire place. For U.S. Postal Service purposes, each building was singled out by its oval number. I think there were nineteen in all, but don't hold me to that. The ovals were connected by a labyrinth of footpaths that looped around and through the acres and acres of identical buildings. It was painfully easy to get lost there if you didn't know exactly where you were going—especially after dark. When I was in college up in Cambridge I had a classmate who'd grown up there and called it a "soul-sucking hell mouth." Apparently, when he was in high school he'd come back late one night tripping on acid and was so wasted that he couldn't find his way home. Just kept wandering from oval to oval until he ended up slumped on a bench, sobbing hysterically. A security guard had to escort him to his building.

Fortunately, Lulu was with me and knew exactly where we were going—she'd been to No. 11 Stuyvesant Oval once before. For Lulu, once is all it takes. So after the cab left us off on First Avenue she headed straight for it without hesitation, ignoring the intersecting paths that were of no use to her. She definitely earned an anchovy treat.

When we arrived at No. 11, I buzzed Tommy and Kathleen O'Brien's apartment, identified myself to the voice that answered the intercom and was buzzed in. The lobby, if you consider a wall of mailboxes and a couple of elevators a lobby, smelled like chicken soup.

The O'Briens lived in a two-bedroom apartment on the third floor. Kathleen was waiting halfway down the hallway for me in front of her open doorway. I'd remembered Tommy's wife as being an attractive, high-spirited redhead with rosy cheeks, sparkly blue eyes and a shapely figure. But I hadn't seen her in several years and time had not been on her side. Just for starters, her head of wavy, flaming red hair was tied back in a tight ponytail that was, well, not red. Dark brown was more like it. She'd dyed her hair red all of those years, I guess. I didn't really feel like thinking about it too much. Her blue eyes were dull, not sparkly, and had bags under them. Her complexion was the color of wet clay. There was also the weight issue, as in she'd put on a lot of it. Exactly how much was hard to tell because she was wearing a baggy Yankees T-shirt and an equally baggy pair of gym shorts, but I'd guess that she was a solid thirty pounds heavier than she'd been when I'd last seen her.

She eyed me suspiciously as she stood there in the hallway. We'd never been close. I was Tommy's hotshot writer friend. The Tommy who yearned to be a hotshot writer himself. The Tommy who'd recently packed his bags and left her. "Stewart Hoag," she said accusingly. "What brings *you* here?"

"I came to tell you he's safe."

"Tommy? Why wouldn't he be?"

"He was mugged on Friday night and disappeared—along with the only two copies in existence of *Tulsa*. Sylvia James has asked me to find him."

"Find *Tulsa*, you mean. Tommy, she could care less about."

"I thought you might be concerned about him."

"Why would I be? We split up. He lives his life, I live mine."

"Be that as it may, we need to talk. May I come in?"

She sniffed at the air. "Does that smelly dog have to come in, too?"

"If you don't mind," I said as Lulu whimpered in protest. "We're a team."

Kathleen peered at me, mystified, before she let out a sigh. "Fine."

It was a bit warm in there—Met Life hadn't wired Stuyvesant Town for air conditioners when they'd built it and stubbornly refused to upgrade. There wasn't a window unit to be found anywhere in the entire complex. But there were shade trees outside of the windows, so it really wasn't too bad with all of the fans that Kathleen had going. It was certainly cooler than my place.

The living room had wall-to-wall carpeting and a decidedly suburban vibe, circa 1962. The floral-patterned sectional sofa and matching armchair had plastic slipcovers over them. So did the lampshades on the end tables. Framed high school graduation photos of the O'Briens' two girls sat atop a TV that was tucked inside a decorative shelving unit. Hardcover copies of the half-dozen most recent Addison James blockbusters were prominently displayed on the shelves. Two framed still lifes, rather awful, hung from the wall over the sofa.

"I take painting classes at the YMCA," Kathleen said defensively as I eyed them. "What the hell else is there to do?"

She led me down a short hall to the eat-in kitchen, where there was a dinette set next to a window with a nice view of the barges going by on the East River. An open box of Entenmann's chocolate doughnuts was parked on the table. She was having herself an afternoon doughnut and coffee break—or perhaps *binge* would be a better way of putting it. Kathleen poured me a cup from the electric percolator on the counter and set it before me.

"Have a doughnut," she said, grabbing one for herself.

"Thanks, I'm all set."

"You take milk in your coffee?"

"Please."

As soon as she started for the refrigerator Lulu parked herself in front of it, gazing up at her beseechingly.

Kathleen frowned down at her. "She wants something?"

"You wouldn't happen to have a jar of anchovies, would you?"

"Your dog likes anchovies?"

"She has unusual eating habits."

"Is that why she smells so awful?"

"No, that has to do with the rain. Her coat is imbued with an oil that—"

"It's okay, I really don't need to know." Kathleen found a jar of anchovies in the refrigerator door, opened it and offered one to Lulu, nearly losing a finger in the transaction. Then Lulu curled up contentedly at my feet.

Kathleen sat down across the table from me and lit a Kent, which had advertised itself on TV commercials back when I was a little kid in the Fabulous Fifties as the only cigarette that featured the "scientific" Micronite filter. Only recently, in 1991, had a huge lawsuit finally unearthed that for several years back in the Fabulous Fifties one of the chief ingredients of the "scientific" Micronite filter had been highly toxic asbestos. Just one of those dirty little secrets that had made the fifties so fabulous.

Kathleen took a deep drag, blowing the smoke toward the window, and studied me in a less than friendly fashion. "Her name is Norma, as you no doubt know. She's an editor at Deep River. She's young, skinny, and for months he swore to me it was strictly business. She was helping him structure his idea for a novel. 'If it's strictly business,' I said to him, 'then why are you coming home at three in the morning with a hickey on your neck?' So I took up with Richie, and Tommy and I were living here under the same roof, leading our separate lives, for six whole months until he decided to move out a few weeks ago. No discussion. No nothing. He just packed some clothes, stuffed his briefcase full of pages, picked up his typewriter and cleared out. I haven't spoken to him since."

"And are you happy with Richie?"

"He's a nice, regular guy," she said, brightening slightly. "We met at the Y. He takes painting classes, too. He's divorced, lives on Oval Seven. He's a cop. Was a cop, I should say. He had to take early retirement because of a medical disability. Got two herniated discs in his back after some crackhead shoved him down a flight of stairs."

"What does he do with himself now?"

"Odd jobs. He's good with his hands. He repairs things for tenants. Drives them to the airport and picks them up. That sort of thing."

"He has a car?"

She nodded. "A Trans Am. Keeps it in that big garage on East 20th. You want to know the best thing about Richie? He actually enjoys being with me. Tommy doesn't anymore."

"What's Richie's last name?"

"Why you asking?"

"Just curious."

"It's Filosi. We have fun together. We go to movies. Go out to dinner. He takes me for drives in the country. We even talk. Tommy and I never talked anymore. He was always locked away in the girls' old room at his desk—eighteen hours a day, seven days a week—working himself into a state of exhaustion for that mean old millionaire who wouldn't give him a nickel or an ounce of respect. I make Richie happy. I haven't made Tommy happy for I don't know how long. I gave him two daughters. Kept a clean apartment. Did the marketing and the cooking, took his mother to the doctor for him, God rest her soul." She reached for another doughnut, munching on it. "As soon as the girls left for college, it was like our life together ended. He acted like I wasn't even here. What's wrong with me, anyhow?"

"Not a thing. Tommy's a writer. We're lost inside of our own heads most of the time. That doesn't make us the easiest people to live with."

"Tell me something I don't already know," she said sharply. "I'm divorcing him. And I'm going to make out plenty okay, too. We're talking infidelity, mental cruelty. Plus I'll bet you he's been socking away more money from that old man than he's been willing to admit to me. It wouldn't surprise me one bit if he's got a safety deposit box somewhere stuffed full of cash."

"Tommy doesn't get a share of Addison's royalties, if that's what you're thinking. Just a straight salary. He's very upset about that, too. It seems that Addison's daughter, Sylvia, promised him coauthor credit and royalty participation for the last three books, and she never intended to keep her promise. She was just stringing him along."

Kathleen sipped her coffee, narrowing her gaze at me. "Did you introduce them?"

"Who?"

"Tommy and *Norma*. I figure it must have been you."

"You figure wrong. I don't know a thing about the two of them."

She stubbed out her Kent and lit another one, gazing at me

through a haze of smoke. "Yeah, you do. You just don't want to tell me."

"Kathleen, I've never even met Norma. I haven't seen Tommy for over six months. And why on earth would I want to break up your marriage?"

"It's no secret that you don't think I'm good enough for him."

"It's certainly a secret to me. I don't know what Tommy has told you about me, but here's my version, okay? He took a creative writing class from me fifteen years ago. I read some of his work. I thought he had real talent. Still do. I liked the guy. Still do. When he was offered the job working for Addison James, I advised him to turn it down. I thought he needed to find his own voice. But he decided to take it."

"We needed the money for the girls. Mary ended up going to Syracuse. Anne's at Seton Hall." Kathleen smoked in silence for a moment, softening slightly. "He loved being a beat reporter. He'd have been happier if he never left the newspaper. We'd have scraped by somehow. You were right. He should have turned it down. The fool's been researching and writing an 800-page book every two years that makes tens of millions for that mean old man and all he gets out of it is $50,000 a year. Never so much as a Christmas bonus. What's a lousy couple of thousand dollars to that cheap old bastard? Nothing. To us it would have meant a week in the Bahamas. A chance for Tommy to breathe a little." Kathleen tilted her head at me, studying me anew. "Why are you here? What do you want from me?"

"The only two existing copies of *Tulsa* have vanished. Tommy told me two street punks snatched his briefcase from him Friday night and a guy with a gun warned him, 'We know where you live.' Tommy's been hiding out ever since, afraid for his life. Mind you, Sylvia's not buying any of that. She thinks that Tommy's holding *Tulsa* for ransom."

"And what do *you* think?"

"Tommy's an old school reporter, not someone who'd cook up a scheme like that. Besides, there are other players in this game."

"Like who?"

"The fewer details you know, the better."

Her eyes crinkled at me with concern. "So you've seen him?"

"I have."

"How is he?"

"Exhausted and terrified. He's tangling with some ruthless people."

"You still haven't told me why you're here."

"I wanted to find out the truth for myself."

"The truth about what?"

"May I see his office?"

She got up and led me down a short hallway. "It used to be the girls' room, but they gave it up when they went away to college."

"Where do they sleep when they're home from school?"

"The living room sofa opens up into a bed. They've always shared a room. Now they share a bed," she said with weary resignation. "Not exactly ideal, but it's just temporary. They'll have their own places soon enough."

The office door was closed, as were the windows. It was hot and stuffy in there. Also cluttered. Kathleen opened the windows a bit, mindful of the rain pattering against the screens. The girls' bedroom furniture had been replaced by a beat-up steel desk and three metal filing cabinets. Lulu made a quick circuit, nose to the rug, then returned to the hallway and stretched out.

I stood in there gazing around. A large wall map of Tulsa,

Oklahoma, dated 1919, was tacked to one wall. On another wall there was a storyboard that had 3-by-5-inch note cards in assorted colors stuck to it with pushpins, a writing technique that I've never understood or found useful. I'm a strict adherent of the late, great Theodore Sturgeon's second law: *The reader can never know where the story is going if the author himself does not know.* But it seems to work for some people. Scribbled on the cards were phrases like *T & T Oil swindle, 1918, Debutante ball, first fistfight, 1926,* and *Birth of Bonita, 1933.* There were also dozens of Polaroid photos tacked to the walls—shots of elegant and not-so-elegant houses, the entrance to a fancy country club, government buildings, shopping districts. There were books piled on the floor. Also shoeboxes filled with dozens of tape cassettes from interviews that Tommy had conducted. One of the shoeboxes was marked "Prof. Henry Thompson, Okla State U," the other "Greg Rollie, columnist, *Tulsa Daily World.*" Notepads were heaped on the desk. So were Tommy's early typewritten drafts, which were piled more than a foot high. I leafed through a few pages, pausing at random to read a snatch from Chapter 1: *Before there was a Tulsa there was the prairie and the Indians and the buffalo who roamed that prairie and sustained the Indians who lived and died there.*

One of the notepads on the desk had been set aside from the others. On its cover Tommy had written ADDISON'S INPUT in big black letters. I flipped it open, glancing at Tommy's notes from his story sessions with the most successful novelist of the past half-century: *A tale of two eras: Pre-oil boom, post-oil boom . . . Keep Indian and settler stories parallel . . . Intertwine by way of Bonita and her baby . . . Brandon is straight arrow, Weath-*

erby a conniving crook . . . Male offspring of Weatherby's Indian mistress doesn't know Weatherby is his father. Lives with his Indian mother. Graduates from law school, enters politics. Is in love with Tulsa's richest society debutante, unaware that they share the same father . . .

To me, Addison's story input came across as if it had been cobbled together from an old Clark Gable/Spencer Tracy MGM movie. But it was also exactly the sort of thing that his millions of readers had been lapping up for decades.

I flipped the pad shut and put it back down on the desk, satisfied. Part of me, the part that suspects the worst and believes nothing, had been wondering if there was no *Tulsa* manuscript and never had been. If Tommy had somehow gotten himself mixed up in an elaborate shell game of Sylvia's devising. He hadn't. The book was real. And worst-case scenario—which is to say if I couldn't recover *Tulsa* from whoever had it—Tommy could conceivably reconstruct his final draft from the earlier ones. Authors lose their final drafts to fires and floods all of the time. Shit happens. But it would take him many months and push back the pub date of *Tulsa* from the summer of '94 to '95, which would constitute a huge financial blow to Guilford House. Could that be why this had happened? To deliver a gut punch to Sylvia and Guilford House? Who would have an interest in doing that, and why?

"He'd lock himself in here every single day," Kathleen said to me in a quiet, strained voice. "He'd come out to eat, pass out for a few hours, then go back to work. He never took a day off. Never even left the apartment unless it was to ride the subway uptown to see Addison. Sometimes I'd wake up in the middle of the night and find him fast asleep facedown on his typewriter with ink all over his stupid face. All he did was work and work. And for what? Why did he push himself so hard?"

"He wants to be a writer."

"He *is* a writer."

"A famous one who is admired and looked up to. Men aren't very complicated. We want to stand out."

"But what about enjoying yourself a little?"

"Writers are a peculiar breed, like I said. We're obsessed. And we're never, ever satisfied."

"*You* seem happy enough."

"Sure I am, aside from the part where I crash-landed for an entire decade."

She glanced down at the desk. "He must have made eight trips to Oklahoma researching the damned thing."

"Do you have his travel and expense receipts?"

"No, he always gave those to Sylvia. Half of the time I never even knew exactly where he was. It's not like he'd call me every night from some motel and say, 'Hi, honey,' and we'd talk over his day. He'd just be gone for weeks at a time and then one day he'd show up here with a suitcase full of dirty laundry and fall into bed. If I asked him how the trip went he'd say, 'I'm tired. Leave me alone.' So I did."

"And now he has Norma and you have Richie."

"That's right," she said, raising her chin at me. "Tell me more about *Norma*. Does he want to marry her?"

"I have no idea. I told you, I didn't know he was seeing another woman."

"And I still don't believe you," Kathleen said defiantly as we stood there in the cluttered office that had once been their daughters' bedroom. "He always talked about you like you were his best friend."

"I'm not."

"Then what are you?"

"You'd have to ask him that."

"He doesn't speak to me anymore, remember?"

"All I know about her is that she's young and a climber."

"So what good can Tommy do her? He's not some famous author and no one's ever mistaken him for Patrick Swayze."

"Kathleen, I truly don't know," I said, suddenly starting to feel trapped and suffocated in there. I backed out into the hall and started toward the front door to fetch my raincoat and fedora. Lulu was already waiting for me. She felt trapped and suffocated, too. "Like I keep trying to tell you, I've never met Norma Fives. But I intend to."

FOR AS LONG as I'd been an aspiring novelist, successful novelist, stoned-out wreck of a novelist and celebrity ghostwriter—which is to say for as long as I'd lived in New York—there'd always been a watering hole somewhere in Midtown Manhattan that was, by unwritten accord, the designated safe haven where literary and theatrical people could meet in public without meeting in public. If a major Broadway producer was cheating on his wife, he could safely meet another woman, or man, for a discreet drink there. If a big-time literary agent was trying to steal another agency's client, the courting would take place there. Once you walked through the door, you became legally blind. If you saw someone you knew you didn't see them and they didn't see you. Gossip columnists like Liz Smith and Cindy Adams respected this understanding and never so much as mentioned the name of the place—which, during most of the 1980s, was Trader Vic's, the dimly lit old-time tiki bar in the basement of the Plaza Hotel. But after the famously sleazy real estate developer/con man/tabloid clown Donald Trump bought the Plaza in 1988, he evicted Trader Vic's on the grounds that he considered it "tacky."

I can pause here for a moment if you'd like to chortle. Virtually everyone in New York did.

After the chortling subsided, a new safe haven had to be found. These days, it was Benny Eng's Wan-Q, a dimly lit retro nonchic Cantonese restaurant on West 56th Street two doors down from the rear entrance to the Essex House. Wan-Q had a burbling Buddha fountain by the front door. It even had a tiki bar motif so that sentimentalists who resented having been evicted from Trader Vic's by the Donald would feel at home.

It was quiet in there at four on a rainy afternoon. Benny Eng, who is a burbling Buddha himself, greeted Lulu and me effusively, took my soaked trench coat and fedora to hang on the rack by the door and led us to a high-backed wooden booth near the rear, where young Norma Fives was seated, sipping a glass of white wine.

I don't know what I was expecting Norma to look like. Actually, that's not true. I was expecting her to be hot. She turned out to be a scrawny, hawk-nosed little woman wearing a pair of thick horn-rimmed glasses. Her blunt chin-length hairdo looked as if she'd cut it herself in the bathroom mirror with a pair of poultry shears. What with the glasses, the hairdo and the boxy, short-sleeved linen dress that she had on, Norma looked eerily like one of those nutso skinny-armed little girls in Roz Chast's *New Yorker* cartoons. Hot she was not. Not unless you consider a young Imogene Coca in horn-rims hot. Calm she was not. In fact, she was so nervous as I approached her that the wineglass shook in her hand, its contents sloshing over the rim. And yet she was *the* most-talked-about young editor in the publishing business. Super smart. Super ambitious. A force to be reckoned with.

And Tommy O'Brien had dynamited his marriage because of her.

She gulped at me. "Mr. Hoag?"

"Make it Hoagy."

"It's an honor to meet you. I admired *Our Family Enterprise* immensely."

"Thank you."

"And Tommy can't say enough great things about you."

"Don't believe any of it." I sat across from her in the booth, ignored the extensive menu of "Tropicocktails" and ordered a Chinese beer for myself and a plate of fried shrimp for Lulu, hold the dipping sauces. Lulu circled around three times under the table and curled up there to wait.

Norma watched her curiously. "So this is the famous Lulu."

"No, I ditched Lulu last year. Too high maintenance. This is her cousin Sweet Emily."

"Tommy warned me you were a kidder. You're teasing me, right?"

"Little bit."

The waiter brought me my beer. I sampled it, found it a bit flat and sprinkled some salt on it to liven up its head as he returned with Lulu's shrimp. She promptly dove in.

Norma studied me in fascinated silence for a moment before she said, "I hear you're working on a new novel and that it's mondo terrific. I'd love to see it when you have something to show."

"Sylvia James has already offered me money for it."

"You haven't signed a contract yet, have you?"

"No, Alberta's considering her offer a floor bid."

"Awesome." Norma smiled at me with vulpine pleasure. "There are very few things in life that make me happier than outbidding Sylvia on a major book."

"Sylvia warned me about you."

Norma took a small, careful sip of her wine. "What did she say?"

"That you were unscrupulous."

She let out a bray of a laugh. "Coming from Sylvia, that's an Olympic-caliber compliment. Did she happen to mention that my first job in publishing was serving as her personal assistant at Guilford House?"

"As a matter of fact she didn't."

"Well, she wouldn't, would she?"

"Meaning . . . ?"

"Have you noticed that ghastly jagged scar directly under her left eye?"

"I have."

"You're looking at the girl who gave it to her," Norma said proudly.

"*You* gave it to her? How?"

"By hurling a Stanley Bostitch stapler across the conference table at her during our weekly editorial meeting. A mere half an inch higher and she could have spent the rest of her life wearing an eye patch just like her crazy father."

"Just out of curiosity, why did . . . ?"

"Why did I throw a Stanley Bostitch stapler at her? Because she screamed at me and called me a 'retarded anorexic cunt' for contradicting her in front of the entire editorial staff. This was after two years of suffering the worst kind of abuse and torment a lowly assistant can be expected to endure. I graduated from Bryn Mawr, same as Sylvia did. My English lit professor was a classmate of hers. When I told her I wanted to get into publishing, she contacted Sylvia and Sylvia took me on as her assistant. My first day at work everyone in the office smirked at me and said, 'Nice knowing you.' I quickly found out why. Sylvia's the single nastiest, most abusive woman I've ever met. She used to berate me until I cried. She also has no sense of professional ethics whatsoever. She's a conniver, a liar and an outright thief."

"But otherwise you like her a lot."

Norma allowed herself a faint smile.

"She stammers, you know."

"Nay, not so. I went through two years of hell with her and not once did I ever hear her stammer."

"That's because you were never in a room with her when she was with her father. She no doubt does everything she can to make sure that no one ever sees the two of them together, but in my case it was unavoidable. And if you think *she's* abusive, you should see the old man in action. It's almost enough to make you feel sorry for her."

"Wait, feel sorry for *Sylvia*?"

"You'll note that I said almost."

Norma took another careful sip of her wine. "That woman tried to break me. It's the only form of pleasure she knows."

"But she didn't break you."

"No way, José. She just made me stronger and stronger until that memorable Monday morning when I called her a deranged bitch in front of everyone and hurled that Stanley Bostitch stapler at her as hard as I could."

"Did she file assault charges against you?"

"Nope, just tried to fire me. I said, 'You can't fire me. I've already quit.' Walked straight to the elevator and never went back. One of my friends brought my purse, coat and personal things down to me in the lobby. Then I went home and made some calls. Two days later I had a job at Deep River."

I sipped my beer, gazing across the table at her. Now that she was done regaling me with her triumphant tale about the Stanley Bostitch stapler she seemed ill at ease again. Squirmy. Couldn't sit still.

"I'm told you're a rising star over there. Hear nothing but good things about you," I said.

"Thank you. That's nice to know."

"So tell me about you and Tommy."

She lowered her gaze, running a finger around the rim of her wineglass. "Just for starters, I never thought that I'd find myself mixed up with a forty-five-year-old married man. I don't see myself as that sort of person."

"What sort of person?"

"A home-wrecking slut. But he told me that he and his wife have an understanding."

"If you call not speaking to each other an understanding, then they have an understanding."

"Tommy calms me down, which is truly major for me. I'm a nervous wreck from the moment I open my eyes in the morning until the moment I try to close them at night. I don't sleep.

Sit up reading most nights until four, five A.M. Tommy's good for me. He makes me feel safe."

"He's not feeling very safe himself right now."

"But he should be okay at your place, shouldn't he?"

"What makes you think he's at my place?"

"He called me from there."

Damn. I'd told him to stay away from the phone.

"Besides, you're that kind of friend."

"What kind is that?"

"The kind who won't bail on him." She took a deep, ragged breath before she said, "He's the first man I've ever loved. I've loved boys. But Tommy's a man. He has genuine life experience. He has depth."

"You sound pretty serious about him."

"I am."

"So why didn't he move in with you when he left Kathleen?"

"Couldn't. I have a tiny studio down on Bank Street that's barely big enough for me and the mice. But we're definitely talking about getting a place together. I have real hopes for us. And for Tommy's career. I think he has tremendous untapped potential. I can help him. I want to help him. In fact, I have a firm deal for serious money that I could offer him right now if he weren't under contract to Addison James for slave wages."

Our waiter returned, retrieved Lulu's cleaned dish and asked us if we wanted another round of drinks. We did.

"What sort of a firm deal?"

"Three years ago I signed up a nifty little thriller by a young copy editor at *People* named Rose Ellen Hartmann for no money, by which I mean $8,000. It was called *The Girl Under the Bed*." Norma paused so that I could let out a suitably awestruck gasp. I don't do suitably awestruck gasps. She sat there with her mouth open, momentarily thrown, before she recovered and kept on going. "We published it in June of last year and it's still on the *New York Times* bestseller list sixty-two weeks later. We've sold the foreign rights in forty-two different countries. Castle Rock paid $1 million for the film rights. The movie, starring Julia Roberts, comes out in December and will send our paperback sales through the roof." Norma hesitated before she added, "Naturally, we signed Rose Ellen to a seven-figure contract to write three more books for us."

"Of course you did."

"But there's been a slight hitch."

"Of course there has. That's what makes publishing such good, clean fun."

Our waiter returned with her wine and my beer. Norma reached for her glass and this time took a large gulp. "Rose Ellen has no second idea. In fact, she sort of crashed and burned after the incredible success of *The Girl Under the Bed*. Had to spend some time in a facility in upstate New York."

"Coke?"

Norma blinked at me. "How did you know?"

"Been there, snorted that."

"Now she's gone home to live with her parents in Maine for a while. She's sort of in hiding, so please don't ask me exactly where in Maine she is."

"Wasn't planning to."

"I want Tommy to ghost her second book for her. I can offer him $250,000 and 25 percent of the royalties."

"Can you get his name on the cover?"

"That I can't do. Deep River thinks Rose Ellen is going to be a franchise author once she gets her head on straight. Still, it's a major pay hike for him and it's royalty participation and . . . you're looking at me dubiously. Why?"

"Does Tommy know how to write a thriller?"

"Did you read *The Girl Under the Bed*?"

"No, I don't go in for that sort of thing."

"What *do* you go in for?" Norma leaned forward, intensely curious.

"Good writing. E. B. White, John O'Hara . . ."

"Who's on your nightstand right now?"

"Shaw."

"George Bernard Shaw?"

"Irwin Shaw."

She looked at me in surprise. "You mean *Rich Man, Poor Man* Irwin Shaw? He was kind of a schlockmeister, wasn't he?"

I reached for a cocktail napkin, uncapped my Waterman fountain pen and wrote Merilee's home phone number on it, pushing it across the table to her. "Go home and read a short story he wrote called 'The Eighty-Yard Run.' Then call me at this number and say, 'Hi, it's Norma, and I'm a big fat idiot.'"

"Okay . . ." She jotted the title down on the napkin before she put it in her shoulder bag. "The point I was trying to make is that Rose Ellen Hartmann will never be mistaken for Daphne du Maurier. The uncredited work that Tommy's been doing for Addison James is of a much higher literary caliber. I have zero doubt he can write an even better thriller than *The Girl Under the Bed*. And when he does, Deep River will owe him big-time. I'll be able to sign him to write the novel he's always dreamed of writing."

"You're trying to set him free, in other words."

Norma nodded her head convulsively. "I'm trying to set him free."

"I assume Tommy told you what's happened to *Tulsa*."

She nodded again, this time unhappily. "Somebody mugged him and it's gone."

"Do you know anything more about it?"

"Why would *I* know anything more about it? And why would you even ask me that?"

"Because Sylvia's hired me to find it."

Norma's eyes widened in shock behind her heavy horn-rims. "I can't believe that a man of your literary stature is working for that awful woman."

"Norma, you're talking to someone who's been ghosting celebrity memoirs for the past decade. I've had to do all sorts of things I never thought I'd be doing. They have a word for that. It's called survival."

"In answer to your question, I don't know anything more than Tommy told me, which was that a couple of young black guys jumped him and stole his briefcase. I told him that he should have called the police, but he said a big scary guy with a gun threatened him."

"And you truly have no idea who's behind this?"

"None. Why do you keep insinuating that I do?"

"Because it's in your financial interest. If Sylvia fires Tommy in a fit of pique—not an unlikely scenario given her volatile personality—then he'll be free to write your Rose Ellen Hartmann thriller. You've already hurled a Stanley Bostitch stapler at Sylvia and nearly blinded her. What's stealing *Tulsa* in the grand scheme of things? You'd not only set Tommy free but totally mess up Guilford House's bottom line for next year."

Norma's thin lips tightened angrily. "I don't know what you've heard about me, but I'm not that sort of person. I don't steal. I don't lie. I love the publishing business. I love working with writers. I'm living my dream. I had absolutely nothing to do with what happened to *Tulsa*. I wouldn't even know how to go about setting up a street mugging or whatever the heck that was." She breathed in and out for a moment, recovering her composure. "Why don't you like me? Is it because Tommy's married?"

"I like you fine. And if you and Tommy love each other, I'm genuinely happy for both of you. But there's more at stake here than just *Tulsa*. Addison James is worth hundreds of millions of dollars. He has a greedy young tootsie of a wife and he has Sylvia around to watch over him like a hawk. I'm fully aware that Sylvia can't be trusted, just as I'm fully aware that Addison is as mad as a hatter. But I'm also convinced that whoever stole *Tulsa* is working some sort of a major scheme, and prior experience tells me that this is going to get a whole lot worse before it gets better. What I am, Norma, is afraid that you may end up exactly where Tommy is."

Norma Fives gazed at me in bewilderment. "Which is where?"

"In way, way over your head."

Chapter Four

The rain had finally let up, leaving behind a stifling blanket of warm, moist air and the exotic scent of Eau de Locker Room that emanated from the overflowing storm drains. Since I'd spent most of the day sitting in a succession of places listening to a succession of people tell me things I really didn't want to hear, I decided to walk through Central Park back to Tommy O'Brien's temporary hideout in my crummy fifth-floor walk-up.

Wan-Q was practically around the block from the park. Lulu and I went in at the 59th Street entrance and strolled along, me inhaling the freshly watered greenery, Lulu the damp soil alongside of the footpath as we made our way uptown past Strawberry Fields, which had been christened in 1985 to memorialize John Lennon's shooting death in 1980 outside of his apartment at the Dakota right across Central Park West. Some sicko named Mark David Chapman shot him. I'd heard the horrible news from none other than Howard Cosell, same as millions of others had. It was Cosell who'd broken it to us during an otherwise routine telecast of a New England Patriots/

Miami Dolphins game on *Monday Night Football*. One of those cultural oddities that you never, ever forget.

We walked, exiting the park at the American Museum of Natural History and working our way west toward Columbus Avenue, then Amsterdam and eventually Broadway, where the Loews 84th Street Cineplex was still showing the summer's biggest hit films—*Sleepless in Seattle*, a treacly romantic comedy starring the erotically charged duo of Tom Hanks and Meg Ryan, *The Firm*, a John Grisham thriller starring that adorable thirtysomething teenager Tom Cruise as a young lawyer who's all tied up with the mob, and *The Fugitive* with Harrison Ford, a blockbuster remake of the 1960s television series that starred David Janssen. The huge box office success of *The Fugitive* worried me. Since Hollywood is incapable of not devouring its own entrails, I couldn't help but wonder what other vintage hit series would soon be headed to the big screen. *The Mod Squad*? *Charlie's Angels*? *My Mother the Car*?

After we'd reached Broadway and West 93rd we turned left, crossed West End Avenue and started toward the river. There were patches of blue sky now and the September sun was still high enough over the New Jersey Palisades that I had to tug at the brim of my fedora and lower my gaze. When Lulu let out a low growl of warning, I looked up. Two blue-and-white squad cars were double-parked outside of my building and twenty or thirty people were clustered on the sidewalk there. My neighbors across the street—most of them Yushies, the Young Urban Shitheads who'd been invading the neighborhood like an army of smug cockroaches—were gathered on their stoops watching what was going on.

I elbowed my way through the crowd and discovered that someone was lying facedown under a blue tarp on the sidewalk there. A man's bare foot stuck out from under the blue tarp, a narrow trail of blood running from his body down to the gutter. A baby-faced cop in uniform stood grim watch over him while two others tried to keep the lookie-loos moving along.

"Something I can do for you?" he asked me.

"I live here. What's happened?"

"Somebody jumped off of the roof, is what's happened. He's got no ID, no keys, no nothing. None of the other tenants seem to know who he is. Mind having a look?"

"Go ahead," I said, trying, and failing, to keep the dread out of my voice.

He pulled back the tarp, and . . . well, it seemed that Tommy and I weren't going to be having that beer and huge laugh at the White Horse after all. He was still dressed in the oversize T-shirt and gym shorts I'd lent him. His nose and cheekbones were flattened from making direct high-impact contact with the pavement. Blood trickled from his nostrils and from the corner of his mouth. But he didn't look too bad. Most of his injuries were internal, I imagined, although I did notice that he also had a raised welt on the back of his head.

Lulu let out a low, unhappy whimper standing there next to me.

"Know who he is?" the young cop asked.

"His name's Tommy O'Brien. He didn't live here. He was crashing at my place for a few days because he and his wife, Kathleen, were having some problems. He lived in Stuyvesant Town. No. 11 Stuyvesant Oval."

"Okay, thanks. And you are . . . ?

"Stewart Hoag, apartment 9."

"He was having marital problems, you said?"

"I did."

"Was he despondent?"

"I've seen him happier."

"Unhappy enough to take his own life?"

"Yo, Procter, open your freaking eyes, will you?" a familiar-sounding voice hollered from behind me. "Dude's got a fresh wallop the size of a golf ball on the back of his bean, yet he's lying facedown. No way he's a jumper. Somebody whacked him and then gave him a helpful shove."

I turned to discover someone who chewed bubble gum with his mouth open standing there astride a racing bike. He was in his twenties, deeply tanned and had a lot of thick black hair, three or four days of stubble, an earring and those soft brown eyes that women get woozy over. I doubt he was more than five feet six, but his biceps and pecs rippled, his thigh muscles bulged and he had an air of hyperintensity about him. His head nodded rhythmically, as if he heard his own rock 'n' roll beat. Clad in his yellow tank top and electric-blue spandex shorts it would have been easy to mistake him for a bike messenger who was mainlining speed. Easy, that is, if he wasn't also wearing a navy blue NYPD windbreaker so that the public couldn't see the shoulder holster that held the Sig Sauer P226 semi-automatic that he and a lot of the new breed had started packing instead of the trusty old Smith & Wesson revolver.

Lulu let out a low whoop and moseyed over to say hi, her tail thumping. He bent down and patted her before he turned his gaze on me, his head nodding, nodding. "Long time no see, dude."

"Very."

He frowned at me. "Yeah, dude?"

"It's been a very long time," I said to Detective Lieutenant Romaine Very, who worked homicides out of the 24th Precinct on the Upper West Side. Officially, that is. Unofficially, he was the top homicide detective in the entire city—especially when there were celebrities involved. He'd achieved that status even though he was not yet thirty because he possessed a rare combination of brains, instincts and guts. Not to mention a BA in astrophysics from Columbia. It also didn't hurt that his rabbi was none other than Inspector Dante Feldman, the man who'd caught Son of Sam and was now the commanding officer of all of Manhattan's homicide detectives.

Romaine Very and I had crossed paths before on what turned out to be the biggest literary hoax in modern publishing history. Four people had ended up dead. Maybe you read about it.

Lulu, who had a real soft spot for him, continued to whoop and moan until he got off his bike, knelt down and gave her jowls and ears a good rub.

"Speaking the real, Procter," he said to the cop in uniform as Lulu tumbled over onto her back and let him scratch her tummy. "If you ever want to get out of your sack into plain clothes, then you need to use all of the sense organs that God gave you, especially your eyes. What do you have for me?"

"We're just getting started, Lieutenant," Procter replied nervously. "Happened maybe twenty minutes ago. Neighbors in the building didn't hear an argument or see anything. And we've got nothing from the neighboring buildings either. Crime scene units and coroner's men are on their way. There's a high-rise apartment building on the corner of Riverside four, five houses down."

"So . . . ?"

"So I'm kind of thinking maybe someone was looking out their window from a high floor and saw activity on the roof."

"Kind of good thinking, Procter. Get some more men over here to canvass the building. Also canvass the top-floor tenants of the brownstones on West 94th, the ones who live in back. They might have seen something."

Procter went off to his blue-and-white to phone it in.

Very shook his head at me irritably. "Half of these guys, they just stand around like department store mannequins waiting for someone to tell them what to do. They have zero initiative." He gave Lulu's tummy a final pat, then stood back up, his jaw working on his bubble gum. "How've you been, dude?"

"I was doing great right up until about ten minutes ago. Merilee and I are getting along really well, and I'm working on a novel."

"Is it good?"

"It's good."

"Super glad to hear that."

"And how are you, Lieutenant?"

Very made a face. "I've got insomnia like you wouldn't believe." Romaine Very paid a heavy price for his hyperintensity. He also suffered from migraines and chronic prostatitis. He rode the bike to try to burn off some of his extra steam. It didn't seem to help. "I need to have a look at your apartment. Stay with me." He carried his lightweight bike through the vestibule and propped it against the wall in the ground-floor hallway. Then we started up the stairs.

"How did Tommy's killer force him up onto the roof from my apartment?" I asked Very as we climbed.

"A gun makes for a pretty good persuader. Was Tommy really having marital problems or was he hiding out here from somebody?"

"Both. He was afraid to go home to the studio in Hell's Kitchen he's been renting since he moved out. The guy who staged the *Tulsa* theft Friday night warned him, 'We know where you live.' And showed him a gun."

"Okay, pull over, dude. I have no idea what we're talking about."

"Tommy was Addison James's ghostwriter."

"Wait, wait . . . *the* Addison James?"

"*The* Addison James, who is seventy-eight, senile and no longer capable of producing pages on his own. Tommy secretly wrote the man's last two bestsellers and had just finished a third, *Tulsa*. He took the only copy of the finished manuscript to a copier place on Broadway Friday evening to make a Xerox to submit to Addison's editor, who happens to be the old geezer's daughter, Sylvia. As soon as Tommy walked out of the door, a couple of street kids snatched his briefcase and handed it off to someone waiting in a cab. Tommy started toward the cab until he was warned not to by the aforementioned guy with the gun. He's been hiding out ever since."

Very grinned. "This is why I like working with you, dude. I can go two, three months without hearing anyone use the word *aforementioned* when they're running a case for me."

"He hid out in a cheap hotel near the Port Authority Bus Terminal for a few nights, then hid out on my roof last night. When I let him in this morning he was soaked and scared to death," I said as we reached the fifth-floor landing. Lulu and I were puffing slightly, Very not at all. The rooftop door was open. So was my apartment door. The lock didn't appear to have been tampered with.

"Jeez, it's hot in here," Very observed, grimacing as he glanced around at my living room.

"Lulu and I prefer tropical climates."

"I take it Tommy didn't report the mugging to the police."

"That's correct."

"Did he know who this gee was? The one with the gun?"

"No, but I may have an idea who he is."

"And this would be because . . . ?"

"Tommy's description—a huge, fleshy guy, maybe fifty, with curly red hair turning gray—matches a PI who works for the South Shore lawyer who's representing Addison's tasty young wife, Yvette. It seems she's trying to get a do-over on her prenup."

"Have you got a name for me?"

"Jocko Conlon."

Very made a face. "Yech."

"Yech?"

"He's slime. Used to be on the job here until he got bounced for being a small-time shakedown artist. You know the type: 'Give me a free three-course dinner or I'll call the health department and tell them I saw mouse droppings.' After that, he went to work for the Nassau County sheriff, where he got bounced yet again. And trust me, you've got to be serious slime to get bounced in Nassau County."

"You think he threw Tommy off the roof?"

"Wouldn't surprise me in the least. Who else besides you knew that Tommy was here?"

"His girlfriend, Norma Fives."

Very thumbed his jaw, his head nodding, nodding. "How?"

"He phoned her. I warned him not to use the phone. I thought there was a chance it might be bugged. But he didn't listen to me. Tell me, if someone with Jocko Conlon's skills wanted to bug my phone, how would he go about doing it?"

"One of two ways. Sophisticated or unsophisticated. The sophisticated way is to splice directly into your phone line down in the basement."

"And the unsophisticated?"

"Pick the lock to your front door when you're out and insert a mike into the mouthpiece of your phone. Those can transmit only two, three hundred yards, so it means he'd have to double-park outside in a van, listening in through a set of headphones. If we're talking Jocko, then I'd wager that's what he did." Very fished a pair of latex gloves from the pocket of his windbreaker, put them on, unscrewed the mouthpiece of my rotary phone and pulled out a small round transmitter. "See? He must've figured Tommy would come to you for help."

I thought this over, my mind working through the progression of steps that might lead Jocko to think Tommy would end up here.

"Did Tommy bring anything with him?" Very asked me.

"His wet clothes were hanging from the back of the bathroom door when I left this morning. His wallet and keys should be in his pants pockets, unless his killer took them. He didn't have anything else."

Very went and had a look. "His clothes are still here. Wallet and keys, too. We'll bag and tag them. I'm afraid this apartment's a crime scene. You'll have to find somewhere else to stay for a couple of days."

"Not a problem."

"Is there anything here that you need?"

"Aside from my sanity? Just some clothes."

"Then throw some stuff together. But first I want to go up top. Stay with me."

We went up the stairs onto the flat tar roof. Two cops in uniform were poking around up there in search of a possible weapon.

I didn't see one. There was nothing up there at all except for rain puddles and a ratty old plastic lounge chair that one of my neighbors sat on sometimes to work on her tan. Lulu sniffed and snorted her way around. Sat down for a moment. Got up, moved over a few feet and sniffed and snorted some more.

Very peered at her. "The hell's she doing?"

"I couldn't say. She doesn't always tell me everything."

"We need to talk this out, dude. I'm starved. Want to grab a burger?"

"Oh, I think we can do better than that."

ROMAINE VERY STOOD there, awestruck, in front of the living room windows gazing out at the sixteenth-floor view of Central Park. It was not yet dusk, but lights were beginning to twinkle in the apartment towers across the park on Fifth Avenue. He'd left his racing bike downstairs in the lobby after showing the doorman his shield. This would be the night doorman, Frank—the one who hated me. Since Very was something of a New York tabloid hero, this meant Frank would now start treating me with a lot more R-E-S-P-E-C-T.

"Dude, you actually used to live here?"

"I actually did." I deposited a suitcase stuffed with more of my clothing and two more garment bags in the master bedroom, where I hung my navy blue blazer in the closet and took off my tie before I rejoined him in the living room. "Right now I'm just house-sitting for Merilee until she gets back from Budapest."

"Sure it's not more than that?" he asked, peering at me.

"We're working at it. We did spend the entire summer together on her farm. Admittedly, I bunked in the guest cottage, but we got along really well. And she's never invited me to stay here before while she was away on location."

"I sure wish I had a woman in my life," he lamented, looking back out at the park. "It's not the part about being horny all of the time that bothers me, although that certainly enters into it."

"As it were."

"It's the not having someone to talk things over with. Someone who actually cares about me."

"I wouldn't think you'd have trouble meeting women."

"And you'd be wrong. What I do scares them off. They hear *homicide detective* and run for the hills."

"Lieutenant, I'll be happy to continue this installment of *Mary Worth* in half a tick, but first I have an important call to make. Please excuse me."

I went back into the master bedroom, sat down on the edge of the bed, called the Algonquin and asked to be connected with Alberta Pryce's table. When the Silver Fox got on the line, I told her that Tommy O'Brien had just been thrown off the roof of my crappy brownstone on West 93rd Street, which was where he'd been hiding out.

Alberta greeted this news with a heavy silence before she said, "Do they have any idea who did it?"

"Not yet, but it'll be on the local TV news soon if it isn't already. I thought you'd want to call Sylvia and tell her about it yourself."

"Yes, I'll do that right now. She's probably still at the office. I'm terribly sorry about your friend, dear boy. I'm also sorry I got you mixed up in this."

"No need to be. My eyes were wide open."

"Please forgive me if I sound like a money-grubbing agent, but have you had any luck finding *Tulsa*?"

"No, but I did find his rough drafts and research materials. If those two copies of the finished manuscript are really, truly gone then it'll be possible for someone—not me—to re-create what he wrote. But it'll be a tedious job and it means Guilford House will have no Addison James blockbuster next year."

Alberta treated me to another moment of heavy silence before she said, "Stay in touch. And, again, I'm terribly sorry."

After I'd hung up, I went into the kitchen and put down Lulu's can of 9Lives mackerel for cats and very weird dogs. Took the fresh mozzarella and hunk of aged Parmesan out of the refrigerator so they'd get to room temperature and opened two cold Bass ales. Very joined me in there.

"Have a seat." I handed him one of the bottles of Bass and rolled up my sleeves. "I'll run it for you while I make us something to eat."

He took a long, grateful gulp before he flopped down at the kitchen table. "I didn't know you could cook."

"Don't tell me you've forgotten how complex and multifaceted I am."

"What I am starting to remember is how annoying you are."

"I'm going to give you a free pass on that one, since it's as plain as the large black nose on Lulu's face that you're not getting nearly enough sleep or sex. I took to gardening this summer on the farm. Helped me sort out my thoughts while I was writing. The best part about it is that you get to eat the results. And if it's fresh out of the ground, you don't have to do much to it."

I grabbed three ripe heirloom tomatoes from the bowl on the table, cut them into slices, did the same to the fresh mozzarella, and arranged them on a platter. Plucked some fragrant basil leaves from their stems, tore them into pieces, scattered them over the cheese and tomatoes, then drizzled the plate with olive oil. The crusty loaf of bread that Merilee had bought was in the bread box. I tore us off a couple of hunks, handed Very a fork and said, "Dig in."

"Jesus, dude, this is unreal," he exclaimed after we'd both devoured several forkfuls.

I got the bags of three different salad greens out of the fridge, grabbed several handfuls from each bag, put them in a big pot and filled it with water. I lifted the greens out carefully so as to leave the dirt behind and put them in a spinner to dry them. Then I put them in an old wooden bowl Merilee and I bought in the Shenandoah Valley shortly after we were married and set them aside.

Lulu finished her dinner and curled up under the kitchen table with her head on Very's foot. He reached down and patted her.

"Yesterday I got a call from my agent to meet with Sylvia James, editor in chief of Guilford House, Addison James's personal editor and only child," I began. "His first wife died many years ago. It was Sylvia who told me that *Tulsa* had been snatched. She hired me to try to get it back. Since Tommy and I were old pals, she thought I'd be able to persuade him to come to his senses."

Very devoured the last of the tomatoes and mozzarella, mopping up the plate with his bread. "Meaning what?"

"Meaning she thought he'd made up the whole mugging story and was basically holding it for ransom until she made good on the lucrative contract he claimed she'd offered him and she claims she didn't."

"And who did we believe?"

"Tommy, most definitely." I squeezed the juice of a lemon through my fingers into a Pyrex measuring cup, discarded the pits, added an equal amount of extra virgin oil, then salt, pepper and a dab of Dijon mustard. "You'd have to hunt far and wide to find a single human being in the publishing world who trusts Sylvia," I said as I whisked the salad dressing. "She's a genuinely horrible human being. Nobody likes her. Not even her famous father, who bullies her with vicious glee."

I found a box of linguine in the cupboard. Got out the Lodge cast-iron skillet. Put a pot of salted water on to boil, then slivered several cloves of fresh garlic. "Sylvia's also the heir to 99.9 percent of her father's estate. He's worth hundreds of millions and owns over half a dozen mansions scattered from Provence to Maui. Plus the royalties from all of his bestselling books, which sell all over the world, pay off like crazy, year after year after year. Only a tiny fraction of what he's worth goes to Yvette, his second wife, due to the ironclad prenuptial agreement Addison forced her to sign. Yvette's thirty-two and you're just going to love her. Sylvia calls her Princess Lemon Jell-O because she's so blond and jiggly. When Yvette got wise that she'd signed the world's worst prenup, she retained a South Shore shyster named Mel Klein, whose firm just so happens to employ a PI named—cue the drum roll—Jocko Conlon."

"Whoa, small world."

"Whoa, isn't it? Yvette puts on the airhead tootsie act but she's no fool." My pasta water had come to a boil. I dropped in half a pound of linguine, stirred it and set the timer. Put the heat on low under the Lodge pan and poured some olive oil in to warm. "I also got a funny hit off of her."

"What kind of a funny hit?"

"The kind that if I were you I'd run a criminal background check on a Phyllis Yvette Rittenaur of Larchmont, New York. R-I-T-T-E-N-A-U-R."

"Consider it done."

I stirred the linguine some more and tossed the slivered garlic in the skillet, keeping the heat low so that it wouldn't burn. Grabbed a fistful of fresh Italian parsley from the fridge and chopped it up. When the timer went off, I drained the linguine into a colander. By now the garlic was golden and filling the entire kitchen with its aroma. I dumped the pasta into the skillet with a half-cup or so of cooking water I'd reserved, stirred it, added more oil and turned off the heat. Dumped in the parsley. Grated a ton of the aged Parmesan over it. Spooned the contents of the skillet onto two plates and added some fresh ground pepper.

"Want another beer or a glass of wine?"

"Another beer's fine by me."

I pulled out a tray, put the plates on it and grabbed us a couple of forks. "Why don't you carry this out to the living room and put it on the coffee table? It'd be a shame to waste that view. I'll bring the salad and two more beers." I poured some of the lemon vinaigrette on the salad, tossed it, opened two more Bass ales and joined him. He was seated in one of the armchairs, anxiously eyeballing our dinner plates.

"No need for formalities here, Lieutenant. Dig in."

He reached for one of the plates and started eating. I sat on the sofa, grabbed my plate and dug in. Lulu stretched out next to me and began to doze contentedly.

"Dude, this is the best dinner I've had in months, no lie," he said as he devoured his linguine, pausing to fork some salad onto his plate and dive into that as well. He sipped his Bass, gazing around at Merilee's magnificent pieces of signed Stickley furniture before his eyes settled on the view of the park again. "I could get used to living here real fast."

"It's not hard at all, trust me."

"So if we run a check on Yvette James, aka Phyllis Yvette Rittenaur, where do you think that's going to lead us?"

"To someone who's not quite who she appears to be, and never has been. It wouldn't surprise me one bit if she's the so-called brains behind this operation. Convinced Mel to mug Tommy and snatch *Tulsa* as big-time leverage in their would-be prenup renegotiation. Mel recruited Jocko to make it happen. Jocko found a couple of street punks to snatch Tommy's briefcase, then threw a scare into Tommy. It worked like a charm—aside from the troublesome fact that Tommy could identify Jocko. That didn't sit too well with Jocko, I'm guessing. So he goes back to Mel and says, 'I don't want this guy to be able to finger me.' Mel says, 'I don't either. Take care of him.' And there you have it. A rat's nest of nasty people, also known as a criminal conspiracy."

Very mulled this over, his head nodding, nodding. "It plays."

"Mind you, it's just one of several scenarios that do. You'll also want to take a good look at Norma Fives, an up-and-comer at Deep River, who is—or I should say was—Tommy's mistress. She's young, ambitious and in big trouble. Can't make good on the follow-up to her huge bestselling thriller of last year, *The Girl Under the Bed*, because it seems that her young unknown author has flipped out. Norma desperately needs someone to ghost it for her and was anxious to throw the job to Tommy. It would have meant a big payday and royalty participation for him. Unfortunately, Tommy was under exclusive contract to Addison. The only way to spring him from that was for Tommy to do something so heinous and unforgivable that Sylvia would have to fire him."

"Something, like, say losing the only two copies of *Tulsa* in existence?"

"Precisely. I should also point out that Norma is Sylvia's former assistant at Guilford House as well as her mortal enemy. Sylvia abused her so relentlessly that Norma blew a gasket in the middle of a weekly editorial meeting and hurled a Stanley Bostitch stapler across the conference table at her. Came within half an inch of blinding her. Near as I can tell, it's one of the proudest moments of Norma's young life. So it's possible that *she's* the one who engineered the snatch of *Tulsa*, although I haven't figured out how she would know Jocko unless I'm missing something, which is entirely possible. I did consume a generous quantity of psychedelics in my youth."

"Was that before or after you snorted your literary career and your marriage up your nose?"

"Before, but thanks large for reminding me."

"You're welcome large. You were saying about Norma . . ."

"She was aware that Tommy was hiding out at my place. He called her from there today, like I told you. So it's possible she paid him a visit right after I met her for a drink in Midtown at four. Lulu and I walked home from there through Central Park. She'd have beaten us there by a half hour if she took the subway. That puts her in play as a suspect. Tommy certainly would have buzzed her in. Trouble is, I can't figure out why she'd want him dead. She loved the guy. She believed in him."

"Maybe he got upset when she told him she engineered the snatch," Very suggested. "Maybe he threatened to call the police on her, being a straight shooter and all."

"That works. Trouble is, she weighs about ninety-five pounds dripping wet, which is an expression I've never understood. No way she could have thrown him off that roof. It's possible she had an accomplice, but if she did, I don't know yet who he might be." I took a sip of my Bass. "And there are some other people you'll want to look at."

"As in . . . ?"

"Sylvia. Maybe she'd had enough of her father's ceaseless abuse. Maybe she wanted, at long last, to be free of him. Arranged the *Tulsa* snatch so as to sabotage the old man's career, quit the publishing business and spend the rest of her days living a life of moneyed leisure. Maybe Tommy got wise to the fact that she was behind it and *she* took care of him. He would have let her into the apartment if she'd buzzed him."

"How would she know he was there?"

"Maybe he called her, too. Can you get a list of the calls that he made from the phone company?"

"I can, but I have to go through proper channels. It'll take a while." Very drank the last of his Bass, considering this. "It would certainly be easy to find out if she left the office shortly before it happened. Someone would have noticed, wouldn't they?"

"Not necessarily. Those places are full of people coming and going. Sylvia could have slipped out for a while without anyone paying attention."

"Is she strong enough to hurl him off of that roof?"

"She's built like a Hubbard squash, to quote her adoring father. Speaking of whom, he's in play, too. He's seventy-eight and doesn't see very well out of his one eye, but he's incredibly fit. Plenty strong enough to throw Tommy off that roof. He also has a temper. Hates that he needs Tommy's help to write his bestselling books. Hates that word might get out that it's actually Tommy who's written the last three. So maybe he strolled ten blocks up Riverside and paid Tommy a visit. Again, Tommy would have buzzed him in."

"The old guy lives in a luxury building. One of the doormen would have noticed if he left, wouldn't he?"

"You'd think so, but doormen can be bribed to keep their mouths shut."

"Not in the middle of a murder investigation, they can't. We'll certainly check that out. You've given me a lot to work with, dude. Thanks." He sat back in his chair, patting his stomach. "And thanks again for the awesome eats. I don't suppose you baked a blueberry pie, too, did you?"

"Sorry, I don't bake. Furthermore, I'm not done yet. There's another thread to tug at. Mighty big one, too."

"Which is . . . ?"

"Kathleen, Tommy's wife, who's enraged that he took up with a younger woman and moved out on her. Which is not to say that Kathleen's pining away, lonely and blue. She's found herself a fellow StuyTown denizen who was on the job until he had to take early retirement due to a medical disability."

"What's his name?"

"Richie Filosi."

Very's face darkened immediately.

"Know him?"

"I know him. He's dirty."

"What kind of dirty?"

"A few years back there was this strange epidemic of cops who suddenly had to take early retirement due to herniated discs. Must have been two dozen men. Oddly enough, all of them had the same doctor. Internal Affairs launched an investigation and caught Richie on videotape playing tennis, golf, handball. When they braced him he came clean. Stayed out of jail but lost his pension benefits, and he has to pay back every cent of those bogus disability payments. He'll be paying them back in monthly installments for years. As for the doctor, he cleared out and operates one of those anti-aging clinics in Miami now."

"That sounds real kosher."

"Doesn't it? I am liking this thread a lot. Richie's broke, needs dough, and listen to this, listen to this . . ."

"I'm listening to this."

"I'm almost positive that he and Jocko worked out of the same house at the same time—mine, the two-four. I'll have to check to make sure about that, but there's zero doubt in my mind that those two sterling specimens know each other." He sat there lost in thought for a moment. "You do realize there's still one more thread, right?"

"What is it, Lieutenant?"

"So far you're selling your boy Tommy as a stand-up guy who just happened to get caught in the cross fire."

"Your point being . . . ?"

"What if *he* engineered it? Hired those street punks himself to steal *Tulsa* so that Sylvia would fire him and he'd be free to make big bucks working for his honey, Norma. How do we know he was clean?"

"We don't," I conceded. "But I don't buy it."

"Why not?"

"Because he worked two grueling years on that book. Flushing it down the proverbial toilet goes against any writer's nature. Especially a writer like Tommy. He was an honest newspaperman."

"People change, Hoagy. Suddenly do things their closest friends and family members never imagined they'd do. Like, say, cheat on their wives."

"Agreed, but I still don't buy it. I just think he fell in with people who were a lot more ruthless than he realized."

"You could be right. You do have amazing instincts when it comes to the horrible things that people will do when they have a shot at fame and fortune. But I still have to take a good hard look at him."

"Of course you do. I'm expecting you to. What's your next move?"

"A chat with Sylvia."

"Why Sylvia?"

"Because Tommy worked for her and because I've never met

a woman who had a Stanley Bostitch stapler hurled across a conference table at her."

"She lives in the northern burbs just past Scarsdale in Willoughby," I offered. "Likes to catch the 6:57 out of Grand Central." I glanced at my grandfather's Benrus. It was 7:30.

"Then let's head on out there."

"You want me to tag along?" Lulu let out a low moan of protest. "*Us* to tag along?"

"Absolutely. You know her. I don't."

"Do you want to make sure she's home before we leave?"

"Never call and warn a suspect that you're on your way. That gives them time to prepare a story. Besides, where else would she be? You said she's the most hated woman in publishing. Has a bad relationship with her father. She'll be home, all right." He got up out of his chair and said, "I have to ride my bike back to the two-four." The precinct house wasn't far—West 100th Street. "I'll throw on some clothes, meet you back here in my Crown Vic in thirty minutes. We good?"

"All good."

LULU LOVES TO ride in police cars, even dented unmarked Ford Crown Vics with no functioning shock absorbers, springs or anything even remotely resembling proper wheel alignment. Very drove pedal to the metal, weaving his way fearlessly through the homebound commuter traffic on the Hutchinson River Parkway, his right hand on the wheel, his left arm hanging out of his open window. Air conditioning? Dream on. Not that Lulu minded. She planted her back paws firmly in my groin and rode with her head stuck out of the passenger window, ears flapping, tail thumping happily.

By the time he'd returned to pick me up, I'd washed and dried our dinner dishes and chosen a fresh pink shirt and burgundy-and-white bow tie to go with my navy blazer. Frank, the night doorman, tipped his hat at me as he held the front door open. Like I said—R-E-S-P-E-C-T. Lulu and I had been waiting downstairs under the awning for precisely two minutes when Very pulled up with a screech and we hopped in and sped off. He'd changed from his bike messenger outfit into a snug-fitting black T-shirt, tight jeans and motorcycle boots.

He made straight for the West Side Highway, which after a while became the Henry Hudson Parkway. Then he caught the Cross County, which merged into the Hutch. As darkness fell we made our way through New Rochelle, where the Petries— Rob, Laura and Ritchie—once lived. From there it was on to Scarsdale, the upscale burb where sixty-nine-year-old Dr. Herman Tarnower, bestselling author of *The Complete Scarsdale Medical Diet*, lived right up until he was shot dead in 1980 by his lover, Jean Harris. After we'd cleared Scarsdale, it was on to Willoughby. Next stop Willoughby.

Very let out a yawn, rubbing his eyes wearily.

"So tell me about this insomnia," I said as we drove. "Is it your energy issue?"

"What energy issue?"

"You have a surfeit of it. Possibly you've noticed."

"Oh, that. No, it's something else." He shot an uncomfortable glance at me before he looked back at the road. "Uneasiness. Dread."

"That sounds to me like anxiety."

"You're familiar with it?"

"I'm a writer, remember? Anxiety is my rocket fuel." I studied him across the seat. "You've seen a lot. Maybe too much. Have you ever considered—?"

"If you're about to say the word *Prozac*, don't."

"Wasn't planning to."

"If I go on meds, I'll lose my edge and then it will be *me* lying facedown on the sidewalk under a blue tarp. And don't say the word *shrink* either. That's a career killer. Besides, I'll sleep much better tonight now that you're around. You drive me nuts, but for some weird reason you also calm me down. Does that make any sense?"

"As much as anything else does. Except I think you've identified the wrong party. It's not me who calms you down. It's Lulu. That's why I keep her around. That and the whole glam thing."

She responded by turning around and licking my face before she stuck her head back out of the window.

Very said, "I had the desk sergeant run a computer check while I was changing clothes. Richie Filosi and Jocko Conlon both served in the two-four at the same time in the early eighties before Jocko got bounced and ended up in Nassau County."

"We know how Jocko's making ends meet. He's a salaried PI for Mel Klein's firm. But I really do wonder how Richie's staying afloat. He can't possibly be making enough doing odd jobs like Kathleen said he was, especially if he's still paying back what he owes the city over that disability scam."

"Maybe Jocko threw a little business his way, one pal to another. Scum does stick together."

"Then again, it could just be a coincidence that the two of them are both potential players in this case."

"Could be," Very said. "Except . . ."

"Except that you don't believe in coincidences. It's one of your bedrock personal tenets, like the right to vote, bear arms and hate the Yankees."

He took the Willoughby exit and eased us through an old-timey shopping district with parking on the diagonal. Kept on going until we'd made our way into Willoughby's residential neighborhoods. The street that Sylvia James lived on was in the deep-pockets district—a wide, tree-lined avenue of stately mansions set far back from the road on deep, wide lots. Hers, No. 14, was a Tudor style, dignified and regal, set behind two giant oak trees. It was quiet and sedate there.

All except for the two Willoughby blue-and-whites, an unmarked sedan, a van and the ambulance with blinking lights crowded in the street out front.

Sylvia's front porch light was on. Her garage door was open. A silver Mercedes 300 SE sedan was parked in the driveway. And another body lay under another blue tarp—this one in the street about twenty feet from the curbside mailbox at the foot of the driveway, or I should say where the curbside mailbox would have been if it hadn't been smashed hard enough to knock it from its post onto the lawn and splinter the post in half. Mail was strewn all over the grass.

Willoughby PD techies were taking photos of the scene. Not my idea of a fun job. Actually, none of this was my idea of a fun job. I wanted to be in my dream office in Merilee's apartment, seated by the windows at my Olympia, working on *The Sweet Season of Madness* while the original vinyl of the Ramones' "Rockaway Beach" blasted on the stereo. But it wasn't to be. Not tonight. Nope.

Not with Sylvia James lying dead under that blue tarp.

Chapter Five

Willoughby was big enough to have a police department with its own violent crime unit. The detective who was at the scene when we arrived was named Sensenbrenner. He was in his late forties and had a narrowly cropped flattop crew cut that I suspected had been his tonsorial choice since he was about twelve. Sensenbrenner was tall and narrowly built. He wore a dark suit with narrow lapels and a white shirt with a narrow tie. Probably lived in a narrow house with a narrow wife, a couple of narrow kids and a narrow cat. Everything about Sensenbrenner was narrow except for his mind, which was keen and supple.

"It plays like this, Lieutenant," he said to Very as Lulu and I looked on, raptly attentive. "Miss James opened the garage door with her remote control device when she pulled into the driveway after her commute home from Manhattan. She arrived at pretty much the same time every evening, according to her neighbor across the lane."

Very frowned. "Sorry, across the what?"

"This is Willoughby. All of the residential streets here are called lanes. You're on Beckwith Lane, one of the nicest, if not *the* nicest. But we all live on lanes. Even overworked, underpaid cops. I live on Sophia Lane."

"I knew a girl in high school named Sophia Lane," I said. "She wore Jean Naté and had the sweetest dimples you ever saw. Married a podiatrist."

Sensenbrenner tilted his narrow head at me. "I'm sorry, you are . . . ?"

"Stewart Hoag. The short-legged one is Lulu."

"They're with me," Very explained. "You were saying . . . ?"

"Miss James had real regular habits, according to the neighbor. Caught the 6:57 out of Grand Central every night, which pulls into the Willoughby train station at 7:52. She'd leave her Mercedes at the station lot, which is a ten-minute drive from here, so she usually arrived home a few minutes after eight unless she had to stop at the grocery store on the way. But she rarely arrived later than eight-thirty. She'd pull in to the driveway, open the garage door with her remote, stop to get out and retrieve her mail from her curbside mailbox, then pull in to the garage, shutting it behind her. There's a door inside the garage that leads into the kitchen. When our first responder got here, the Mercedes's engine was still running, the transmission set in park. My guess? Someone was idling one or two houses over just waiting for her. As soon as she opened her mailbox, he floored it, plowed right into her and ran over her body. Then he hit the brakes hard. See these skid marks on the pavement?" He walked us past Sylvia's body under the blue tarp, using his flashlight so we could get a better look. "Then he put it in reverse and backed over her as she lay here in the lane. Hit the brakes yet again.

See that second set of skid marks? Then he ran over her a third time. Our medical examiner isn't here yet, but the EMT people swear that whoever did this broke every bone in her body. You name it, he crushed it. Wanted to make good and sure she was dead, I guess," Sensenbrenner said as Very crouched in the street, studying the tire marks.

"No, this was more than that," I said. "It was pure, sadistic pleasure."

"You think?" Sensenbrenner raised a narrow eyebrow at me. "Who in the heck would hate Miss James that much?"

"Pretty much everyone in the publishing business who knew her."

"Are you saying she wasn't well liked professionally?"

"That's putting it mildly."

"I'm completely unaware of that aspect of her life. Just the life she led here."

Very lifted a corner of the blue tarp and had a look at her body, his eyes scanning her from head to toe. "Jeez, she looks like she jumped out of a plane without a parachute. Want to have a look?" he asked me.

"No, thanks. One dead body a day is my official limit."

Sensenbrenner peered at Very curiously. "Mind if I ask what brought you fellows out here this evening?"

"One of her writers, Tommy O'Brien, was murdered late this afternoon," Very answered. "Shoved off the roof of an apartment building. Hoagy's apartment building. An extremely valuable manuscript, one of her father's, was stolen from O'Brien on Friday. Miss James hired Hoagy to get it back."

"Are you a PI?" he asked me, peering at me.

"No, Tommy happened to be an old friend of mine. I was acting as a go-between. Sylvia thought that he was behind the theft."

"Is that what you think?"

"No, I don't. I think he was collateral damage. He showed up at my place this morning, soaking wet and terrified, and told me that the manuscript had been stolen from him. Also that his life had been threatened. I gave him some dry clothes and a bed. When I got home this afternoon he was lying face-down on the sidewalk out front under a blue tarp."

"I'm working the case," Very said. "Wanted to sound her out about it."

Sensenbrenner pondered this, thumbing his narrow chin. "Are we working the same case?"

"I'd be surprised if we're not," Very responded. "Although I don't have any idea how. Not yet. But I'll be happy to keep you in the loop if you'll clue me in on what you find out from your end."

"You bet. Anything I can do to help."

The two of them exchanged business cards before Very turned and looked at the pavement by the blue tarp that covered Sylvia's body. "Can your people read anything from those skid marks?"

"It's possible we'll get a match on the make and model number of the tire treads. Also paint residue from the car off the mailbox or the post, which might tell us its make and year." He paused, scratching his narrow head. "The trouble is, the car was probably stolen."

Very nodded. "I hear you. No way anyone would take the chance of using his own car. He'd steal one and ditch it somewhere. None of the neighbors saw it happen?"

"Not a one. The folks we've spoken to were either having supper or tidying up in the kitchen. They weren't looking out their front windows. Besides, it all happened in a span of about ten seconds. Her next-door neighbor, the one who phoned it in, heard the initial smash. He and his wife were taking a dip in their pool. But by the time he toweled off and made it to his front door, Miss James was lying dead in the street and her killer was long gone. We'll canvass the gas stations and convenience stores near the on-ramps to the Hutch, see if anyone spotted a car hightailing it out of town some time between eight-fifteen and eight-thirty. But I'm not holding my breath. I'd wager he observed the speed limits and blended in after he got two blocks from here."

"Was the house entered?" Very asked.

"It was not. No windows or doors were tampered with. He wasn't after jewelry or silver. He was after *her.*"

"What about the mail that's scattered about?" I asked.

"Glanced at it, haven't opened it. There isn't anything that looks like a ransom demand or any such thing, if that's what you're wondering. Just the usual catalogues and bills."

Very stood there for a moment, his head nodding, his jaw working on a fresh piece of bubble gum. "He knew her routine. That means he followed her home from the train station several times. I'm betting he also camped out here a few evenings before she got home, using a different car every time, to see if he'd have a regular dog walker or jogger to contend with. This was carefully worked out by somebody who knew what he was doing."

"An out-of-towner, if you want my opinion," Sensenbrenner said. "No one around here had an ax to grind with Miss James. She was a kind, highly respected person in Willoughby."

I tugged at my ear. "We're talking about *Sylvia* James, right? Daughter of Addison James, the bestselling author?"

"We are," Sensenbrenner said. "Like I said, I know nothing about her professional life in New York City. But here in Willoughby Miss James was legendary for her generosity. She donated $50,000 to our public library last year when it needed renovations. She endowed a college scholarship program at Willoughby High. Wrote a $20,000 check every year for our volunteer fire department. She was a private person. Kept to herself. Never threw her weight around. The only time we ever heard from her was a couple of winters ago when she found a dead fox in her backyard. Our Animal Control officer took care of it. Animal Control got a check in the mail for $10,000 from her the next day."

Lulu moseyed over toward the edge of the pavement near the gutter about ten feet from the blue tarp and began snuffling and snorting—until she abruptly stopped and let out a low woof.

"Why is she doing that?" Sensenbrenner asked me.

"She generally has a pretty good reason."

"Let's have a look." Sensenbrenner shined his flashlight on Lulu's find, which was a slightly dented piece of tan plastic tubing, maybe an inch long. He took a ballpoint pen from his narrow shirt pocket, inserted it in the plastic and picked it up, examining it in the light. "I wonder what the heck this is?"

I said, "Remember those TV commercials when a shapely, scantily clad cigarette girl would sashay around a fancy nightclub cooing, 'Cigars, cigarettes, Tiparillos . . .'"

"Sure I do," Sensenbrenner said. "So?"

"So that's a plastic Tiparillo tip."

"Could have been sitting there for days," Very said. "Weeks."

"Don't think so," I said. "If that was the case, then Lulu wouldn't think it's important. And I never doubt her instincts."

Sensenbrenner said, "You're suggesting her killer tossed it there?"

"Her killer or whoever else might have been in the car with him."

He scratched his narrow head again. "This sure qualifies as a first for me. I've never collected a potentially critical piece of crime scene evidence from a dog before."

"Can your people bag and tag it?" Very asked him. "Might get a fingerprint off it."

"You bet." Sensenbrenner waved down one of his crime scene techies, who took charge of it. Then the three of us stood there in thoughtful silence for a moment before he confessed, "You've got one person dead in New York City this afternoon and another one dead in Willoughby this evening, all because of some book. What's the point? It's just a book."

Lulu bared her teeth at him, growling.

He eyed her warily. "Did I say something wrong?"

"Hoagy's an author," Very explained. "Rather prominent one, in fact."

"Sorry, Mr. Hoag. I'm not familiar with your name. Not much of a reader. Just the occasional Louis L'Amour."

I told Lulu to chill out. She did so, grudgingly.

Very said, "We're just about done here, dude. Why don't you and Lulu hop in my ride while Detective Sensenbrenner and I wrap things up?"

We got into his battered Crown Vic while Very and the narrow detective exchanged a few more words. Then they shook hands and Very climbed in behind the wheel, bristling with anger.

"Something wrong, Lieutenant?"

"That elongated bastard just dissed me," he said, biting off the words before he started up the car, made a screeching U-turn and sped back toward the Hutch.

"Dissed you as in . . . ?"

"Quote: 'We don't expect these sorts of things to happen in a place like Willoughby.'"

"Wait, wait, I know how the rest of this one goes. Quote: 'It's more like the sort of thing that you expect to happen in New York City.' Unquote. Am I right?"

"How'd you know?" he acknowledged sourly.

"I just spent a bloody summer in small-town Connecticut, remember? These sorts of things never, ever happen there either."

"When you dis my city, you're dissing me and the job that I do," he fumed. "He's lucky I didn't punch him in the face."

"You know, maybe you *should* think about Prozac."

"Will you shut the fuck up about Prozac?"

He got back on the Hutch and floored it back toward the city while Lulu stood in my lap with her nose stuck out of the window and I tried to ignore the back spasms that I was developing from his car's total lack of shocks and springs.

Very's two-way radio squawked at him from the dash. He yanked it from its bracket, held it close to his mouth. "This is Very. Go."

A voice at the other end responded, accompanied by so much static and distortion I don't know how he understood a word of what was being said. But he did. "Gotcha. What else? . . . No shit? Oh, this just keeps getting better and better. And how about the old man? . . . Got it. Got it. Got it. Solid." He returned the two-way radio to its bracket and wove his way through the late evening traffic in thoughtful silence, his left arm hanging out his open window.

I looked over at him, mystified.

He glanced at me, frowning. "What?"

"You sign off by saying 'Solid'?"

"Why, you got a problem with that?"

"Broderick Crawford always said 'Ten-four' on *Highway Patrol*. I thought that was de rigueur."

"Well, I say 'Solid.' Seriously, are you planning to annoy me the whole way home?"

"Can't say. Is it okay if I get back to you on that?"

He shot a concerned look at me. Something he'd heard in my voice. "You okay, dude?"

"Considering that in the past few hours I've encountered the bone-crushed bodies of two people whom I knew rather well, I think I'm doing just dandy. What did the man on that squawk box thingy have to say?"

"They got a list from the phone company of the calls Tommy O'Brien made and received on your phone today. At 10:55 A.M. he called Guilford House and spoke to his editor, Sylvia James, who is now dead in the street."

"Dead in the *lane*. Who else?"

"At 11:33 he received a call from Mel Klein's private line at the law offices of Klein, Walker and Pignatano in Babylon, Long Island. At 12:38 P.M. he called Deep River Press and spoke to his girlfriend and would-be editor, Norma Fives, who I understand once threw a Stanley Bostitch stapler at Sylvia and nearly blinded her. At 2:07 P.M. he called the big man himself, Addison James, at his penthouse on Riverside. And last but not least, at 2:39 P.M. he called his wife, Kathleen, at their apartment in Stuyvesant Town. So far that makes five people who potentially knew that he was hiding out at your place. Six if Yvette James overheard their conversation or her husband told her."

"I wonder why Mel Klein called him."

"That makes two of us."

"I also wonder why Tommy called Addison. Can't imagine what he had to say to him."

"We could always ask the old guy."

I glanced at Grandfather's Benrus. It was nearly ten P.M. "Tonight?"

"In the morning. It'll be too late by the time we get back to the city."

"I assume someone has informed him about Sylvia?"

"Two Homicide officers were with him until a half hour ago."

"How did he take it?"

"He totally creeped them out. Kept quizzing them on exactly how many times the car ran over her and which bones were broken. Then he pulled a bottle of Dom Pérignon out of his office fridge, popped it open and poured himself a glass."

"Was Yvette with him?"

"Right by his side. She tried to give him a hug when he got the bad news. He told her to leave him the hell alone."

"Yeah, it's one of those warm, fuzzy marriages."

"I understand he was a spook during the Second World War."

"An original spook. OSS."

"You figure he killed people?"

"I don't figure it. I'm sure of it." I glanced across the seat at Very. "Any idea where Addison was this evening?"

"He and the missus dined at home. Check this out, a chef from Peter Luger came over and made them an aged porterhouse for two in their kitchen. Can you imagine being so rich that a chef from Peter Luger comes to you?"

"When you're that rich, he'll even cut your meat for you."

Very shook his head. "This sure does go off in a whole lot of different directions, am I right?"

"Very."

He frowned at me. "Yeah, dude?"

"It goes off in a whole lot of different directions. We know that Yvette James is hooked up with Mel Klein, whose law firm employs Jocko Conlon . . ."

"Yech."

"Jocko could certainly have accompanied Yvette to my place, whacked Tommy over the head and thrown him off my roof. We know that Tommy's bitter, estranged wife, Kathleen, is hooked up with Richie Filosi, who has no herniated discs in his back and could certainly have accompanied Kathleen to my place, whacked Tommy over the head and thrown him off of my roof. We know that Sylvia, before all of the bones in her body were crushed, was a substantially built woman. If she thought Tommy was behind the *Tulsa* snatch I have no doubt that *she* could have whacked him over the head and thrown him off my roof."

"I got to say, if it turns out that your boy Tommy did steal *Tulsa* to use it as leverage, he sure didn't have much of an exit strategy."

"He didn't. Steal it, I mean. He was just a useful putz. Nothing more."

Very glanced over at me. Once again he'd heard something in my voice that he didn't care for. "What happened to him isn't on you. It's not your fault that he's in the morgue."

"Yes it is, Lieutenant."

"How do you figure it that way?"

"Because he came to me for help and . . ." I trailed off, staring straight ahead at the road in front of us.

"And what, dude?"

"And I failed him."

Chapter Six

When I awoke the next morning in the middle of that king-size bed in Merilee's lavish bedroom, my mouth tasting vaguely of library paste, I had no idea where I was. It took me a second to remember. Lulu was sprawled out next to me, fast asleep, tongue lolling from the side of her mouth, which is vastly preferable to when she sleeps on my head. You'll just have to take my word for that. She stirred as I began to move around in the bed and seemed a bit confused herself as to why we were in Merilee's apartment but Merilee wasn't. Not that she was complaining. She likes her creature comforts same as I do.

Groaning from an ache in my lower back, I climbed out of bed, put on my silk target-dot dressing gown and staggered to the front door of the apartment. That morning's newspapers awaited me in the hallway on a small table outside of the door. Just one of the perks of living in a full-service luxury building.

I scanned them as I drank my orange juice while Merilee's shmancy espresso machine did its schmancy thing and Lulu put away her 9Lives mackerel. BOOK 'EM was the non-clever banner headline on the front page of the *Daily News*. The

Post had opted for the even more non-clever LITERARY SPLAT. No question about it, the deaths of Sylvia James and Tommy O'Brien were major tabloid news. Huge enough for the *News* to bump the story of Janet Jackson appearing topless on the September cover of *Rolling Stone* to an inside page, and to relegate the earth-shattering Johnny Depp/Winona Ryder breakup to Page Six of the *Post*. The sober, proper *Times* featured the story on the front page of its Metro section under the sober, proper headline: DISTINGUISHED PUBLISHER VICTIM OF VEHICULAR HOMICIDE. The subheading read: *Bestselling Author's Research Assistant Found Dead from Rooftop Fall.* As was typical with the *Times*, I had to read between the lines while I drank my first cup of espresso to grasp that there was the slightest potential connection between the two violent deaths, since both the NYPD and the Willoughby police spokesmen had taken pains to point out that there *was* no evidence of a connection, even though the timing and the fact that Thomas O'Brien had worked for Sylvia's legendary father had to lead anyone who had the approximate IQ of a melted ice cube to wonder.

I toasted a baguette and slathered it with some of the blackberry jam from the wild bushes that grow on Merilee's farm, munching on it with my second cup of espresso. The weather forecast was for a humid day in the upper 80s. There was also a 20 percent chance of widely scattered showers, which is the sort of weather forecast that I've always found exceptionally helpful. After I showered, I stropped Grandfather's razor, shaved, powdered my neck with Floris No. 89 talc and dressed in the slate-gray linen suit from Strickland & Sons, a contrasting pale gray shirt and a powder-blue knit tie. I was trying to decide whether I should go with my trilby or my Panama fedora when Very buzzed me from the lobby. I went with the trilby.

When Lulu and I emerged from the elevator, Very was waiting outside at the curb leaning against his battered cruiser, wearing his trademark black T-shirt, jeans and motorcycle boots, his jaw working on a piece of bubble gum. It was already warm and hazy out.

"How did you sleep?" I asked him.

"Like a log. Best night's sleep I've had in months. Thanks, Lulu. You work wonders."

She let out a woof in response.

"That was her way of saying 'No problemo, amigo,'" I translated for him.

"So she speaks Spanish?"

"Little bit. But her French is terrible."

"We tossed Tommy O'Brien's studio apartment in Hell's Kitchen," he informed me. "Place is a real dive. He was living on the cheap."

"I don't suppose you're about to tell me that you found two copies of a 783-page opus called *Tulsa*, are you?"

"Nope, just cockroaches. Really big ones, like out of a fifties horror movie."

"There's no chance the book's hidden there somewhere?"

"We didn't tear up the floorboards, but the place was searched good and thorough. The book's not there, dude. Where are you going with this?"

"Lieutenant, I haven't figured out much yet, but there's one thing of which I'm absolutely certain. Everything that happened yesterday goes back to what did or didn't happen to

Tommy outside of that copier shop on Friday night. When we find *Tulsa*, we'll find out what this mess is really about."

He got in behind the wheel and started up the Crown Vic, revving its engine impatiently. I opened the passenger door. Lulu jumped in ahead of me as I got in, my lower back reminding me how many hours we'd spent bouncing around in it last night. "What's the plan for this morning?"

Very made a shockingly illegal U-turn and headed west on West 83rd Street. "We pay a visit to Addison and Yvette James, then Kathleen O'Brien and her boyfriend, Richie, okay?"

"Fine. Tell me something I don't know from reading the morning papers."

"No prob. For starters, our canvass of the high-rise building on the corner near your building turned up nothing. No one saw anything happen on your roof. Neither did the fifth-floor rear residents on West 94th. The ME has confirmed that prior to his fall, Tommy was hit on the back of the head with an extremely hard object, like a piece of pipe. Therefore, his death has been officially classified as a homicide, as opposed to a suicide. We conducted a thorough search of the stairwell as well as the trash cans up and down the block. Zilch. His killer took the weapon with him."

"So you have nothing."

"Slow down, I'm not done yet. A couple of my men spoke to Addison James's doorman. He says that the old gent left the building approximately two hours before Tommy's murder and went strolling off dressed in a white linen suit. He was carrying a walking stick but no umbrella."

"It was still pouring rain."

"Which my men pointed out to the doorman."

"And . . . ?"

"And Mr. James told him that the rain reminds him of Maui. He owns a lavish estate there, I gather."

I mulled this over as we went spelunking in and out of the potholes on West 83rd. "So Addison's in play?"

"Most def. Who gets them when he dies?"

"Gets what, Lieutenant?"

"Those multimillion-dollar retreats that he has scattered all over the place."

"Sylvia would have, presumably. But now that she's gone, you'd figure Yvette will come into them, unless there's something in his will that specifies otherwise."

"Does that sound like a motive or am I crazy?"

"Sounds like one to me. Although you *are* crazy."

"Thanks, dude. I really needed to hear that."

"You would have been disappointed if I hadn't said it, admit it."

He weaved his way around the cabs, bike messengers and jaywalkers in our path as he sped along, his jaw working on his gum. "After we talk to Kathleen and Richie, I also want to talk to Mel Klein, Esquire, out in Babylon. And Jocko Conlon. And much as it pains me to say it, you make up for your annoying personality with your amazing instincts. Real, dude, I'm in awe."

"I appreciate the kind words . . . I think. But will you kindly tell me what you're not telling me?"

"Before Phyllis Yvette Rittenaur—who by the way is thirty-six, not thirty-two—moved from Larchmont to New York City to seek show biz fame and fortune, she'd been busted numerous times."

"Really? Do tell."

"When she was fourteen, she was heavy into shoplifting. And

I'm not just talking about lifting a pair of sunglasses from the corner drugstore. She got nailed for trying to walk out the door of a department store wearing an entire outfit that she hadn't paid for—expensive shearling winter coat, cashmere sweater, flannel slacks, ankle boots, the works. Store security nailed her and called the Larchmont PD, but she was so little and cute and wept so pitifully that they sent her home with a stern warning. By the time she was sixteen she'd graduated to blackmail. She used to babysit little kids, okay? When the father would drive her home, she'd rip her blouse and tell him she'd claim he'd tried to attack her if he didn't give her a hundred bucks. Got away with it several times, too, until she picked the wrong dad—a law professor—who called the cops on her. She was nailed for extortion, but she was so little and cute and wept so pitifully that the judge let her off with probation and community service." Very came to a jarring stop at a red light on Broadway. "That's when she went to secretarial school and learned how to type."

"This is the part of the story where I have to ask you what sort of parents she had."

"She didn't. Her father ran off with another woman before she was born, never to be seen again, and her mother deserted her when she was four. Left her with an aunt, who was a barmaid-slash-hooker. I'm surprised that little Phyllis didn't end up hooking herself. But she had her sights set higher than that. By age eighteen she'd partnered up with Mick the Quick Rafferty, age twenty-three, a high-stepping two-time loser out of Bayonne. The pair of them got busted for trying to lift a diamond engagement ring from a jewelry store in Nyack. Mick the Quick played Sir Galahad and took the whole rap—ten to fourteen for armed robbery. It seems he was packing a gun, just to round things out in the stupidity department. They let him out after eight." The light turned green and off he sped. "By then little Phyllis Rittenaur was now calling herself Yvette Ritt and had moved to New York City."

"I take it she never studied drama at LIU."

"Long Island University has no record of her ever being enrolled there."

"And also that she made up the part about being Joe Heller's typist."

"No, that part's true. She typed for him for two years. But he hit a dry patch and had no work for her, so he passed her along to Addison. Heller was really, really sorry to see her go, he told my officer."

"I'll bet he was."

"She started working for Addison part time but eventually became his full-time typist and bed partner, despite the fact that Sylvia hated her. School me, do you think the old guy knows the real deal about her past?"

"I have zero doubt. I also have zero doubt that he's ever cared. He was a spook, remember? He has no illusions about people. Do you have any idea where Yvette was when Tommy was getting thrown off my roof?"

"Excellent question."

"Thank you, I try."

"The doorman of their building put her in a cab at three. She went to Guillaume's on West 56th Street, where she had a 3:30 appointment to have her hair and nails done. She also had a facial. Was there until shortly after five. From there she tried on about twenty pairs of shoes around the corner at the Gucci store on Fifth Avenue. They know her well there. She's a regular customer. Bought two pairs. Came home in a cab with her Gucci bag at around six o'clock, according to the doorman, who told our people she never comes home without at least one new pair of shoes. The doormen call her Imelda Marcos."

By now we'd reached Addison and Yvette's building on Riverside Drive. A patrol car was stationed there to keep the press away. Two cops in uniform were on the door. Undaunted, several local TV reporters were doing stand-ups from across the street, using the building as a backdrop.

Very double-parked his Crown Vic out front, which is one of the genuine pleasures of driving around New York City with a cop, and in we went. The doorman phoned the penthouse and up to the twenty-fourth floor we rode in the Jameses' private elevator. Once again, I buzzed the door for guests. Once again, it was Yvette who answered it.

I truly did think that Yvette was going to faint when she set her huge baby blues on Very. They seemed to roll back in her head, and she teetered slightly on her pampered bare feet. She wore a new color of polish on her toenails and fingernails today—oxblood. Her hair had been so expertly trimmed by Guillaume that I couldn't tell that it had been trimmed at all, except for a slight tapering at the neck. She was not dressed in a mourning ensemble out of respect for Sylvia's violent death. Not unless you consider a skintight bright pink sheath with nothing underneath it a mourning ensemble.

Romaine Very, who I happened to know hadn't been very active in the female department lately, was rendered momentarily goggle-eyed himself as he stood there gaping at her cleavage, nipples and belly button.

"Hello again, Hoagy," Yvette said finally, her voice quavering slightly. "And, wait, don't tell me, the short one was . . . Lulu, wasn't it?"

"Still is."

"Forgive me if I seem a bit thrown. I'm still in a state of shock over Sylvia and Tommy." She turned her blue-eyed gaze back to Very. "Are you the detective who's investigating their murders? We were told to expect someone."

"I'm Detective Lieutenant Romaine Very. And I'm sorry for your losses, Mrs. James."

"Call me Yvette, please. And do come in. Addy's on the phone upstairs in his office," she informed us as she padded her way up the grand curving staircase, all curves and wiggles and jiggles in that tight, thin sheath. "Reporters have been calling all morning nonstop. His attorney, Mark Kaplan, is with him."

"So are you still in touch with Mick, Yvette?" Very asked as we followed her.

"Mick who?"

"Mick the Quick, your partner. The one who took the fall on the jewelry heist in Nyack."

She halted on the stairs and turned around, her face drawn tight, her gaze chilly. "I'm not that person anymore."

"So you've made a clean break with the past?"

"Exactly, Lieutenant."

"I understand you've retained a Babylon lawyer named Mel Klein."

"What of it? He's a fine, reputable attorney and a gentleman."

Very let out a laugh. "I've never heard a South Shore shyster called either of those things before. I'll have to pass that one along to the boys at One P.P. They'll get a real kick out of it."

Yvette glared at him. "You're not a very nice person, are you?"

"They don't pay me to be nice."

"That's a shame, because with your looks you'd be fighting the girls off with a stick."

"Even you?"

"Especially me." She reached over and ran a small manicured finger along his stubbly jaw. "If you play nice, you'll find out that I'm worth it."

"Is Mel playing nice?"

"Our relationship is strictly business," Yvette said curtly, resuming her climb up the stairs.

She led us down the long parquet-floored hallway past her suite, where she'd been listening to Mariah Carey try to bring up a lung. It was becoming clear to me that Yvette's taste in music was not my idea of music.

"You and your husband have separate rooms?" Very asked her.

"We prefer it that way. We both value our privacy."

The big oak pocket doors at the end of the hall were closed. She knocked.

Addison yelled, "Enter!"

We entered.

He was on the phone with a reporter, it appeared. "For the *eighth* time, I have nothing more to say about yesterday's events!" he roared. It also appeared as if he'd just completed his Royal Canadian Air Force exercises. He was standing at his desk stripped down to his jockstrap, eye patch and combat boots, covered with sweat. "And now this is me hanging up on you!" Which he did, slamming the phone down hard before he fetched a towel from the bathroom, mopped himself dry and put on his terry cloth robe. Then he grabbed a bottle of Perrier from the refrigerator and took several huge gulps.

His attorney, Mark Kaplan, was seated at the partners desk in the non-rolling chair. He seemed very calm, composed and dignified, if you go in for that sort of thing.

"Addy, this is Detective Lieutenant Very," Yvette informed him. "He's the homicide investigator you were expecting."

"Come on in, Lieutenant," he said to Very. "Yvette, go away."

"You sure you don't want me to stay?"

"Quite sure," he said testily.

She slid the door shut, pouting slightly.

Addison acknowledged me with a nod before he studied Very with his one not-so-good eye. "I was expecting a schlub in a rumpled suit, not some kid in a T-shirt and jeans. And yet I'm told you're Dante Feldman's best man."

"I just try to do my job, sir," Very said.

"Say hello to Mark Kaplan. He handles my legal and business affairs. Mark, the tall one is the writer I was telling you about, Stewart Hoag, who seems to go everywhere with that dog."

Kaplan got to his feet. He was an athletically built man of about sixty, so sleekly put together that he bordered on senatorial. He had gleaming silver hair, a long narrow blade of a nose, a high forehead, and a strong, decisive jaw. He wore a beautifully tailored navy blue pinstripe suit, a red tie and a spread collar white shirt with French cuffs and silver horseshoe cuff links. Since he was a Park Avenue lawyer and not a racetrack tout, I took that to mean he was a horseman who weekended up in Bedford along with the posh likes of Ralph Lauren.

"Pleased to meet you, gentlemen," he said in a rich burgundy voice as he shook each of our hands. His grip was firm and calloused. Definitely a horseman. He smiled down at Lulu and said, "I've always wanted a basset, but my wife claims they have a reputation for being stubborn."

"That's actually a bum rap—they're as compliant as little lambs," I assured him. After all, the man was a lawyer. I was entitled to amuse myself.

"Good to know. Thanks."

"My pleasure."

He raised his gaze back to Very. "Is this an official visit, Lieutenant?"

Very frowned. "Official as in . . . ?"

"An interrogation."

"Not at all. It's a conversation."

Kaplan thumbed his jaw thoughtfully. "Still, perhaps I ought to stick around, Addison."

"No need," Addison said, waving him off. "You can go."

"I think I should stay. This *is* why you pay me, after all."

"And I just told you to go," Addison shot back. "So go!"

Kaplan let out a courtly sigh. "Very well. I gave up trying to argue with you twenty years ago."

"You'll see to Sylvia's affairs?" Addison asked him.

"I shall. We drew up her will together two years ago and it's fairly straightforward. She wished to leave the bulk of her estate to her alma mater, Bryn Mawr. The proceeds of the sale of her home in Willoughby will go toward endowing a Sylvia James Memorial Scholarship Fund at the local high school. The town's public library will come into some money as well." Kaplan hesitated before he added, "Would you like me to contact anyone for you?"

"Such as who?" Addison demanded.

"Your physician. You've had quite a shock. Perhaps he ought to swing by and check your blood pressure."

"There's nothing wrong with my blood pressure. I'm fine."

"Of course. Whatever you say." Kaplan turned back to us and said, "Gentlemen, nice meeting you. Sorry it couldn't have been under happier circumstances." Then he picked up his leather briefcase, one of those accordion numbers designed to hold a multitude of legal briefs, and strode briskly out, sliding the pocket door shut behind him.

Very watched him go, noticing the old man's collection of exotic walking sticks that were in a copper stand by the door. He moseyed over and admired them. "You've got some real beauties here, sir."

"Why, thank you, Lieutenant," Addison said, moving toward him. "They're the fruits of my travels. Do not mistake them for mere souvenirs. Nearly lost my left leg in the war and I've used them one and all. This one here is still my favorite, because it was my first. Pure hickory. They gave it to me in the military hospital in Asheville, North Carolina." He pulled it out so that Very could have a better look at it, then shoved it back in with the others. "This one with the knob at the top is called a shille-lagh. I got it in Dublin many years ago. It's made of blackthorn. This is a Malacca, a Malay stick made of rattan palm. I got that one in Burma. This is a makila, a Basque walking stick, made of medlar. And this one here is a whangee, made of bamboo. Which one do you think I used to whack Tommy O'Brien on the back of the head before I hurled the worthless son of a bitch off the roof of Hoagy's brownstone?"

Very studied him coolly. "How did you know he was hit

on the back of the head? That information hasn't been made public."

"Reporter from the *New York Post* just told me. It's in the coroner's report. And I most certainly am."

"Are what, Mr. James?"

"Fit enough to climb the five flights of stairs to Hoagy's apartment. I'm in tip-top condition. I'm also at your complete disposal. How I can help with your investigation?"

Addison sat at the giant partners desk in his rolling desk chair. I sat in the junior partner's chair with Lulu at my feet. Very didn't sit. He preferred to pace the office like a panther, his jaw working on his gum. Addison smiled faintly as he watched him pace back and forth, back and forth.

"Mr. James, someone put a tap on Hoagy's phone. I understand from our trace that one of the people who Tommy called yesterday was you."

Addison nodded his shaved pink head vigorously. "Correct."

"What was the purpose of his call?"

"The purpose?"

"What did the two of you talk about?"

The old man sat there in silence for a moment, gazing out at the summer haze that hung low over the Hudson. "Everything. Nothing."

Very came to a halt. "All due respect, can you be more specific?"

"He called to tell me he didn't have *Tulsa* and that the fellow who stole it from him had threatened his life. He sounded frightened. Guess he had reason to be, considering what ended up happening to him." Addison peered at Very, shaking a long, crooked finger at him. "Now I remember."

"Remember what, sir?"

"Slinker Raab. *That's* who you remind me of. We came out of Yale together. He was a brilliant mathematician. We called him Slinker because he had such a strange, slinky way of walking. We both ended up working for Wild Bill in Europe. He liked dogs same as you, Hoagy. Had a wire-haired terrier named Victor. Funny how the human mind works. I can remember that dog's name, but I can't remember what I had for dinner last night."

"An aged porterhouse from Peter Luger with creamed spinach and hash browns," Very told him.

"Have you been checking up on me, Lieutenant?"

"You and everyone else. It's nothing personal."

"Slinker bought it parachuting into Yugoslavia. Had the same dark eyes and coloring that you have, Lieutenant, though he was a good deal taller than you. My God, he'd be an old fart now just like I am, wouldn't he?"

"Yes sir, I suppose he would."

Addison let out a mournful sigh. "So many friends lost. I was one of the lucky ones. All I lost was an eye. Those poor bastards lost their whole futures. They're for *them*, you know."

"What are, Mr. James?" I asked.

"All of those gaudy homes that I own from Aspen to Maui. I'm leaving them to the Veterans Administration to be repurposed as recovery hospitals, same as the one in Asheville where I recuperated after I was wounded. They came home from Desert Storm by the thousands. The Pentagon talked about our 'surgical strike' in Kuwait as if there weren't men getting limbs and chunks of their brains blown to bits. And there'll be more, mark my word. Saddam Hussein backed off this time, but I guarantee you within ten years we'll go into Iraq and take him out. It'll be a colossal mistake, but we'll do it anyway because we're a nation that's led by unbelievably stupid men. Saddam's a thug, I'll grant you, but he's *our* thug. His soldiers are fighting with weapons that *we* supplied them with. The unlucky ones will come home in coffins. The lucky ones will come home like I did, missing pieces of themselves. And when they do they'll be cared for at one of my retreats at no cost to the American taxpayer. I'm leaving the VA the income from all of my book royalties to make sure of that. It's all spelled out in my will, chapter and verse. Chapter and . . ." He trailed off for a moment before he roused himself and said, "Have you figured out who killed Sylvia, Lieutenant?"

"No, sir, just that it was carefully planned by someone who was waiting there for her and ran her over multiple times when she went to get her mail."

"How many, Lieutenant?"

"Excuse me?"

"How many times was she run over? Was it two times, three, four . . . ?"

"Why does that matter?"

"Two times would signify someone who had a mission and was being thorough. Three or four times, that's more a sign of outright hatred. She hated *me*, you know. I gave her a prominent publishing career, not to mention as much money as anyone could ever dream of, and yet she hated me."

"I doubt that very much, sir," Very said.

"And you'd be wrong. I'm a cruel bastard. Rode her mercilessly because she was a fat cow who wouldn't stand up straight and look you in the eye. She also picked her scalp. Truly disgusting habit. Couldn't stand to look at her when she . . ." He trailed off again, gazing out the window. "I don't think I ever saw Sylvia smile. Not once."

"Was she aware that you intended to leave your houses to the VA?" I asked him. "Or was she expecting to inherit them?"

Addison studied me across the partners desk with his one not-so-good eye. "Why are you asking me that?"

"Just curious."

"You're curious about a lot of things. I still can't decide whether you're keenly perceptive or simply the possessor of a mediocre wandering mind." He waited for me to react to his attempt to goad me. When I didn't, he said, "No, she didn't know. It was none of her damned business. They're *my* houses."

"And she was your daughter."

"Wasn't a family matter. It was personal. I worked it out several years ago with Kaplan. He has all of the paperwork." Addison sat back in his rolling chair. "He handles all of my publishing deals, too. Foreign rights, movie sales, all of it. I don't have a literary agent. Why should I give an agent ten percent of everything I earn when I can simply pay Kaplan by the hour?"

Very studied him, his head nodding. "Is it true that Tommy O'Brien wrote your last three books for you?"

The old man flared instantly. "That's bullshit. Stop. Backspace. Erase. That's *total* bullshit. Our arrangement was the same as always. I'd give him the broad strokes of the story. He'd do the research that I'd need to give it authenticity and flavor. Then I'd get it down on paper with my trusty old machine," he said, patting his Underwood next to him.

"So it's not true that Sylvia had promised him coauthor credit and a share of the royalties?" I asked.

Addison turned and looked at me, his eye narrowing slightly. "If that's what Tommy told you, it's a goddamned lie."

"Do you think he lied about the mugging, too? That he was using *Tulsa* as a bargaining chip?"

"I really wouldn't know."

"Mr. James, who do *you* think took it?" Very asked.

"I really wouldn't know," he repeated with a casual wave of his hand.

"And what about Mrs. James?"

"Yvette? What about her?"

"Does she know that you intend to leave your homes to the VA?"

"No reason for her to. I spelled things out very clearly to her in our prenuptial agreement. When I'm gone, she'll get this apartment and a monthly income. Should she choose to sell this place and move somewhere else, she's free to do so. But she has no claim to any of my money, royalties or houses. She's well aware of that. Cheeses her off, too. She's even hired some lawyer who thinks he can talk me into drafting a more generous agreement."

"Can he?"

"Not a chance, sonny boy. He knows it, too, unless he's a complete idiot. He's just trying to get in her pants. It's not very hard, I'm told."

"By . . . ?"

"Excuse me, Lieutenant?"

"You're told by whom?"

"The doormen. They've witnessed her slipping out late at night for years. She usually returns shortly before dawn, unless she decides to go away with her latest beau for a week or two.

She doesn't go in for long-term relationships. I think her record is one month. That was two years ago, maybe three. I was told he was a professional poker player from Atlantic City. Yvette is partial to low-class greaseballs who like to live on the edge. No surprise there. She lived that way herself before she met me."

"So she was candid about her past when she came to work for you?"

"Didn't have to be. I can read people instantly. It was my job to read people. I was damned good at it, too. That's why I'm still alive and Slinker isn't. Still am good at it, even with one eye. You, for instance, Lieutenant."

"What about me?" Very asked him.

"You're wondering if this senescent gasbag is capable of masterminding the deaths of two people very close to him, and if so, why I would."

"Okay, I'll bite. Why would you?"

"No reason. Tommy was as loyal and hardworking as they come. I'll never find as good a legman. As for Sylvia, I was right here at the time of her murder. That would mean I had to go to the trouble of hiring someone to run her over. What possible reason would I have for doing that? There is none."

"Sure there is," I said. "Because you'd become convinced that *she* was going to kill *you*."

"Why would Sylvia want to kill me?"

"Well, for starters, she hated you . . ."

"Boo hoo."

"And maybe because she wanted your country estates right now. The ones you'd neglected to tell her you were donating to the Veterans Administration. Maybe she didn't want to wait around for another six or eight years for you to kick off. Maybe she wanted to get away from publishing—and you—right now and enjoy life for a change."

"Nice little yarn," Addison said. "Mind if I steal it for my next book?"

"It's yours. I'm still curious about one thing. If you knew that Yvette was a fake, why did you hire her?"

"She was a good typist. Easy on the eyes, too. Or eye, in my case."

"And why did you marry her?"

"Have you *seen* that ass?"

"She's an attractive woman," Very acknowledged.

"Attractive doesn't begin to describe it, Lieutenant. That creature oozes eroticism. When I married her, I could still rise to the occasion with some regularity. Her sort of woman is what it takes for a man of my years to get it up, and they are not easy to find. I married her because I didn't want to lose her."

"Yet you don't treat her very well," I pointed out.

He looked at me in astonishment. "Why would you say that?"

"You hurled a Perrier bottle at her yesterday, remember? You could have injured her badly if you'd hit her."

"That was nothing. I'm just a mean old bastard. Is that a crime, Lieutenant?"

"Wasn't the last time I looked." Very resumed pacing. Lulu lifted her head and watched him, then let out a low grumble and went back to dozing. "As it happens, it's quite plausible."

Addison shook his head at him. "What is?"

"That you strolled your way up to West 93rd and killed Tommy O'Brien yourself. I understand from one of the door-men that you went out for a walk in the rain two hours before he was murdered. Didn't return until well after he was thrown from Hoagy's roof."

"All true. I love walking in the rain. Would you believe that *Maui* still remains my bestselling title even though I wrote it more than twenty years ago?"

"People," I said, "want to believe that there's such a thing as paradise."

"People," he said, "are idiots."

"Where did you walk to?" Very asked him.

"Zabar's."

"That fancy deli on Broadway?"

"It's not a deli, Lieutenant." He tut-tutted. "It's the closest thing we have to a European food hall. They sell everything there. Smoked fish. Fresh ground coffee beans. Exotic spices. I love to stroll around in Zabar's and inhale all of the scents. Smell is such a powerful sense memory, especially when your sight is failing. When I'm in Zabar's, I'm back in Paris in 1952 with my whole life ahead of me—unlike now. Mind you, my doctor says my health is excellent for a man my age. My greatest fear is that I'll suffer a stroke and end up imprisoned in some nursing home, sitting in a wheelchair all day in a puddle of my own urine."

"Better your own than someone else's," I pointed out.

"I'd blow my brains out if it came to that."

"Do you keep a weapon?" Very asked him.

Addison patted the desk with his right hand. "In my top drawer—a .38-caliber Ruger Service Six revolver."

"Loaded?"

"No point in having it there if it's not."

"Got a license for it?"

"Haven't the slightest idea."

Very studied him curiously. "Do you mind if I make a personal observation, sir?"

Addison heaved an impatient sigh. "If you must."

"You don't seem particularly upset about what's gone down. In fact, I'm getting no emotional hit off you at all. Sylvia was your only child and your editor. Tommy was your researcher and collaborator. Between them, they were your support system. Now they're both dead, yet you don't seem to care."

The old man shook his bald pink head at him. "You have no idea what it's like, do you? War, I mean."

"No sir, I don't," Very conceded.

"If I allow myself to care I'll lose my fighting edge and then . . ." He snapped his fingers. "I'll be dead, too. I'm here, they're not. That's the stark reality of it. So I have to keep going."

"Keep writing, you mean?" I asked him.

"Absolutely. I'm still under contract. Still have to keep producing new books. But first I have to get that damned *Tulsa* manuscript back."

"Do you think you will?" Very asked him.

"I know I will. Whoever took it wants money for it. Everything's about money. As soon as they contact me, they'll get their money, I'll get my manuscript back and you'll arrest them, won't you, Lieutenant?"

"I certainly hope so."

"Besides, I still have a support system. I have Yvette, who's been screening my calls today. I have Mark Kaplan. Furthermore, I'm not the helpless, doddering old fool that you seem to think I am. Is there anything else I can do for you?"

"No, we're good," Very said.

"Then please excuse me. Yvette has prepared a list of phone calls from journalists that I have to return. A nuisance, but when the likes of *The New York Times* and *The Washington Post* call, they mustn't be ignored." Addison reached for the phone, squinted at Yvette's list and began dialing a number. As far as he was concerned, we weren't there anymore. He'd dismissed us.

We left, sliding the pocket door shut behind us.

"Can't say I've ever encountered a cooler customer," Very murmured as we strolled down the hall. "I wonder if that was all just an act for our benefit and he's in there sobbing like a baby right now."

"You keep forgetting that he was one of Wild Bill's boys."

"Meaning . . . ?"

"Meaning it was no act. He's killed plenty of people."

"That was during the war."

"Don't be so sure. I have no doubt he was capable of killing Tommy."

"If he went to Zabar's like he said, it'll be easy to check out."

"He still could have gone to my place from there and killed him. Same as he could have hired someone to run Sylvia down."

"Someone like who?"

"Good question."

Yvette heard our voices as we neared her suite and intercepted us from her open doorway. "Was Addy able to tell you anything?"

"Not very much, Mrs. James," Very said politely.

"It's Yvette, hon. He say anything about me?"

"Such as . . . ?"

"He's not going to throw me out, is he?"

"Why would he do that?"

"He's crazy, didn't you notice? Plus he's been sore at me ever since I retained Mel."

"Actually, he said you were a vital part of his support team. He was highly complimentary. Isn't that right, Hoagy?"

"Absolutely."

"For real?" she asked us, sounding woeful and helpless. Or trying to. She didn't quite pull it off. "Wow, that's sure a load off my mind. Hang on one sec, will you, Lieutenant? I want to give you my direct line." She darted into her sitting room, scribbled her phone number on a piece of notepaper and handed it to Very same as she'd handed it to me yesterday. "If there's *any-thing* I can do, call me, okay? Day or night."

"Sure thing," he said, pocketing it.

She looked him over with those huge blue eyes of hers. "You got a girlfriend?"

"Not presently, no."

"So call me."

"I don't usually date married women."

She gazed up at him through her eyelashes. "But for me you'll make an exception, won't you?" Then she got up on her tiptoes, plastered her barely sheathed assets against his chest and kissed him smack on the mouth. I'm not talking about any kindergarten kiss either. I'm talking about a long, slow, wet one. When she finally pulled away, her eyes twinkled at him mischievously.

"I'll certainly think about it," Very responded, his voice sounding admirably close to normal.

"You do that, hon. You think about it."

Chapter Seven

I hate this place," Very fumed as we followed Lulu down one of the labyrinthine paths toward No. 11 Stuyvesant Oval. The day was becoming stiflingly humid, with not so much as a trace of a breeze. The heavy air smelled strongly of the fetid East River. "I had a thing with a Barnard girl for a while when I was at Columbia. She lived at home in Oval No. 7. I was always a half hour late when I came to pick her up because I always got lost trying to find her building. She decided I was an inconsiderate prick and dumped me."

"I can't find my way around here either. I think they laid it out this way on purpose to dissuade 'undesirables' from wandering about. Did you know they banned blacks from living here until 1950?"

"I did not. Gives me another good reason to hate it."

"What you need is a basset hound. Lulu always remembers the way."

"Dude, what I need is a complete and total absence of professional ethics for thirty minutes. Hell, I'd settle for twenty."

"During which time you would . . . ?"

"Rip that dress off Yvette James and ravage the hell out of her, what else? I mean, she is *the* hottest babe I've been around in months." He let out a pained sigh. "I wonder if she knew she was giving me a boner."

"I'd say Yvette was well aware that she was getting a rise out of you."

"Why do you think she did that?"

"People respond to grief and loss in different ways. Some can't stop crying. Others have an overwhelming urge to find out whether the detective investigating the case still has his tonsils."

"Dude, I'm being serious here."

"To disarm you. She wants you docile and in her corner."

"Sometimes I wish I had just a teeny-tiny Richie Filosi streak in me, you know? Richie's kind would have made a date with her on the spot and not given it a second thought."

"But that's not you?"

"She's a person of interest in two homicides. No way I can allow myself to get personally involved with her. Besides, she's not my type."

"You have a type?"

"Oh, most def. Brainy. I'm attracted to brainy women of high integrity, a concept that's not even on Richie Filosi's radar screen. He didn't see anything wrong with faking a disability and bilking the taxpayers out of their hard-earned money. His sort make me sick."

"I'm glad you're not like Richie, Lieutenant—even if it does consign you to a state of pulsating tumescence."

"Oh yeah? Why's that?"

"Because if you were, then we wouldn't be friends."

He shot a glance over at me. "We're friends?"

"Aren't we?"

He shrugged his rippling shoulders in his tight black T-shirt. "I don't really know. Don't have many friends. I seem to rub people the wrong way."

"As do I. See? We have a lot in common, setting aside that I'm the superior dresser, not to mention the first major new literary voice of the 1980s."

"Dude, these are the nineties."

"Thank you large for pointing that out."

"You're welcome large."

Lulu led us directly to the building. I buzzed. Kathleen let us in. She was waiting for us in the corridor outside of the apartment, wearing a baggy T-shirt, baggy shorts and flip-flops. She looked exhausted and emotionally drained.

"Kathleen O'Brien, this is Detective Lieutenant Romaine Very, the city's top homicide investigator. They've sent you the best."

"I'm sorry for your loss, Mrs. O'Brien."

"What loss?" she said to him bitterly. "He'd dumped me. Took up with a young babe."

I said, "You and Tommy were married for twenty-two years and have two beautiful girls. The love doesn't go away."

"No, it doesn't," she acknowledged morosely. "Come on in."

The living room wasn't nearly as spotless as it had been yesterday. The coffee table was strewn with empty coffee mugs and cans of Ballantine ale, which I happen to think tastes remarkably like soapy dishwater. Newspapers were scattered on the sofa.

She led us into the kitchen, where a fresh box of Entenmann's doughnuts was parked on the table and another person was parked in a chair there, drinking hot coffee and smoking a Marlboro. The muggy air was heavy with cigarette smoke.

"This is my friend Richie," Kathleen said. "Richie, this is Tommy's friend Stewart Hoag and Lieutenant Very, who's investigating his murder."

Richie Filosi got up out of his chair with a grunt, reeking of Aqua Velva. He was a big, thickly built guy in his late forties with a droopy salt-and-pepper mustache. Wore his thinning strands of hair in a comb-over that I can't imagine fooled anyone except himself. Richie was dressed in a horizontal-striped tank top that did an excellent job of accentuating his beer gut, blue jean cutoffs, and dark blue Pumas with a pair of knee-high striped tube socks that were all the rage back when Earl "The Pearl" Monroe was wowing Knick fans at Madison Square Garden. The man was into gold. He wore a heavy gold chain around his neck with some kind of pendant on it that meant nothing to me, a gold ID bracelet on his right wrist and a gold watch on his left that I would have said was a Rolex knock-off except that he was a bent cop, so it just may have been a real one that he confiscated in a raid and kept. He had a tan, but it wasn't a healthy one. You could see the broken blood vessels of a heavy drinker in his puffy face.

He threw his shoulders back and stuck out his chin, sizing Very up. "So you're Dante Feldman's boy," he said in a raspy voice.

"I'm not anybody's boy," Very shot back, bristling.

"Cool off, brother. I didn't mean anything by that."

"Sure you did. You're trying to piss me off so I'll ask you to leave. Not a chance, Richie. Sit the hell down. Oh, and I'm not your brother." This was a side of Very I'd never seen. He was polite and deferential around celebrities. But he was dealing with one of his own now. One of his own whom he considered a lowlife. "So tell me, Richie, how are you getting by without your pension?"

Kathleen looked at Richie in surprise. "What does he mean by that? You told me you collect a pension *and* your disability payments."

"My lawyer's working at getting them restored," Richie assured her. "Just a slight technicality."

Very let out a harsh laugh. "Is that what you call faking an injury in the line of duty? A slight technicality?"

"I served," he said defensively. "I ought to be eligible to collect my retiree benefits."

"If it were up to me, you'd be eligible for jail time," Very said with total contempt as Kathleen watched them go at it, wide-eyed.

"I do odd jobs here and there," Richie said.

Very glared at him. "What?"

"That's how I get by, in answer to your question."

"You mean like running over a middle-aged lady who was out getting her mail?"

"I had nothing to do with what went down in Willoughby last night. You can't pin that on me. I don't care how much juice you have at One P.P. What I meant was, I install screen doors, paint kitchens . . ."

"That must be hard with those herniated discs in your back."

"You just going to keep busting my chops?" Richie demanded angrily.

"I don't know. Haven't made up my mind yet."

Lulu had made up her mind. She went to the fridge, sat and stared at it.

"Does that mean she wants another anchovy?" Kathleen asked me.

"I'm afraid so."

Kathleen fetched her one from the jar in the door of the fridge, once again nearly losing a finger in the transaction, before she sat back down and lit a Kent, dragging on it deeply.

Richie looked at me in amazement. "Your dog eats *anchovies*? What is she, weird?"

Lulu bared her teeth at him, growling.

He eyed her warily. "Why's she doing that?"

"She seems to have taken an instant dislike to you."

"How come?"

"Saves time," Very said.

"Possibly because you're wearing Aqua Velva. She was once kicked in the ribs by a guy who was wearing Aqua Velva."

"But that wasn't me," Richie pointed out.

Then again, I reflected, maybe her large, wet black nose had detected the brawny, urinal-cake scent of Aqua Velva in my apartment. I hadn't, but I'm not a scent hound. Maybe it was Richie who'd picked my lock and bugged my phone. Maybe his old pal Jocko from the two-four had thrown the job his way.

Kathleen swiped at the tears that had welled up suddenly in her eyes. "I still can't believe Tommy's gone. I've known him since we were nine years old. We grew up in the same building."

"Are your girls coming home from school to be with you?" I asked.

"This afternoon. The fall semester just started, too. But they don't care. They're both so upset."

"I'm just glad I could be here," Richie said, patting her hand. "You shouldn't be alone at a time like this."

"Somebody put a tap on Hoagy's phone," Very said to Kathleen. "Tommy made several calls from there yesterday. One of them was to you."

"Yes." Her voice was almost a whisper. "Not long after Hoagy was here. He told me not to believe what people were saying. That he hadn't stolen *Tulsa*."

"How did he sound?"

"Scared. I'd never heard Tommy sound so frightened." To me she said, "He told me I could trust you. I told him you'd already been here and had looked around in his office."

"How did he react to that?" I asked.

"He said, 'Good, at least he knows it's not a hoax. I busted my butt on that damned book.' I said, 'Tommy, what's going to happen?' And he said, 'Don't worry, Hoagy will make everything right.' Except you didn't, did you?"

I sighed inwardly. "No, I didn't. I'm truly sorry I let him down, Kathleen, but the lieutenant will figure out who killed him and why. And I *will* clear Tommy's name. You have my word."

"He was a good guy," Richie put in. "I always liked him."

"Shut up, Richie," Very snapped.

Richie reddened. "I've had just about all I'm going to take from you, *Romaine*. How about we step outside and settle this like men?"

"Happy to," Very said calmly. "Only I should warn you that it means you'll end up with a rearranged face and a half-dozen fewer teeth."

"Guys, come on," Kathleen said pleadingly.

"Sorry, hon," Richie said. "But I don't care for this punk's attitude."

"And I feel just sick about it, Richie." Very glowered across the table at him. "Where were *you* at the time of Tommy's death?"

"This would have been when?"

"Maybe five o'clock."

"Right here," he said as Kathleen's eyes widened in surprise. "Kathleen was watching that Oprah Winfrey on the tube. I was dozing on the sofa. Warm, rainy days like that I can barely keep my eyes open."

"You can back that up?" Very asked her.

Kathleen lowered her eyes, swallowing. "Uh-huh," she murmured in a barely audible voice. Unlike Richie, she was not a practiced liar. And Richie was clearly lying. That look on her face had said so.

"And how about at seven-thirty, eight o'clock? Where were you then?"

"Still right here, except for when I strolled over to First Avenue and got us some Chinese. The owner will remember me. I'm a regular. Beef with broccoli and moo shu pork. My Trans Am never left the garage."

"Oh, hey, are you still in contact with Jocko Conlon?"

Richie blinked at him. "Jocko? Nah, not for years. Last I heard he was peeping through keyholes on the South Shore. Why you asking?"

"There's really no need for you to know why I'm asking, Richie. And it's not too late. Not yet, anyhow."

"Not too late for what?"

"For you to change your story."

Richie shook his head at him disgustedly. "I was a good cop. Do you honestly think I'd have anything to do with what went down yesterday?"

"You and I both know that more than half of the professional hits in this city are performed by retired cops," Very responded. "If someone's looking to take out a no-good spouse or business partner, who do they come looking for? An ex-cop with money problems. How's your bank account these days, Richie?"

"I'm scraping by. That lawyer of mine ain't cheap."

"Whoever took out Sylvia James in Willoughby was no amateur. It was planned and executed by a careful professional."

"Well, it wasn't me," Richie insisted. "Neither was what happened to Tommy. I'm telling you the god's honest truth, I swear."

"Is that right?" Very leaned over the table toward him. "Then help me out here, Richie, because I've got a problem. Why am I having so much trouble believing you?"

"*DO* YOU BELIEVE him?"

"He's a lying schmuck," Very responded as I worked the Jag through the traffic on the Sunrise Highway, gateway to Long Island's South Shore.

I'd insisted upon fetching the Jag from its garage on Columbus Avenue because my sacroiliac, kidneys and possibly spleen refused to make another long trip in Very's cruiser. The lieutenant hadn't resisted. It was a hot late-summer day and we were heading for the shore. Who wouldn't want to drive there in a vintage red XK150 roadster with its top down? I love that car.

Whenever I'm behind the wheel, I'm *me* again. Lulu loves it, too. She sat up happily in Very's lap with her head stuck out the open window, ears flapping.

"I don't like him hanging around that woman either," Very added.

"Nor do I, but that's none of our business. Kathleen told me they have a good time together. Take art classes at the Y, go to the movies . . ."

"Big whoop."

Once the Sunrise Highway made its way from Queens out to Long Island, it began to pass through the dreary, sunbaked South Shore suburbs that snooty Hamptonites long ago dubbed Queens by the Sea. We sped our way past Valley Stream, Freeport and then Massapequa, which had become famous a year earlier when a teenaged girl named Amy Fisher rang her married boyfriend Joey's front doorbell. When Joey's wife opened the door, Amy shot her in the face. The wife survived. The tabloids quickly dubbed Amy the "Long Island Lolita," and Joey, who ran an auto body shop, achieved third-tier celebrity status judging wet T-shirt contests on MTV. Me, I still say the story would have gotten zero traction if Joey's last name hadn't been Buttafuoco.

Babylon, best known by Manhattanites as the last stop on the Long Island Rail Road before Bay Shore, gateway to the Fire Island ferries, had some very nice sections down near the water. There were yacht clubs and lavish beach houses. But if you found yourself a few miles inland you encountered that same flat, cheap, sunbaked suburban sprawl that was true of most of the South Shore.

The law offices of Klein, Walker and Pignatano were located

in a cinder-block building in an unglamorous strip mall next to a beauty salon and a video rental store. This was no fancy Park Avenue law firm filled with elegantly tailored Yale and Harvard Law School types like Mark Kaplan. It was a regular-Joe law firm with regular-Joe lawyers out of schools like St. John's and Fordham.

"So what's Klein's deal?" Very asked me as I pulled the Jag into the parking lot.

"He's been giving Yvette legal advice on how to get a more favorable prenup out of Addison. She told me he's working strictly on a contingency basis."

"Meaning she's giving him a taste?"

"Yvette insists she's not, though I have no doubt she's convinced him that she will."

"She's married to a multimillionaire. Why didn't she hire herself a big-leaguer?"

"I wondered about that myself. Yvette's no dummy. She could have driven a harder bargain when she signed that prenup. Yet she chose not to, meaning she had a bigger scheme in mind—something truly down and dirty—in which case a low-rent shyster like Mel Klein might be exactly who she needs."

It was bright and hot in the parking lot. I put the Jag's top up so the biscuit-colored leather seats wouldn't fry and in we went. The lobby of Klein, Walker and Pignatano, Attorneys at Law, was small, unadorned and chilled to about 55 degrees. It was also empty. No one sat in the waiting area waiting to see anyone. A trim gray-haired woman sat at a reception desk. She had a blue IBM Selectric typewriter on a typing table next to her. Behind her, on a credenza, there was an office computer, as well as a fax machine that was busy churning, churning. She did not look up when we came in. She was too busy chatting with the guy who stood next to the fax machine that was churning, churning. He was a huge, fleshy guy in his fifties with curly red hair that was starting to gray. He wore a pair of tan permanent press slacks and a loose-fitting aqua Ban-Lon shirt that did nothing to hide the horror that Mr. Gravity was doing to his sagging man boobs.

He looked up at us, his face freckled and sunburned, and tilted his head mockingly. "Wait, don't tell me, it's Romaine Very, Dante Feldman's wonder boy. Am I right?"

Very nodded. "And you're none other than the famous Jocko Conlon, king of the shakedown artists. Am *I* right?"

Jocko's eyes narrowed. "You should watch your mouth, kid."

"Yeah, I'll have to do that some time. Richie Filosi sends his regards."

Jocko's face gave away nothing. "Richie? He's a good guy. Sure does love his Ballantine ale. How's he doing?"

"Scraping by. See much of him lately?"

"Nah. Haven't bumped into him in years."

"You sure about that, Jocko?"

"Plenty sure," he said with a distinct cooling in his voice. "What are you doing out here in Babyland?" Which was what some people derisively called Babylon. "Bit out of your jurisdiction, aren't you?"

"Need to talk to one of the partners."

"Which one?"

Very turned to the receptionist. "Mel Klein, please."

"I'm not sure Mr. Klein is available right now," she said hesitantly.

Very flashed his shield and his smile. "Tell him that Detective Lieutenant Romaine Very of the NYPD would appreciate a few minutes of his time in connection with a multiple homicide investigation."

"Of course, Lieutenant." She swiveled in her chair and buzzed Klein. When he answered, she spoke to him in a low, discreet voice.

Jocko was busy eyeballing me. "Who's Beau Brummell here?"

"He's with me," Very said curtly.

"And what do you want with Mel?"

"To talk to him, like I said."

"What about?"

"That would fall under the category of none of your damned business."

"Don't get your panties in a twist. Just curious."

"That makes two of us."

Jocko tilted his head at him again. "How so?"

"What exactly do you do around here?"

"Take a whole lot of photos of married men shtupping their girlfriends out on their boats."

"Do you shake the husbands down for the photos or do you actually bring them back to the office?"

Jocko's face tightened. "I got a PI license. I do legit work for a legit law firm."

"You wouldn't know a legit job if it fell on you like an anvil. Spend any time in the city lately, Jocko?"

"Nah. The city's a cesspool. I like it out here. Everything's nice and clean."

Very nodded. "True that. Everything except for you."

"You've got a real mouth on you for such a little punk."

"So I've been told. Bugs the hell out of me."

The receptionist hung up the phone and sat there with her hands folded before her on the desk. "He'll be happy to see you, Lieutenant. It's the third door on the right."

He thanked her and we started down the hall.

"Excuse me, sir?" she called after me. "There are no dogs allowed in the office."

"We're going to pretend we didn't hear that," I said as we kept on going.

The office of Mel Klein, attorney at law, wasn't much of an office. Eight by ten, and I'm being generous. A cheapo wooden veneer desk. A filing cabinet. A window with venetian blinds that enjoyed a splendid view of the parking lot. The only thing noteworthy about it, other than its air of small-time failure, was what sat on the floor behind his desk—a thirty-inch-square solid steel Honeywell safe with a combination lock.

Mel wasn't much himself as he got up from behind his desk to greet us. He was fortyish, stood five five tops, was concave-chested, and weighed no more than 140 pounds. His wire-framed glasses were crooked and needed attending to, and his close-cropped black hair had a definite dandruff problem that needed attending to. He wore a shirt in that shade of pale green that doesn't look good on anyone, not even me, a striped tie and tan suit trousers that rode too low in the seat. The jacket was on a hanger on a coatrack by the door. Loosey-goosey Mel was not. The man was so jittery he trembled like a little Chihuahua. He also had an unhealthy grayish pallor. Looked as if he lived in a subterranean cavern, not a beach town.

"Lieutenant Very of the NYPD, is it?" he said, his manner hovering somewhere between obsequious and unctuous.

"Thank you for taking the time to see us, Mr. Klein."

"My pleasure, I assure you. And please call me Mel. Everyone does."

"Mel, this is my friend Stewart Hoag."

Mel raised his eyebrows. "The author?"

"I'm afraid so," I said.

"This is a real honor for me. I thought the world of your first novel."

"Thank you. The short-legged one is Lulu."

She took a quick exploratory lap around the office before pausing at the wastebasket next to his desk, sniffing at it.

He watched her curiously before he sat, his hands flat on the desk before him. "Please have a seat and tell me how I can help you."

"Hoagy was close friends with Tommy O'Brien," Very said as we sat.

Mel's face fell. "Are we talking about the Tommy O'Brien who was pushed off that brownstone roof on the Upper West Side yesterday?"

"We are. It was Hoagy's brownstone, in fact. Tommy was hiding out in his apartment."

"Hiding out? Why was he doing that?"

"He'd gotten himself caught in the middle of something and was frightened. When we searched Hoagy's apartment, we discovered that someone had placed a tap on his phone. Tommy made several phone calls yesterday. And received one from here on your private office line at 11:33 A.M."

Mel looked unhappily at the phone on his desk before he nodded his head, considering his next words carefully. He slid open the top drawer of his desk and removed a Tiparillo from its small, flat box. Stuck it in his mouth and lit it with a Ronson lighter that he also kept in the top drawer. He took a few puffs before he slid the drawer shut. "My pacifier," he explained with a nervous chuckle. "Hope you don't mind the smoke."

"Not at all," Very assured him.

Lulu sat on my foot and nudged my knee with her head, which was her way of telling me she was eligible for an anchovy treat.

"Why did you call Tommy, Mel?" Very asked.

"Another client of mine who I was assisting with a contractual matter had asked me if I might be able to help him out."

"Had you spoken to him before yesterday?"

"No, I hadn't."

"Never met him?"

"Never met him."

"This other client you mentioned. Would that be Yvette James?"

Mel stubbed out his Tiparillo in a glass ashtray. "I'm under no obligation to answer that particular question, but I've always tried to cooperate with the police, and since the poor man's dead, I'll be candid with you. Yes, it was Mrs. James. She'd spoken to Mr. O'Brien about the disadvantageous prenuptial agreement she'd signed when she married Addison. And Mr. O'Brien had spoken to her about his own contractual issues with the James family."

"I didn't realize they were confidantes," I said. "She certainly didn't give me that impression."

"My own impression? They weren't close friends. But don't forget that they shared a common foe in Sylvia James, who I understand was run over by a car right outside her own home last evening. I saw it on the eleven o'clock news. Ugly business."

"Yeah, that whole getting murdered thing pretty much always is," Very said. "What was the gist of your phone conversation with Tommy O'Brien?"

"He told me that he had a chance to sign a lucrative contract with a different publisher, one that would also offer him royalty participation. Apparently, his contract with Addison James made him nothing more than a salaried employee. I told him I'd have to take a good hard look at his contract, but that if he had a firm offer for higher-paying employment elsewhere, these sorts of situations could usually be worked out to everyone's satisfaction. Slavery *was* abolished, after all." Mel let out a nervous chuckle. "I suggested we try to set up a meeting next week. I could come into the city or he could come out here."

"I see," Very said.

Me, I was staring at the steel safe behind Mel's desk.

Mel's gaze followed mine. "We keep a safety deposit box at the bank, but we need to store documents, deeds and so forth in there from time to time."

"Is it fireproof?"

"It most certainly is. Waterproof, too. Weighs 295 pounds. It took a pair of burly men with a hand truck to get it in here."

"My brownstone on West 93rd is a firetrap. Whenever I go out for more than an hour I always stash whatever I'm working on in the vegetable bin of my refrigerator."

Mel frowned at me, puzzled. "You don't back up your work?"

"Um, okay, I don't know what those words just meant."

"Store it on a floppy disc that you could take with you when you leave."

"I write on a 1958 solid steel Olympia portable."

"Oh, I see, a traditionalist." Mel smiled slightly. His teeth were small, pointy and yellow. "In that case, my advice is that you ought to invest in a good fireproof strongbox. It wouldn't cost you nearly as much as a safe. And it would do the job for you."

"A strongbox. Interesting idea. I hadn't thought of that. Where would I get one of those?"

"I imagine a good office supply store in Midtown would carry them. If not, they could certainly point you in the right direction."

"I'll look into that. Thanks."

"My pleasure."

"Do you mind telling us how you met Yvette James?" Very asked him.

"Not at all, Lieutenant. A few weeks ago I successfully settled a case involving a landlord who was trying to take advantage of a commercial tenant. I decided to treat myself to a vodka martini at the bar at the American Hotel in Sag Harbor."

"You live out that way?"

"Who, me? Heck, no. I live in Amityville in a two-bedroom condo that I got for a song in a foreclosure. But I'd settled a case, like I said, and sometimes I feel like rubbing shoulders with that rich Sag Harbor summer crowd. My God, I sure do love to look at those fancy women with their tanned, toned figures and designer clothes. I always wonder just exactly how tall and rich a guy would have to be to attract a woman like that. So I sat down at the bar, bought myself a vodka martini, had a sip, and suddenly a voice next to me said, 'Whattaya drinking, hon?' I turned around and, I am not exaggerating, almost fell off of my stool. You've . . . met Mrs. James?"

"We have," Very said. "Nice-looking woman."

"I would call that a bit of an understatement, Lieutenant. She's absolutely *the* most gorgeous creature I've ever met in my life. My God, those blue eyes of hers had me mesmerized instantly. She was wearing a halter top, short shorts and high-heeled sandals. Every guy in the bar was checking her out. Rich, good-looking guys. And yet she'd plopped herself down on the stool right next to mine and asked *me* what I was drinking. I cleared my throat and somehow managed to convey to her that it was a vodka martini. 'I never had one of those before. Would you buy me one?' she said to me. I told her I'd be happy to. When it arrived, we toasted each other and she said, 'I'm Yvette. You're Mel, right? My friend Shauna said I'd find you here, because you settled her case for her today and you have a ritual about coming here. I adore rituals. I have all kinds myself. Like whenever I get sad, I paint my toenails a new color. Right now they're Ballet Slipper.' And with that she proceeded to kick off her sandal and plop her bare foot in my lap right there at the bar, wiggling her succulent toes in the air. Can you imagine?"

"Unbelievable," I said, shaking my head in amazement.

"Anyway," Mel continued, "she said that her friend Shauna—"

"Last name?" Very pulled his notepad from the back pocket of his jeans.

"Reininger. Shauna Reininger, who runs East Hampton's top beauty salon and does Mrs. James's hair and nails whenever she's out there. It was Shauna's case that I'd settled that day. She'd been trying to get out of her lease and move elsewhere because her landlord had failed to make good on the improvements he'd promised. He was trying to hold her up for an entire year's rent. Mrs. James said, 'Shauna told me you argued that bastard down to one month's rent and also spoke to her in plain English so you didn't make her feel stupid.'"

"Just to be clear," I said, "was her bare foot still in your lap at this point?"

"Uh, no. She'd put her sandal back on."

Very shot an irritated look at me. "Please go on, Mel."

"Mrs. James is married to a much, much older man. An *extremely* wealthy one at that. And she's not what I'd call thorough when it comes to examining fine print. Consequently, it seems that Mr. James convinced her to sign a truly awful prenuptial agreement, which basically stipulates that upon his death she will inherit none of his vast fortune, not a single one of his numerous country retreats nor so much as one cent of the royalties of his many bestselling books, which run into countless millions of dollars per year. It was really quite a deplorable agreement, in my view. We're talking about a man who's worth in excess of $200 million and owns prestige properties scattered from Provence to Maui, including the $4.5 million shorefront mansion on Lily Pond Lane in East Hampton, where Mrs. James has summered ever since they got married. Yet upon his death, the mansion on Lily Pond Lane would have passed to Sylvia, not to her."

"Except it turns out that he's still alive and Sylvia's the one who's dead," Very pointed out. "How does that affect Yvette?"

"I can't help you there. I'm not privy to the terms of Mr. James's will. I just know that when Mrs. James came to me, the likelihood was that Mr. James would predecease Sylvia, that Sylvia would inherit the Lily Pond Lane mansion and that Mrs. James would end up out on her fanny."

"And a cute little fanny it is," I said.

"Yes, it is," Mel agreed, coloring slightly.

"I don't mean to get personal," Very said, "but is your relationship with Yvette James strictly business?"

Mel was blushing like a bashful schoolboy now. "Of course it is. She's a client. It would be unethical for our relationship to be anything but business."

"Have a girlfriend, Mel?"

"Our receptionist, Miss Leto, and I have gone out to dinner together a few times, but she's made it clear she thinks of me as more of a friend."

"Getting back to Tommy O'Brien . . ."

"Absolutely. What else can I tell you about him?" Mel asked, eager to help out—and to get off of the subject of Yvette's cute little fanny.

"Your only contact with him was that one phone call yesterday?"

"Correct, the one phone call. He said he'd be back in touch as soon as he was able to set up a date and time, but I take it that the poor fellow died a few hours later. Horrible thing. Just horrible." Mel glanced at his watch, which was a slim rose-gold Patek Philippe Calatrava with an alligator band. Mighty expensive watch for a small-time South Shore lawyer. I wondered if it had been a gift from a certain client. "And now, if you gentlemen will please excuse me, I'm due at the county courthouse."

"I STILL DON'T get it," Very said as I lowered the Jag's top and we got in, Lulu jumping into his lap. "This dude's strictly a small-timer. Why didn't Yvette hire herself a stud?"

"Don't be fooled by Mel's appearance or manner, Lieutenant.

I've been around dozens of pint-size Hollywood agents who come across like total nebbishes same as he does. They're not. They'd stab you in the jugular vein with a Bic pen to protect their client's interests. And if he's got Jocko around the place, then we know he's a shyster. Also, don't forget that Yvette has been skating on the edge of the law most of her life. She's right at home here at the law offices of Klein, Walker and Pignatano. Besides, she's got Mel wrapped around her pinkie toe." I was about to start up the Jag's engine when I stopped. "We've got company."

Jocko Conlon had followed us out there. He moved slowly in the bright sunlight, massaging his thick right shoulder with his left hand like an aging sore-armed relief pitcher trying to hang on for one more season.

"Nice ride," he said to me admiringly as he approached us.

"Thanks, I like it."

"I'm concerned about something," he said to Very. "Figured I ought to mention it to you."

"That's real thoughtful of you," Very said to him dryly. "Mention away."

"I hope you don't think Richie Filosi had anything to do with Tommy O'Brien's murder."

"Why would I be thinking that?"

"Because I read in the *New York Post* that he's been seeing Tommy's wife. But Richie hasn't got a mean bone in his body. In fact, I always thought he was too nice a guy for the job. A cop has to be willing to put a scare into people sometimes. Maybe even rough 'em up a little. I don't need to tell you that, do I?"

Very let that one slide on by. Just sat there in silence waiting for Jocko to speak his piece.

"But Richie wasn't like that. Anyway, just thought you should know."

"Okay, now I know. Thanks for the advice."

"Can I give you some more advice?" Jocko edged closer to the Jag, his voice distinctly more threatening now. "Go easy on the little guy."

"You mean Mel?"

"He's the sensitive type."

"You say that like it's a bad thing," I put in. "I'm the sensitive type myself, but I've got everything I need. I'm an artist, and I don't look back." On his blank stare I added, "Not a big Zimmy fan, I take it."

He shook his head at me. "Why can't I understand a single fucking word you're saying?"

"I could tell you, but I don't think you'd like the answer."

"You trying to pick a fight with me?" he demanded angrily.

Lulu immediately bared her teeth at him, letting out a low growl.

Jocko watched her in amusement. "And I don't understand the deal with the dog."

"You make it sound as if there are things you *do* understand," I said.

"Listen, you're making a big mistake if you push me, pal."

"I'm not your pal. And excuse me, but did you just threaten me in front of a police officer?"

"No, that was friendly advice. Same as I just gave *Romaine*."

"What advice was that again?" Very asked him. "I've forgotten already."

"Go easy on the little guy," Jocko repeated, biting off the

words this time. Then he turned and started back toward the cinder-block law offices of Klein, Walker and Pignatano, moving slowly and heavily. He had a rolling gait, as if the ground was shifting under his feet.

Maybe it was.

Chapter Eight

W e stopped off at a diner on our way back to the Sunrise Highway. It was one of those places that had huge, well-padded booths, huge, well-padded menus and very few customers. Also one of those rotating glass display cases laden with shelves of gooey cakes and pies that looked as if they'd been going around and around in there for weeks. The creepy Muzak version of "Raindrops Keep Fallin' on My Head" that was playing as the perky young hostess led us to our booth segued to an even creepier Muzak version of Donovan's "Mellow Yellow," which I was unable to get out of my head for several hours no matter how hard I tried. When our waitress came, we both ordered cheeseburgers, fries and chocolate shakes. Lulu had a tuna melt, hold the toast. I resisted the urge to tell our waitress to hold the toast between her knees, just in case she wasn't a Jack Nicholson fan, hadn't seen *Five Easy Pieces* and would order us to vacate the premises at once. Slowly, ever so slowly, I am maturing.

"What's your thinking, dude? Is Yvette James shtupping Mel?"

"Did you see that Patek Philippe he had on? If she can keep him happy with a wristwatch, then that means she hasn't had to sleep with him. But I guarantee you he'll do *anything* if he thinks he has a shot at getting naked with her."

"Including flattening Sylvia James with a car?"

"Hey, the plastic Tiparillo tip that Lulu found didn't wind up at the crime scene by accident."

"I was wondering when you were going to bring that up."

"And now you're going to tell me that it doesn't prove Mel was there."

"That's exactly what I'm going to tell you. Not unless the Willoughby PD crime lab turns up a fingerprint on it that matches Mel's. If they don't, then anyone could have tossed it there. Hell, it could have been sitting in that gutter for a week."

"I'd call that a pretty humongous coincidence."

"Call it whatever you like. Just don't call it proof."

The waitress placed our cheeseburgers, fries and shakes before us and slid Lulu's tuna melt under the table.

"Personally, I agree with you," Very admitted as he took a huge bite out of his cheeseburger. "But professionally, I have to deal in hard evidence that a DA can walk into a courtroom with."

I took a bite of my own burger and found it passable— although something about our visit with Mel Klein in his dreary little office had made my stomach tighten up. Jocko Conlon hadn't done much for my appetite either.

"Go easy on the little guy."

We ate in silence for a moment. Or at least Very and I did. Lulu has never learned how to eat tuna melts quietly. She slurps them. Sounds like a drain unstopping.

Very popped a couple of fries in his mouth, munching on them. "School me—why were you going on and on about that safe in Mel's office? I've never heard so much gum flapping about office safes. You even got him to offer you a crash course on metal strongboxes. What were you doing?"

"My job. It may have gotten lost in the carnage of the past eighteen hours, but I was hired by Guilford House to find *Tulsa*. If it was Jocko who staged that snatch and grab outside of the copier store—and he certainly matches Tommy's description of the guy who threatened him—then there'd be no better place to stash two copies of the newest Addison James saga than inside his employer's fireproof office safe. You'll notice that Mel didn't offer to open it so as to show me how roomy and luxurious it was inside."

"I did notice," Very said grudgingly. "You think he's got *Tulsa* stashed in there?"

"Don't you?"

"For whose benefit? Who's behind this?"

"I wish I knew, but there are still too many moving pieces. Tell me, Lieutenant, do you think Mel could have done it?"

"Done what?"

"Shoved Tommy off my roof. Tommy was five eight and a solid 165."

Very mulled it over as he munched on his burger. "Don't see why not. If he'd already whacked him over the head, then all it would have taken was one good push. You liking him for it? Because I'm not."

"Why not?"

"The Mel Kleins of the world get other people to do their dirty work for them."

"People like Jocko?"

"People like Jocko." Very took a gulp of his shake. "Were you gas-facing Mel or do you really stash your manuscript in the vegetable bin of your refrigerator?"

"I absolutely do. My building's a firetrap. And believe me, I'm not alone. Isaac Bashevis Singer's manuscripts always smelled like rotting onions. He was famous for it. Also Norman Mailer, Maxwell Taylor . . ."

Very looked at me, puzzled. "Maxwell *who*?"

"I take it you're not a Zimmy fan either," I said as the sound system gave way to a relentlessly cheery Muzak version of Jimi Hendrix's "Hey Joe." There's a reason I don't own a handgun. I just never know when I might go on a rampage, shoot up a diner's sound system and end up with my wild-eyed mug shot plastered on the front page of the *New York Post*.

"Mel's right," Very said. "You should get a metal strongbox."

"I'd much rather move back in with Merilee."

"Yeah, that would work, too."

"Lieutenant, I have an incredibly stupid question for you."

"I'll do my best not to give you an incredibly stupid answer."

"Did the same person who killed Tommy kill Sylvia? Or is it possible that we're looking at two different killers?"

"Based on my experience, it'll turn out to be the same person." He polished off the last of his burger. "But don't go by me. It's not as if I'm an expert or anything. I only do this for a living."

IT WAS MIDAFTERNOON by the time we got back to the garage on Columbus Avenue, swapped out the Jag for Very's Crown Vic and careened our way down to Sixth Avenue in Midtown to see Norma Fives, noted ninety-five-pound rising star of Deep River and former lover of Tommy O'Brien.

Not that it was easy. In order to see Norma without an appointment Very had to flash his shield at the supremely stuck-up receptionist and inform her that it was an urgent police matter. She spoke to someone on the phone in a low voice and then asked us to wait.

We waited. Lulu dozed. Very paced. After twenty minutes or so, the door next to the reception desk finally opened and an exceptionally tall, athletically built young man emerged to usher us in. He was dressed in Brooks Brothers from head to toe, minus his suit jacket. He wore his striped repp tie tucked in between the second and third buttons of his white shirt so as to keep it from getting caught in his typewriter. That's a Dartmouth thing. My idea of lame, but it's better than the way Princetonians oh-so-casually throw their tie over their shoulder.

"I'm Bart, Norma's assistant," he informed us. "Please follow me."

So we followed him through the door, where he made a sharp right turn, then a left turn, then a second left before he opened another door that led us to a long, narrow corridor. Bart was not easy to keep up with. He was at least six six and had the springy, loping stride that I can remember having had fifteen years ago myself and don't anymore. The corridor's walls were lined with the cover art of Deep River's current top-selling books, many of which appeared to be romance novels featuring heroines with large, heaving breasts and heroes who resembled Fabio. Bodice rippers, they call them in the trade. There were spine-tingling thrillers for readers who like spine-tingling thrillers. I don't. My

real life is already spine tingling enough. Deep River also published several prestige highbrow novelists as well as a Pulitzer
Prize–winning *Washington Post* foreign correspondent who'd
just written a major bestseller about the Iran-Contra Affair.

The editorial assistants were parked at cubicles outside of
the editors' offices. The lower-ranking editors had small win-
dowless offices on our left. The senior editors and rising stars
such as Norma had larger offices on our right with windows
that looked out over Sixth Avenue.

"Norma's conferring with one of her authors on the phone,"
Bart said apologetically when we arrived at his cubicle to find
her office door closed. "She'll just be another minute."

Very asked him if he could use his phone.

"No problem, Lieutenant. Let me get you an outside line."
Bart punched a button, then swiveled the phone around and
handed it to him.

Very thanked him and made his call.

I studied Bart, who had neatly trimmed light brown hair
and a sincere, boyish face. "What's your last name, Bart?"

"It's, um, Shackleford," he replied, slightly ill at ease.

"Thought so. You played small forward for Dartmouth,
didn't you?" I asked him as Very spoke to someone on the
phone about Shauna Reininger. He wanted a man to locate her
and confirm Mel's story. "You're a southpaw. Used to fire long-
range jumpers from way deep in the corner. Whenever you hit
nothing but net, the home crowd would yell 'Swish!'"

Bart nodded his head. "Graduated two years ago. You must
be a real fan of Ivy League sports."

"Chucked a spear or two for the Crimson back in my day."

Very hung up the phone and said, "Hoagy's being modest,

which I have to say is shocking the hell out of me. This man right here was the fourth-best javelin hurler in the entire Ivy League."

"Third best," I corrected him.

Now Bart was staring at me with his mouth open. "My God, you're Stewart Hoag. And that must be Lulu."

"I'm afraid so."

"Wow, this a huge honor for me. May I shake your hand, Mr. Hoag?"

"Make it Hoagy," I said, waiting patiently for the numbness in my fingers to subside. Bart had huge hands and a powerful grip.

"I am such a huge fan of *Our Family Enterprise*. I've read it four times. Are you working on anything new? Please say you are."

"I are."

"Wow, that's the best news I've heard in weeks."

Norma's office door opened. She shook my hand with her small ice-cold one and ushered us in—us as in Lulu and me. Very was making another call and held up one finger to let us know he'd join us in a second.

Norma's windowed office was insanely cluttered. There were white metal bookcases bursting with manuscripts, bound galleys and recently published hardcovers. Her desk was heaped with piles of manuscripts. So was the carpeted floor.

She sat down behind her desk. There was one other chair in there—piled with books, naturally. I put them on the floor and sat down, looking her over. She had dark circles under her eyes and seemed emotionally wrung out. She was wearing a different drab, shapeless linen dress. Same limp hair. Same horn-rimmed glasses.

"How are you, Norma?"

"Not great."

"I'm truly sorry about Tommy."

She said nothing in response. Just watched Lulu sniffing delicately at the piles of manuscripts on the floor, possibly in search of one that smelled like a bestseller. Trust me, her guess was as good as 90 percent of the editors in New York.

Very joined us now, closing the door behind him, his eyes widening as he gazed across the desk at Norma. He seemed startled . . . or something.

So did Norma as she gazed back across the desk at him. She gulped. She definitely gulped. Was I witnessing an instant attraction? Was bony little Norma Fives Very's type? She *was* brainy. He said he liked brainy. But was a hyper, rock 'n' roll homicide detective *her* type? Such a love match would never have occurred to me before, but ever since Julia Roberts and Lyle Lovett tied the knot that summer, I'd decided I knew nothing about what drew two people together.

"Norma Fives, say hello to Detective Lieutenant Romaine Very of the NYPD. He's investigating Tommy's death. Also Sylvia's."

Again Norma gulped. "Pleased to meet you, Lieutenant. Well, not pleased. There's nothing to be pleased about, is there? But if there's anything I can . . ." She glanced around at the office. "Sorry, I don't seem to have another chair. I'll have Bart get you one."

"Please don't bother," he said, leaning against the closed door, his muscular arms crossed in front him, right knee jiggling. "I've been sitting all day. Just have a few quick questions for you anyhow."

"All right. What is it that you wish to know?"

"I understand you and Tommy O'Brien had a romantic relationship."

She shrugged her narrow shoulders. "Of a sort," she said glumly.

"Meaning . . . ?"

"Tommy was a married man. My first. I'm told that every sophisticated professional woman in New York must have at least one affair with a married man. Tommy was mine. I don't intend to have another one. Absolutely nothing good came of it. He left his wife and moved into a fleabag studio apartment in Hell's Kitchen. He was miserable. His wife was miserable. And I spent most of my time crying. What's so sophisticated about that?"

"Why didn't Tommy move in with you when he left his wife?"

"I have a tiny studio on Bank Street that's barely big enough for one person. And we weren't ready to make that sort of commitment."

"Did you ever spend the night at his place in Hell's Kitchen?"

Norma shook her head. "Never even saw it."

"Why not?"

"He didn't want me to. Told me it was a dump."

"Well, he wasn't lying to you about that. We tossed it yesterday."

"Is that routine procedure?"

"Pretty much. Plus we were looking for *Tulsa*."

"Did you have any luck?"

"Afraid not. *You* don't have it, do you?"

Norma looked at him surprised. "You think *I* hired someone to steal *Tulsa*?"

He looked around at the heaps of manuscripts in her office. "This would be a perfect place to hide it—in plain sight. Am I right, dude?"

"Yes, you are. We could be staring directly at it."

"Except you're not," she insisted. "Besides, why would I want to steal *Tulsa*?"

"To hose Sylvia James, who I understand you once nearly blinded with a Stanley Bostitch stapler," Very said. "And to get Tommy fired so you could hire him to take on a more lucrative project for you."

"Well, I don't have it," she stated defensively. "And I have no idea where it is. But you're right. I was hoping to sign Tommy. Addison and Sylvia treated him very shabbily. He deserved better. He was a talented writer and a good man." She paused, her mouth tightening. "He told me that he and his wife were talking about getting a divorce. That's not something I'm very proud of. I've never broken up a marriage."

"You didn't break up this one," Very assured her. "Unless, that is, you're the one who shoved him off Hoagy's roof."

Norma blinked at him in surprise. "You're kidding, right? I'm an editor, not a killer."

"Real world? All kinds of people are killers. Doctors, lawyers, certified public accountants, notary publics . . ."

"How would I have done it?"

"Done what?"

"Shoved Tommy off of that roof. I'm not strong enough."

"So you had a helper. Your assistant, Bart, looks strong."

"Very," I agreed, nodding.

He frowned at me. "Yeah, dude?"

"He looks very strong."

"You got that right."

"Next I suppose you're going to tell me I drove out to Willoughby and ran Sylvia over," Norma said to him coldly.

"Did you?"

"Of course not. I don't even own a car."

"That's why God invented car rental agencies."

"I didn't rent a car."

"We can check all of the rental agencies."

"Go right ahead," she dared him.

"Then again, maybe you've got a friend who has one." Very stepped away from the door, swung it open and gestured to Bart, who came loping in, instantly filling the office with his giant frame. Very closed the door, gazing up at him. "Own a car, dude?"

"Yeah, I do, Lieutenant. A BMW 325i."

"Nice car."

"It's not brand-new or anything. It's an '89."

"Still a nice car. Where were you last evening, Bart?"

"Home."

"Where's home?"

"I have a floor-through in a brownstone on East 73rd."

Very let out a low whistle, impressed. "You can afford that on what they pay you around here?"

"I, um, have some family money," Bart said uncomfortably.

"You live alone?"

"I have for the past month or so, yeah."

"Meaning you just broke up with someone?"

"That's the general idea."

"What'd you do last evening?"

"I read a submission for Norma that a top agent at ICM had sent over."

"Were you alone all evening?"

"Yes."

"Did you go out to eat?"

"No, I picked up a pizza on my way home from work."

"Talk to anyone on the phone?"

"Yes, I talked to Norma."

"What about?"

"The submission, after I finished reading it."

"Did you like it?"

"I thought it was pretentious crap."

Very turned to Norma. "So I guess that means you were home, too."

"Yes."

"Alone?"

"Yes. The man I've been seeing was murdered yesterday, remember?"

"Trust me, I haven't forgotten." Very swung the door back open. "Thanks, Bart. We're good."

Bart returned to his cubicle, Very closing the door behind him.

"Is there anything you want to tell us about him?" I asked Norma.

She arched an eyebrow at me curiously. "Such as what?"

I didn't bother to respond. Just stared across the crowded desk at her.

"Well, his full name is Bart Shackleford."

"Already know that," I said. "And . . . ?"

"Where are you going with this?"

"You know exactly where I'm going with this, Norma. *And* . . . ?"

She heaved a sigh. "And his father was Gerrard Shackleford."

"As in *the* Gerrard Shackleford?"

"As in *the* Gerrard Shackleford," she confirmed with a nod of her head.

"Okay, help me out here," Very said. "Who was Gerrard Shackleford?"

"One of the true giants of the hard-boiled detective fiction world, Lieutenant. He wrote with genuine depth, wit and style. His name doesn't ring a bell because in real life he was a federal appellate court judge in Trenton, so he published under the pseudonym of Tucker Maxwell."

Very's eyes widened. "Tucker Maxwell? I've read him. He was great."

"You're right, he was," I said. "And guess what? His editor was none other than Sylvia James at Guilford House. He must have written a dozen books for her."

"Fourteen," Norma said softly.

"Until, that is, his sales started to dip a bit. This was, when, four years ago? You were still working there, weren't you, Norma?"

"I was," she said, her voice barely more than a whisper.

"Instead of offering Judge Shackleford a new contract for a tad less money, which would have been the classy thing to do given his elite status in the crime fiction world, what did Sylvia do?"

"She dropped him."

"You may remember what happened next, Lieutenant. It made the newspapers. Bart's dad drove his car to a rest stop on the New Jersey Turnpike, parked and downed a fifth of vodka with a Drano chaser."

"I do remember," Very said quietly. "Ugly way to die."

"Is that why you hired Bart as your assistant?" I asked Norma. "Because of what Sylvia did to his father?"

"It's certainly one of the reasons. He's also good at his job. Smart, talented, works hard."

"Does he have the writing bug himself?"

"Every editorial assistant in this place does. They all want to grow up to become you."

"They wouldn't if they knew me better. Did Sylvia know you hired him?"

"Naturally. This is publishing. Everybody knows everybody's business."

Very popped a fresh piece of bubble gum in his mouth and stood there chewing it, his head nodding, nodding. "So Bart owns a car and has a motive of his own for murdering Sylvia. Interesting. Do you know anyone else who owns a car?" he asked Norma.

"My cousin Meg does."

"Where does she live?"

"In a high-rise on First Avenue."

"I'll need her contact info."

"Whatever for?"

"So we can check to find out whether you borrowed her car last night."

Norma glared at him. "You're being adversarial and accusatory, Lieutenant, if you don't mind me saying so."

"I don't mind. That's my job. It's what I do."

"It's true, it is," I told her. "I've seen him in action several times. Lieutenant Very happens to be the NYPD's top homicide investigator. He also has a BA from Columbia in astrophysics."

She shook her head at me. "And you're telling me this be-cause . . . ?"

"I sensed you were curious."

"You should take your sensor in and get it recalibrated. I wasn't."

Lulu was done sniffing her way around the office. Went over and put her head on Norma's knee.

Norma was taken aback. "Why is she doing that?"

"She wants you to pet her."

"Oh." Norma patted her gingerly on the head. "We never had pets when I was growing up. My parents didn't believe in them."

"What a shame," I said. "A house without a pet is a home without a soul."

"That sounds familiar. Who said that?"

"The Dalai Lama, I believe. Either the Dalai Lama or Soupy Sales."

Lulu moved away and curled up at my feet with a grunt.

Very crossed his arms in front of his chest again, narrowing his gaze at Norma. "Why did you hurl a Bostitch stapler across a conference table at Sylvia?"

"Because she humiliated me in front of the entire editorial department and I couldn't take it anymore. I snapped."

"You were lucky, you know. She could have filed criminal assault charges against you. Instead she just fired you."

"She didn't fire me, I quit. But you're right. I was very lucky. I've always been lucky. Ask anyone. They'll tell you just how incredibly damned lucky I am," Norma said, gazing morosely out the window at the traffic on Sixth.

"Were you in love with Tommy O'Brien?" Very asked her.

She turned and studied him. "Why is that important?"

"It may not be. Then again, it may be the linchpin of the entire case. I merely collect information. That's what an investigator does."

"I don't know if loved him, Lieutenant. I'm not sure if I've ever been in love. I've had my share of boyfriends. We've talked literature, consumed tremendous quantities of wine, had sex that ranged from unexciting to awkward to just plain awful. But I've never experienced that 'running barefoot through the park with balloons' kind of love. Maybe there is no such thing. Maybe that's just movie love." She paused, considering her next words carefully. "Tommy made me feel safe. I had feelings of affection for him. But he wasn't my soul mate. Maybe there is no such thing as one of those either. Maybe that's movie love, too."

Very nodded. "Fair enough. Where were you when he was getting thrown off Hoagy's roof?"

"What time did it happen?"

"Around five."

"I was having drinks at the Algonquin with one of our romance authors. I need someone to write the follow-up to *The Girl Under the Bed*. I'd been hoping it would be Tommy, but I had to have a Plan B in case he couldn't get out of his contract with Addison."

"And this author's name is . . . ?"

"Morris Needleman. He writes under the name Madeira Corso."

"And how about when Sylvia was run over? Where were you then?"

Norma let out an exasperated sigh. "I just told you. I was home."

"Doing what?"

"Drinking a bottle of Sancerre and crying my eyes out. I spoke to Bart, as you already know. I called my sister, Lauren, in Santa Cruz. I called my college roommate, Andrea Lorenz, who now lives in Minnesota, has three kids and is married to a metallurgist named Pete. I called my first boyfriend from high school, Steve Portigal, who works in the art department at *Sports Illustrated* and lives in Park Slope with a woman from Ecuador."

"We can run a trace on all of those calls, you know."

"Go right ahead. You don't actually consider me a suspect, do you?"

"I consider you a person of interest."

She frowned at him. "Do I need a lawyer?"

"If you need a lawyer, I'll be the first to tell you," he said, easing himself away from the door. "Well, okay then . . ."

"What is that supposed to mean?"

"It means we're done here," I translated, getting up out of my chair.

"Thanks for your time," Very said. "Oh, hey, I almost forgot to give you my card." He plucked one from the wallet in the back pocket of his jeans and handed it across the desk to her.

She took it, peering at it. "Do you want one of mine?"

"I wouldn't say no."

She reached into the top drawer of her desk for one and gave it to him.

"Your hands are ice cold," he pointed out.

"They keep the AC in this place cranked up for the men, who are never cold."

"You should be wearing a sweater. You got a sweater?"

"There's one around here somewhere . . ."

Lulu found it—tossed carelessly over a box of books. Very grabbed it for her. Not surprisingly, it was a shapeless cotton cardigan that was the color of Malt-O-Meal.

Very held it open for her. "Here, put this on. You'll catch cold. You're under a lot of stress, and you look like you haven't eaten a decent meal in a year."

"Who are you, my long-lost Jewish mother? Because you're not exactly what I was picturing."

"Put it on, will you?"

"I'm perfectly comfortable, Lieutenant. And I've always been this thin. But thanks for your concern."

"Let's get one thing straight. I'm not leaving until you put this sweater on. Now stand up, will you?"

She stood up, coloring ever so slightly, and slid her skinny arms into the boxy sleeves. "I do know how to button it myself," she assured him as he started to work on the buttons.

"Suit yourself," Very said. "You may hear from me again. Then again, you may not. Depends on how it all shakes out. But you have my card. If you think of anything that slipped your mind, don't hesitate to call."

"I won't. Now, if you'll please excuse me, I really need to get back to work. Bart will escort you to the elevators."

Very closed her door behind us and said, "I'll run you home, dude."

"No need. I can catch a cab."

"Nah, I'll drive you home."

"Okay, thanks. There may be a couple of Bass ales in the refrigerator, if that's of any interest."

"A great deal of interest, now that you mention it."

Bart got his towering self up from behind his desk and said, "Let me show you gentlemen how to get back to the elevators."

"Did he just call us gentlemen?" Very said to me.

"Must have us confused with a different pair of guys."

As we started from Bart's cubicle his phone rang. He stopped to answer it. "Naomi Fives's office . . . Why, yes, he's right here. You just caught him." He held the phone out to Very. "It's for you, Lieutenant."

He took the phone from Bart and said, "It's Very. What's up?" He face fell. "Uh-huh . . . Uh-huh . . . Okay, I'm on it." Then he handed Bart the phone, thanked him and went charging down the corridor.

"Where's he going?" Bart wondered.

"Somewhere in a big hurry. Lulu will show us the way out, not to worry. Nice meeting you, Bart. I was a big admirer of your father's work. That was a terrible thing, what happened to him."

"Yes, it was," he said quietly, his jaw tightening. "Thank you."

Lulu had already rambled her way down the hall and caught up with Very so he wouldn't get lost. She's not quick off the blocks, but she can scoot once she gets up a full head of steam. I had to practically sprint to catch up with them as editorial assistants up and down both sides of the corridor eyeballed us with a mix of curiosity and fascination.

"What's up?" I called out to Very.

"It's contagious, that's what," he answered over his shoulder.

"What is?"

"We got a bulletin from the Nassau County sheriff. Mel Klein's neighbor in his condominium complex in Amityville just found him in their parking garage shot through the head."

"No way . . ."

"Yes way. The little guy's gone."

MEL'S CONDO COMPLEX was two blocks from a marina. There were several of them on the block, all newly built. Townhouse-style condos, with underground parking garages. Perfect for up-scale singles. The half-dozen cars that were parked in the garage of Mel's complex were shiny high-end late model Acuras, Audis and the like—with the exception of Mel's relatively modest and not very late model black Volvo 740 station wagon, which suited his personality perfectly. He was just the sort who wouldn't want his clients to think that he was getting rich off them.

Instead, he'd just gotten dead.

He was seated snugly behind the wheel in his harness seat belt with his window rolled down. His complexion in death wasn't much different than it had been in life, although he did look utterly shocked and his face was distorted from the entry wound in the side of his head directly over his left ear. Plus there was the issue of all of the blood splatter and brain tissue that were congealing on his neck and the shoulders of his green shirt.

Nassau County sheriff's cars were clustered out front along with an unmarked Crown Vic, an EMT van and a couple of crime scene vans. A bald, tubby middle-aged detective named Meade was the lead officer.

After he and Very exchanged terse greetings, Very said, "I was told that a neighbor found him when she got home and pulled into the garage. Nobody heard the shot and phoned it in?"

"Nobody," Meade answered wearily. "And I'm right there with you, Lieutenant. You fire off a weapon in a basement ga-

rage like this one, it's going to make such a *boom* that people
will hear it halfway down the street."

"Meaning his shooter used a silencer," Very said.

"Must have," Meade grunted. "Victim's got what appears to
be a 9-millimeter entry wound in the side of his head. And the
weapon had enough muzzle velocity for the bullet to go straight
through his head, shatter the passenger-side widow and embed
itself pretty damned deep in the garage wall twenty feet away.
We're not talking about your ordinary personal protection
handgun."

"I'm down with that," Very agreed. "I'd make it a .357 Magnum. Professional hit."

"Me, too," Meade said, noticing me standing nearby with
Lulu right at my heel. She's learned to not wander off and potentially contaminate a crime scene when there's been a violent
death. She has a lot of experience with violent deaths. We both
have. Too damned much, if you ask me. Not that you did.

Very followed Meade's gaze. "This is Stewart Hoag. He was
hired to find a missing Addison James manuscript that may or
may not be at the center of this."

Meade came over and shook my hand. "You a PI, Hoag?"

"Novelist, actually."

Meade furrowed his brow, bewildered, then glanced down
at Lulu, who gazed up at him quizzically, which left him looking even more bewildered. He turned back to Very. "I understand you paid a call on the victim at his office this afternoon."

"That's correct."

"Mind if I ask why?"

"Klein was providing legal advice to two people connected
to a case I'm working. One of those people, Tommy O'Brien,

was thrown off of an Upper West Side brownstone roof yesterday. Hoagy's roof, as a matter of fact. O'Brien worked for Addison James, the bestselling author. The other person Klein was advising was James's wife, Yvette."

"Any idea what kind of advice Mrs. James was seeking?"

"She wasn't happy with the prenup she signed when she married him. She was hoping Klein could arrange to have it redrafted."

"Addison James is a pretty big name, isn't he?" Meade said.

"He's the wealthiest author in America," I said. "Worth hundreds of millions of dollars."

"So why'd his wife retain a Babylon small-timer like Klein?"

"Klein had helped a friend of hers," I said. "She also told me she felt comfortable with him because he didn't talk down to her." I glanced over at him, seated there behind the wheel of his modest Volvo in his blood- and brain-splattered green shirt. "Do you think he knew his killer?"

Meade thumbed his chin. "What makes you ask that?"

"The absence of shattered glass. It's a hot day. He had his AC on, yet he'd rolled down his window. The passenger-side window was still rolled up—hence all of that shattered glass over there."

"Maybe he needed a key card to open the door to the garage," Very said.

Meade shook his head. "Remote control device. It's on the passenger seat."

"Then I'm right there with Hoagy," Very said. "Somebody he knew must have approached him."

"A neighbor?" Meade wondered.

"A neighbor who then proceeded to shoot him at point-blank range with a .357 Magnum equipped with a silencer?" Very said doubtfully.

"You make a good point," Meade acknowledged.

"Did you know Klein?" Very asked him.

"Not personally. I knew of him. He had a good reputation. Decent low-key guy who did a decent low-key job. Quiet bachelor who steered clear of the marina party crowd. We're searching his apartment now. And I want to sit down with his firm's PI, Jocko Conlon, to see what he knows."

"You haven't talked to him yet?"

"Just briefly on the phone. He's holding down the fort at the office. The receptionist there, a Roseanne Leto, is real upset, apparently."

"Are you acquainted with Jocko?"

"More than acquainted," Meade responded, his tubby face breaking into a grin. "He was my partner out here when he went to work for the Nassau County sheriff. Best cop I've ever worked with. But he got fed up with having to fill out a form in triplicate every time he had to take a piss, so he decided to go private. Keeps telling me I ought to join him. Believe me, Lieutenant Very, if anyone can help us nail Klein's shooter, it'll be Jocko."

"I see . . ." Very said gloomily.

Meade studied him curiously. "You see what, Lieutenant?"

"Nothing. Don't mind me. I'm just feeling kind of fed up with the world right now."

"Sure, I hear you. Appreciate you making the drive back out here. Is there anything else I can tell you?"

"Nah, I think we're good," Very said.

"Then if you'll excuse me I'd better get back to working this."

"Yeah, you'd better do that."

"HOW ON EARTH could Meade possibly say that Jocko Conlon was a good cop?" I asked Very as he steered his cruiser back toward the Sunrise Highway, Lulu curled up on the seat between us with her head in my lap.

"And here I thought you were supposed to be a brainy dude."

"So, what, you're telling me he's as crooked as Jocko?"

"That's exactly what I'm telling you."

"Meaning that if it turns out Jocko had anything to do with this . . ."

"Then Meade will do everything he can to gum up the investigation. He's scum. A total waste of skin. Every breath he takes he's using up somebody else's oxygen."

"I'm sensing the man didn't make a good impression on you."

"Ya think?"

"There's something that my mind keeps circling back to, Lieutenant."

"Which is . . . ?"

"When Jocko was on the job in the city he worked out of the two-four with Richie Filosi, and Richie is short on funds."

"I've had a man on Richie all day. He and Kathleen went to a two o'clock W. C. Fields double bill at the Film Forum."

I glanced over at him admiringly. "Nothing gets past you, does it?"

"Not true, dude," he said, turning gloomy again. "This whole case is getting past me. No matter which direction I turn, somebody ends up dead."

"So what's your next move?"

"Good question." He got back on the highway and floored it, his jaw working on a fresh piece of bubble gum, his mind working the case. He was silent for a long time before he said, "I know, way deep down inside, that I'm going to be sorry for the words that are about to come out of my mouth."

"What words are those?"

"Dude, have you got any ideas?"

"Funny you should mention that, Lieutenant. As a matter of fact I have."

Chapter Nine

Addison was seated at the partners desk in his huge office gazing stubbornly out the window at his view of the Hudson. Darkness had fallen over the river and lights blazed in the windows of the waterfront apartment towers across the river on the New Jersey Palisades. Addison wore his eye patch, a plain white T-shirt, white linen drawstring pants, huaraches and a highly petulant expression on his face. He was in a churlish mood.

I couldn't exactly blame him.

His personal space had been invaded by people who were seated on his leather sofas and armchairs or were just milling about, and he wanted nothing to do with any of them. Just wanted to sit drinking his goblet of Dom Pérignon and staring out at the river. The office was warm, what with the presence of so many people and the absence of air conditioning. There was also a definite edge of tension in the quiet conversations that were taking place.

This was no party. This was no disco. This was no fooling around. We were gathered there because someone in this room had murdered three people and we all knew it. We just didn't know who that someone was. Check that—one of us knew. The killer among us.

Addison did swivel around in his chair when he saw the reflection of Very and me in the window standing by his desk, Lulu at my side. "What are all of these people doing in my office?" he demanded angrily. "And why is that dog here again?"

"She's with me, as I've told you, Mr. James."

He shook his bald pink head, overwhelmed. It was a bit much for him to take in. "And what's with all of this *food*, Yvette?" he roared. "Why am I feeding these people? I don't even know them."

"I thought it would make things more pleasant," Yvette explained breathlessly, rushing over to him. She was wearing an exceptionally clingy pink sheath with a pair of gold leather flip-flops and seemed bright-eyed and excited to have company. Yvette seldom entertained, I gathered, and had spared no expense. She'd arranged for three banquet tables to be set up in the middle of the room, and a catered spread from Zabar's filled every square inch of them. There were platters, platters and more platters. For those who wanted fish, there was an entire nova salmon, smoked sable, whitefish, a bowl of pickled herring—which was of particular interest to Lulu—along with plain cream cheese, cream cheese with scallions and a basket filled with a half-dozen different kinds of bagels. For those who wanted deli, there were immense platters laden with sliced rare roast beef, corned beef, pastrami, salami and a selection of cheeses. There were bowls of potato salad, coleslaw and pickles, and another basket that was filled with sliced loaves of rye bread and pumpernickel. For those who wanted sweets there were three—count 'em, three—different kinds of cheesecake—plain, chocolate and strawberry. Coolers were filled with soda, beer, white wine and mineral water. There was also a huge coffee urn.

Yvette had even retained two maids for the evening to escort the guests upstairs when they arrived and to make sure there were no dirty plates or glasses left lying around.

"That is really quite some spread," I said to her admiringly. "Why, I'll bet it's even bigger than the old Velveeta Spread."

Yvette gazed up at me blankly.

"Not a fan of *Mad* magazine in your youth, I gather. That's an iconic line from their takeoff of *Bonanza*. I believe they called it 'Bananaz,' but I'm not positive about that. I took a lot of psychedelics in college and they poke strange holes in your memory."

"No offense, hon, but for such a smart, cute guy you don't make a whole lot of sense sometimes."

"Thank you, it's something I work very hard at. I see you went with real plates and silverware. Classy."

"I hate, hate paper plates. Plastic forks, too. They're tacky. I've done everything I can to eliminate tacky from my life."

"And you have. In fact, I'd call you a consummate success."

She studied me suspiciously. "Are you being sarcastic?"

"No, I'm perfectly serious."

"Well then, that was a sweet thing to say."

"Mind you, your taste in music could use some refining."

"Why, what's wrong with it?" she demanded.

"It doesn't actually qualify as music. Tell you what, I'll put together a playlist for you." Then I turned back to Addison and said, "I thought a relaxed mood would prove more effective than hauling people downtown and having Lieutenant Very grill everyone by shining bright lights in their eyes."

"Dude, we haven't done that since the fifties," Very said. "We don't whack people over the head with the Manhattan Yellow Pages anymore either."

"The lieutenant concurred. And in answer to your question, Mr. James, 'these people' are here to help out."

"These people" being Kathleen O'Brien, Richie Filosi, Norma Fives and her assistant, Bart Shackleford. "These people" being Sensenbrenner, the narrow detective from Willoughby, and Meade, the tubby detective from Nassau County. All were partaking of Yvette's spread and acting extremely ill at ease. Two others, Jocko Conlon and Mark Kaplan, Addison's sleek personal attorney, had yet to arrive.

"Help out how?" Addison demanded as Yvette bustled off to make absolutely sure the buffet table was in order.

"For starters, we're trying to figure out who killed your daughter," Very replied.

"What the hell good will that do?"

Very peered at him, mystified. "Don't you want to know?"

"Not particularly. I suppose I ought to care that she's dead, but I don't."

"Well, I *do* care," Very said to him, his right knee jiggling. "It's my job to care, and to bring her killer to justice. Not to mention whoever killed Tommy O'Brien and Mel Klein."

The old writer stared at Very with his one not-so-good eye. "Mel *who*?"

"Klein. He was an attorney on the South Shore. Babylon. His name doesn't ring a bell?"

"Klein, Klein . . ." Addison searched his memory. "I do remember an Irwin 'King Kong' Klein who was the starting center for NYU's basketball team back before the war when NYU was a sports powerhouse. He was also an All-American on their football team. One of the great two sports athletes of all time. But no, I don't believe I knew a Mel Klein. Should I?"

"He was your wife's lawyer," Very said.

"Yvette had a lawyer? Why'd she have a lawyer?" Addison seemed genuinely baffled. "Was she planning to divorce me?"

"He wasn't that kind of lawyer."

"Well then, what the hell kind was he?"

"Contracts. He was working with her on the prenuptial agreement she signed when you two got married. She thinks she got a raw deal. He agreed. Are you telling us you didn't know about this?"

"I don't concern myself with such matters," he said with a dismissive wave of his hand. His champagne goblet was empty. He reached for the bottle of Dom Pérignon on his desk, hefting it. "There's no champagne in my champagne." Got up and fetched a new bottle from his refrigerator, limping ever so slightly, and sat back down with it. Popped its cork and refilled his glass. It didn't occur to him to offer us any.

I left him with Very and moseyed over to the buffet table, where I opened a cold Moosehead ale and prepared a small plate of pickled herring for Lulu. Yvette was busy rearranging the basket of rye bread so that the slices were all in a neat row. Then she neatened the stack of napkins. Cloth napkins, not paper.

"By the way, Yvette, I meant to tell you how sorry I am for your loss."

"Loss?" Her huge blue eyes studied me. "What loss?"

"Mel Klein. Somebody shot him this afternoon."

"Oh, Mel. Yeah, I saw it on *Eyewitness News*. Tell me, what am I supposed to do now?"

"How do you mean?"

"Do I contact another lawyer and ask him to take over my case? And what happens to all of Mel's paperwork? Will his office hand it over to my new lawyer?"

"You'll have to authorize it, but that's generally how it works," I said, intrigued by her complete absence of emotion. The little guy was history. She'd moved on. "You're a pretty cool customer, aren't you?"

"What's that supposed to mean?"

"It was my impression that the two of you had formed an emotional bond. Something stronger than a typical lawyer-client relationship."

"Where'd you get that impression?"

"From Mel."

Her eyes avoided mine now. "What, you met him?"

"Lieutenant Very and I had a good long talk with him in his office this afternoon. Two hours later, he was dead."

She neatened the same stack of napkins again. No one had touched them since she'd neatened them before. "I wasn't sleeping with him. I told you that already. I felt sorry for him is all. He was such a sad, lonely little schlemiel. And he was sweet to me. You tall, good-looking bastards never are. Mel treated me like I was special. Plus he wasn't a typical asshole lawyer. Not that I mean to bad-mouth lawyers."

"You can go ahead and bad-mouth them all you want. That was a very nice wristwatch you gave him."

"He *told* you?"

"He didn't have to."

"I like to show people my gratitude. We understood each other. Spoke the same language."

"And now he's dead."

Yvette's soft round face tightened. "Who in the heck would want to shoot him in the head? I mean, it sounded like a gangland hit or something. It's kinda freaky, don't you think?"

"I do. I think it's extremely freaky. Mel told us that you'd spoken to Tommy O'Brien about him. Tommy phoned his office from my apartment before someone threw him off the roof. The two of them were planning to get together to talk about his contract with Sylvia."

"Yeah, Tommy told me he'd lined up a better job somewhere else. More bucks, more credit. Only he'd signed a piece of paper that made him like an indentured servant to Addy. I thought maybe Mel could help him."

"Somewhat weird, both of them turning up dead, don't you think?"

She studied me with her huge blue eyes again. "Hoagy, I really don't know what to think except . . ."

"Except what?"

"Somebody's gone loco."

"I don't think so."

"You don't think this is loco?"

"Oh, it's plenty loco. But it's also been carefully planned. None of this has been haphazard or spontaneous, starting with the theft of *Tulsa* last Friday. That's what makes it so mystifying."

One of the pocket doors slid open and Mark Kaplan came in, elegantly tailored and brimming with upper-crust certitude— everything that Mel Klein hadn't been.

He made his way straight for Yvette with a caring, fatherly expression on his face. "Terrible business about Mel Klein."

"Ya think?" she said in tight-lipped response.

"I was sorry to hear about it."

"You and me both. Excuse me," she said, darting back over to the desk to check on Addison.

"Couldn't get away from me fast enough," Kaplan observed wryly. "She actively detests me. I wonder why."

"It might have something to do with the prenup that you drew up."

"I was simply fulfilling Addison's wishes. I do what my clients ask. Have you had any luck securing the return of *Tulsa*?"

"Plenty. All of it the wrong kind."

"That's too bad," he said, helping himself to a mug of coffee from the urn. He poured some milk in and stirred it. He wore a worsted wool navy blue suit, a pale blue broadcloth shirt with French cuffs and those same silver horseshoe cuff links. "I'm afraid that this is turning into what my son, Mark Jr., refers to as a 'total shit storm.'"

"I'm afraid your son, Mark Jr., is right."

Kaplan smiled at me faintly before he excused himself and went over to greet his client.

I prepared a second plate of pickled herring for Lulu before I went to visit Kathleen and Richie, who were seated on one of the leather sofas with plates of food in their laps, looking out of place in their tank tops, shorts and sneakers. They were dressed for a summer picnic in the park, not an elegant two-story penthouse in a doorman building on Riverside Drive.

Lulu had growled at Richie again when he and Kathleen got there, Richie reeking of Aqua Velva. Again, I wondered if he'd been the one who'd bugged the phone in my apartment and whether Lulu had smelled the residue of his cologne. Was this her way of trying to tip me off? Or did she simply not like the guy? Having a nonverbal sidekick can be a bit confounding sometimes.

Kathleen seemed downcast, seated there with her plate of lox and bagels. Richie was busy devouring a pastrami sandwich and sneaking looks at the delectable Yvette across the room. The way he was ogling her led me to believe he'd never set eyes on her before, which may or may not have meant something.

"Nice to see you folks again," I said, perching on the arm of the sofa. Lulu came over and sat at my feet, watching Richie balefully.

"I sure do wish I knew what we were doing here," Kathleen said.

"Me, too," echoed Richie, as he continued to eyeball Yvette. Subtle he was not. "I ain't complaining, mind you. We don't get invited to places like this every day. The doorman told me that the Bambino used to live in this very building. Is that for real?"

"I believe it is," I said, studying Kathleen. "How are you doing?"

"I'm hanging in. That's all I can do, right?"

"Have your daughters made it to town?"

"They should be at the apartment when we get home."

"What did you folks do today? Something fun, I hope."

"Richie took me for a ride on the Staten Island Ferry this morning . . ."

"Cheap date," he said, winking at me. "And then we saw a W. C. Fields twin bill at the Film Forum."

"Really? Which of his movies did you see?"

"Um, *The Bank Dick* and *It's a Gift*, right, hon?"

She nodded her head ever so slightly.

"I love *It's a Gift*," I said. "Especially that scene when he's trying to fall asleep on the covered porch and that loudmouthed guy comes around looking for someone named Carl LaFong: 'Capital *L*, small *a*, capital *F*, small *o*, small *n*, small *g*. LaFong. Carl LaFong.'"

Richie looked at me blankly before he said, "Yeah, they were funny movies." Then his gaze swiveled to the pocket doors, where Jocko Conlon had just come in, wearing that same loose-fitting, non-flattering aqua Ban-Lon shirt he'd had on earlier that afternoon. Unless, that is, he had an entire collection of them in the same color with the same armpit sweat stains. "Oh, hey, that's an old buddy of mine from the job. Would you excuse me for a sec, hon?"

"Of course," Kathleen said, her eyes never leaving her plate.

Richie got up and went to say hello, shaking Jocko's hand and patting his meaty shoulder. Jocko grinned and murmured something in Richie's ear. The two of them chuckled. Gave every impression of being comrades-in-arms who hadn't seen each other in a good long while. Unless, that is, they were giving a performance for our benefit.

Romaine Very went over and joined them. Both men, I noticed, immediately became much more guarded.

Kathleen's eyes were still on her plate. "The reason Richie gave you such a funny look just now," she said in a hushed voice, "is that he only stayed for *The Bank Dick*. He didn't watch one second of *It's a Gift*. Said he had something to take care of for a friend and left me there. I stayed and watched it by myself. You're right, it *was* a funny movie. And it felt good to laugh."

She raised her eyes to meet mine. "That's the second time he's lied to you."

"He wasn't taking a nap on your sofa yesterday afternoon while you were watching *Oprah*, was he?"

"No, he wasn't," she acknowledged.

"Did a friend need him then, too?"

"He didn't say. Just took off. I'm about ready to go insane, Hoagy, I swear. I just . . . I just wish I knew what the hell's going on."

"So do I, Kathleen," I said before I moved to the other end of the sofa to join Norma Fives and Bart Shackleford. Norma, who wasn't eating, was gazing around in childlike awe at the floor-to-ceiling bookshelves filled with all of the different editions and translations of Addison's novels. Bart was devouring a corned beef and Swiss cheese sandwich, washing it down with a Coke and doing the same thing Richie had been doing—ogling Yvette, who was still standing on the other side of the room attending to Addison.

"I can't even wrap my mind around that old man's output," Norma said to me in amazement. "*Forty-two* novels, all of them translated into more than thirty languages. He keeps Guilford House afloat all by himself, you know. His earnings keep the lights on and pay everyone's salaries."

"Pretty incredible," Bart agreed. "To be able to produce that much, I mean."

"Indeed," I said. "I've been at it for ten years and I'm still trying to come up with my second book."

"Alberta told me your first three chapters are thrilling," Norma said to me. "That's not a word she throws around loosely. I meant what I said before, Hoagy. I'd love to see them.

And now that Sylvia's out of the picture I won't have to outbid her for it, as delightful as that would have been."

"Just out of curiosity, Norma, are you ever *not* working?"

"No," Bart answered.

"I'm truly a fan of your work," she plowed ahead. The woman was a ninety-five-pound juggernaut. "Honestly, it's a major loss to American literature that you haven't been writing."

"I've been writing," I said.

"Ghosting other people's memoirs doesn't count. They're not in your voice. Your voice . . ."

"What about my voice, Norma?"

"It needs to be heard. You *know* that. Listen, if you ever want to bounce ideas off of someone . . ."

"I'm not much of an idea bouncer."

"Or just talk about writing, *please* call me. And for god's sake, get that horrified look off of your face. I'm not hitting on you."

"I know you're not. If you were, Lulu would be growling at you right now."

Instead, Lulu was just gazing up at Norma quizzically. She'd never encountered anyone quite so single-minded.

"A lot of authors seek me out when they're in between books. We drink wine. We lie on the grass in Central Park. We talk about serious things, silly things. Sometimes it helps. I'm just sorry that . . . I wish I were old enough that I could have been here for you ten years ago."

"Trust me, you wouldn't have been able to help me. Not unless you were dealing coke on the side."

She looked at me with a hurt expression on her face. "You have *so* much talent. Pissing it away on celebrity memoirs is a sin."

"I couldn't agree more. And I thank you for your interest in my career. I really do. I'll make sure Alberta shows you the manuscript when it's ready."

"You promise?"

"Scout's honor. By the way, you ought to talk to Lieutenant Very if you get a chance. You two have a lot in common."

She looked at me in surprise. "We do?"

It was time for me to keep working the room. I moved back over to the buffet spread, where Jocko Conlon was building a mammoth pastrami sandwich and heaping his plate with potato salad and coleslaw. Richie had rejoined Kathleen, who was giving him a chilly reception. Very was busy using the phone on Addison's desk. Addison continued to sit with his back to everyone, sipping Dom Pérignon and staring out the window at the Hudson. Yvette stood there next to him with her soft little hand resting on his shoulder.

"I was sorry to hear about Mel," I said to Jocko. "He seemed like a decent guy."

Jocko eyed me up and down gruffly. "I didn't know him real well, tell you the truth. I mostly work divorce cases. But I did track down a contact or two for him, and I always liked the little guy. He seemed decent, like you say. Something tells me he got in over his head with *that* one," he said, gesturing with his chin toward Yvette. "She'd drive any man nuts. Seriously, have you taken a good look at that ass?"

"Hard to miss it."

Very hung up the phone and gestured to me. I excused myself and made my way over to him as he moved away from Addison and Yvette at the desk.

"I was just getting the preliminary report from the Nassau

County crime scene people on Mel Klein's condo," he told me in a low voice.

"Did they find anything?"

"Bubkes."

"No sign of forced entry?"

"See above, re bubkes. A cleaning lady came in every Friday morning, but she said he barely needed her. The little guy kept the place neat as a pin on his own. As far as she could tell, no one ever set foot in there except for Mel and her. He slept alone, as in the bedsheets *never* got a workout. She did say he got a bunch of new clothes lately. Gave his old ones to her for her husband, who's also a little guy."

"Hold on, are you telling me that green shirt of his was *new*?"

"Dude, you obsess over the strangest things."

"Stupid question, Lieutenant. Couldn't you have gotten this information directly from Detective Meade over there?"

"You're right, I could have," he acknowledged.

"I take that to mean you don't trust Meade as far as you can throw him."

"Right again."

Meade was seated on the other leather sofa across the coffee table from Kathleen, Richie, Norma and Bart. Jocko had settled himself next to Meade with his huge plate of food. The two of them were murmuring quietly to each other. Sensenbrenner, the narrow Willoughby detective, was sharing the sofa with them, but they were ignoring him completely. He sat there in patient silence, narrow legs crossed, sipping from a mug of coffee and checking out those battered olive drab Army footlockers that served as Addison's coffee table.

Norma Fives got up, moved her scrawny self over toward the

buffet spread and began poking around there, thinking about possibly helping herself to something.

"You should go talk to her," I said to Very. "You two have a lot in common."

"We do?" He frowned at me. "Such as . . . ?"

"Just go talk to her," I said, nudging him toward the buffet table.

"Okay, but stop shoving me, will ya?" Very joined her and said, "You're not partaking?"

Norma shook her head. "I don't eat much. I have a nervous stomach."

"I know what you mean. I had an ulcer a few years ago."

"She also suffers from insomnia," I informed Very.

His eyes widened. "Really? If I can drop off for two hours that's a good night's sleep for me."

"God, I'd kill for two hours," she said. "All I do is sit up and read manuscripts until dawn."

"How did Tommy feel about that?" I asked her.

Norma narrowed her gaze at me. "He understood."

"You didn't keep him awake at night flipping through those manuscript pages, hour after hour, with the light on?"

Norma shook her head. "Nothing kept him awake. He slept like a stone." She studied me curiously. "Why are you asking about that?"

"Don't mind me. I ask all sorts of things."

"Actually, I'm not super hungry myself," Very interjected, glancing at Norma. "I don't suppose you'd split a lox and bagel with me, would you?"

Norma pondered his question seriously. "Plain or scallion cream cheese?"

"Scallion, most def."

"What kind of bagel?"

"There's no point in eating a bagel unless it's an onion bagel."

"You passed the test, Lieutenant. It's a deal. I'll fix it."

"I can do it."

"No, you'll slather too much cream cheese on it. Men always do."

I left them to it and eased on over to the partners desk to visit with Addison, who was alone. Apparently, Mark Kaplan had no time to give him. The attorney was seated in a leather armchair poring over a file from his briefcase and marking it up with a red pencil. Yvette was helping a maid gather up the dirty dishes.

The old man was still sipping champagne and gazing out the window, lost in his thoughts. He seemed a million miles away. Possibly he was preparing to jump out of a plane into German-occupied France.

"Are you ready, Mr. James?" I asked.

It took him a long moment to come back from wherever he was and turn to look at me. "Ready for what?"

"To figure this out."

"It's your gambit, young fellow, not mine. I'm just the resident senile old man. Do what you will. I won't stand in your way."

"Thank you, sir." I stood with my back to the desk and Lulu seated at my feet, faced the assembled guests and in a loud, clear voice said, "Could I have everyone's attention, please?"

Norma returned to the sofa with her half bagel and sat with Bart. Yvette came over and sat at the partners desk across from her husband. She'd prepared herself a bagel with sable and cream cheese and was taking little nibbles from it, delicately licking the cream cheese from her fingers for the benefit of Richie, Jocko and Bart, who absolutely could not take their eyes off her. Very remained standing at the buffet table, the better to watch everyone.

"Quite a lot has happened to all of us," I began. "The only two copies in existence of Addison James's latest manuscript, *Tulsa*, have been stolen and are currently missing. Addison's associate, Tommy O'Brien, the writer from whom they were stolen, was thrown from the roof of my brownstone on West 93rd yesterday afternoon after first suffering a nasty blow to the back of his head. Last evening, Addison's daughter, Sylvia, the manuscript's editor, was run over by a car in front of her house in Willoughby. Run over so many times that virtually every bone in her body was broken. And this afternoon, Mel Klein, an attorney who'd been retained by Yvette James and had also been contacted by Tommy, who was anxious to get out of his contract with Addison, was found in—"

"Tommy wanted to *quit*?" Addison demanded indignantly. "Why that ungrateful, no-talent hack."

"If I may continue . . ."

"Do whatever you want," he huffed. "I don't give a crap."

"Mel was found shot dead in the parking garage of his condo complex in Babylon. Not only are three people dead, but Guilford House has lost its editor in chief as well as next summer's biggest moneymaker, since *Tulsa* has vanished and it would take a highly skilled writer—not me—at least a year to put it back together again from Tommy's early drafts and notes. Meanwhile, Tommy's lover, Norma Fives of Deep River . . ."

"Wait, Tommy was banging that little mouse in horn-rims?" Addison interjected. "What on earth for?"

"Hush, Addy," Yvette whispered to him.

Norma reddened, as did Kathleen. Richie reached over and gripped Kathleen's hand.

"Norma was anxious to pry him from his contract with Addison so that Tommy could write her a thriller for considerably more money as well as royalty participation, which Sylvia refused to give him on any of the last three novels that he secretly authored for Addison, who isn't quite up to the job anymore. Norma felt that Addison and Sylvia were taking advantage of Tommy. She was ready to hand him a whole new career."

"When she wasn't busy having sex with him, you mean," Kathleen said bitterly.

Norma sat there, tight-lipped and pale. "*Must* we talk about this?"

"I'm afraid so. I apologize if this will make more than a few of you uncomfortable." I turned to Bart. "I should also mention that Norma's editorial assistant, Bart Shackleford, is the son of the late author Gerrard Shackleford, who wrote under the name of Tucker Maxwell."

Addison immediately perked up. "Is that right, young fellow?"

Bart lowered his eyes. "Yes, sir."

"That son of a bitch was a hard-boiled genius," Addison said, shaking a long bony finger at him. "Hell, I'd put him right up there with Cornell Woolrich and Jim Thompson. I loved his work. Loved it. What was that great line the killer said in *Smoke on the Water*? 'The first man you kill is hard. The second is easier. The third is so much fun you wonder why murder hasn't surpassed baseball as America's favorite pastime.' God, I wish I'd written that line."

"Okay, I'm getting confused," Yvette confessed. "Why are we talking about him?"

"Because Gerrard Shackleford was a Guilford House author for nearly twenty years," I explained. "And when his sales dipped a few years back Sylvia dropped him. She could have kept him on out of professional respect and loyalty, considering that he'd written fourteen books for Guilford House and had been voted a Grand Master by the members of the Mystery Writers of America, which is their highest honor. But such things meant nothing to Sylvia. Plus she had a personal issue with him. Apparently she had a couple too many eggnogs at the annual Guilford House Christmas party, the only social event she ever attended, and made a pass at him. He politely declined, but Sylvia was positive he'd gloat about it all over town. So, Sylvia being Sylvia, she not only didn't renew his contract but made sure he'd be unable to get a deal anywhere else."

"That was my dear sweet Sylvia for you," Addison recalled. "It wasn't enough for her to cut him loose. She also had to destroy him."

"When his agent tried to find him another publisher," I continued, "she discovered that she was too late. Sylvia had already told every top editor in New York that his last several books had required total rewrites because he'd become a hopeless alcoholic."

"Which was a flat-out lie," Bart said heatedly. "My father was a federal appellate judge in Trenton. He hardly drank at all. He was clearheaded, alert and highly respected by everyone who knew him."

"The kid's right," Mark Kaplan spoke up. "Judge Shackleford had a sterling reputation in the legal community. Furthermore, it was my pleasure to sit next to him at a charity banquet the year before he died. He was a class act. A gentleman."

Bart looked across the room at me, his jaw muscles tightening. "How do you know all of this, Mr. Hoag?"

"My agent told me. She knows everything that goes on. How do *you* know about it?"

"I told him," Norma said. "It was still watercooler talk when I started working at Guilford House."

"So I'm guessing you weren't a big Sylvia fan, were you, Bart?" I said.

"I hated her with every fiber of my being," he responded angrily.

"If Judge Shackleford had sought my counsel," Kaplan said, "I would have advised him to sue Sylvia for slander."

"Instead, he drank a bottle of Drano," Addison recalled disgustedly.

"Indeed he did," I said. "Which, in a way, makes him our first casualty. And now there are a whole lot more of them." I fixed my gaze on Richie Filosi, whose eyes avoided mine guiltily.

Then I looked at Jocko Conlon, who warned me, "You better not be thinking about dumping this pile of crap in *my* lap."

"We already know that you're into it deep," Very told him bluntly.

"I'm a licensed operative of a legit law firm," Jocko fired back. "I get paid to do a job. Well paid. I've got a sweet setup at Klein, Walker and Pignatano, and I want to hold on to it. So when a partner tells me to do something, I do it." His face darkened. "You see, back when I was on the job, there was always one tight-ass boss after another who had it in for me. So I . . . I have a couple of black marks on my record, understand?"

"Are you done?" Very demanded.

"I'm just saying I've got to look out for myself, don't I? All these years I've been working and I've got nothing to show for it. That's nobody's fault but my own. I admit that. I went in on an Irish pub with a pal of mine a couple of years ago and lost every penny I'd saved. So now I'm fifty-two years old and I've got no nest egg and who knows how many good years left. There's a spot on my left lung that the doctors are watching. I'm on medication for high blood pressure. I have to use special eye drops for glaucoma. Plus I've got a prostate gland the size of a freaking beach ball. I'm damned lucky to be with that firm. I'd have a real hard time hooking up with another one. Probably have to go out on my own, which would mean scraping by month to month, waiting for the phone to ring, taking whatever crapola case comes along." He let out a defeated sigh. "I'd probably end up bunking on my office sofa, showering at the YMCA and living on cat food."

"I understand that 9Lives canned mackerel is very tasty," I said. "Just remember to brush after every meal."

Jocko glowered at me. "What the fuck are you talking about?" To Very he said, "Do *you* know what the fuck he's talking about?"

Very just stared at him. "*Now* are you done?"

"What in the hell do you want from me, Lieutenant?"

"For starters, to let you in on a little something. There's an officer of the NYPD standing in the hall right outside of those doors and two more parked downstairs in the living room."

Jocko shrugged his meaty shoulders. "So?"

"So just tell us how it went down. Tell it plain and tell it straight."

"I want a lawyer," Jocko declared.

"What for?" Very demanded. "I haven't charged you with anything. I just want to know what you know, that's all."

Jocko looked over at Mark Kaplan. "What do *you* think?"

"As a caveat, I must preface my remarks by pointing out that I'm not a criminal attorney," Kaplan answered carefully. "But from where I sit, the lieutenant is correct. Technically, he hasn't charged you with a crime, although his allusion to you 'being into it deep' does suggest that he may, at some future point, elect to press charges against you. Then again he may not. I'm not privy to his intentions."

Jocko rolled his eyes. "Typical Park Avenue lawyer. Lots of smooth words and none of them make any goddamned sense." To Very he said, "Forget it. I'm not talking."

"Fine, then let's go find ourselves a nice, private interrogation room up at the two-four," Very said brusquely, starting across the office toward him. "I'm pretty sure we've got a Manhattan Yellow Pages lying around somewhere. It'll give me a tremendous amount of personal satisfaction to turn that skull of yours into a soft gelatinous mass. Let's go, Jocko. We're out of here."

Jocko stayed planted on the sofa, his eyes widening with fear. He did not, repeat not, wish to be hauled off to the precinct house. He was much better off right here, surrounded by all of these other people, and he knew it. "Take it easy, will ya?" he said appeasingly. "Just slow down a sec and let me think."

"Call me crazy, Lieutenant," I interjected, "but I get the feeling that Jocko wants to cooperate. He's a smart individual. He realizes what's at stake here."

Jocko peered across the office at me. "Meaning what exactly?"

"Meaning that if you're cooperative, there's a decent chance you won't get charged as anything more than ... what, Lieutenant? Aiding and abetting under extreme duress?"

Very nodded. "Sounds reasonable."

"But if you don't cooperate, there's an equally good chance that all three murders will land right on top of you and stay there," I said. "That wouldn't exactly be an ideal scenario for you, Jocko. You'll be put away in a maximum security prison with other violent offenders, and they absolutely detest ex-cops. Plus the odds are not in your favor."

Jocko frowned at me. "Odds? What odds?"

"The chances are pretty good that one or two of them ended up there because you put them there back when you were on the job. Wouldn't you think so, Lieutenant?"

"I would," Very said, nodding. "Most def."

"Which means they'll be harboring an extreme personal grievance against you, Jocko. Hell, you'll probably get shanked less than an hour after you arrive."

Jocko swallowed, his eyes widening with fear again. "Can't we work something out?"

"Sure, we can," Very said easily. "Just tell us what you know."

"About *what*?"

"For starters, who snatched *Tulsa*?" I asked him. "You were standing right there on the sidewalk outside of the copier shop when it happened. Don't bother to deny it. Tommy described you right down to your boxer shorts. Actually, he didn't say you were wearing boxer shorts, but I just really, really don't want to picture you in a pair of briefs."

Jocko sat there in charged silence. Twenty-five floors below on Riverside Drive I could hear fire trucks go by, their sirens wailing, big horns honking. "It was Mel's scheme," he finally said. "Mel thought that if he had *Tulsa* he could pressure Sylvia into convincing the old man to give Yvette the prenup that she wanted. He figured she'd do anything to get *Tulsa* back."

Addison peered thoughtfully across the desk at Yvette, who continued to take tiny nibbles of her bagel and lick her fingers. She didn't react at all to what Jocko had said. It was as if he were talking about someone else.

"So you knowingly broke the law," Very said to him.

Jocko let out a scornful laugh. "Don't jerk me off. You and I both know that the law's elastic. You can bend it, twist it, stretch it. The law is whatever you want it to be."

Very wouldn't go near that. Just looked at Jocko with distaste. "How did it go down?"

"I offered a couple of street punks who I've known for years a C-note apiece to snatch O'Brien's briefcase. I fingered him for them. Then they dashed down the street, handed his briefcase into a waiting cab, collected their money and were gone with the wind."

"Was it Mel who was waiting in the cab for them?"

Jocko made a face. "Mel? No way. 'I'm an officer of the court,' he told me. Plus he was a major wuss. No, I gave an old buddy a C-note to help me handle it."

Kathleen immediately shot a glance at Richie next to her on the sofa.

"And I bought him a steak dinner with all of the trimmings when we got home," Jocko added.

Very said, "I gather we're talking about Detective Meade, your partner from your days on the job in Nassau County."

Meade shifted on the sofa in rumpled, uncomfortable silence.

"Why would you think that?" Jocko wondered.

"Because when we were at the crime scene today he couldn't stop talking about what a great guy you are. Am I right, Hoagy?"

"Yes, you are. It was kind of nauseating, actually."

"I don't know what kind of game you two clowns are playing," Jocko said. "But I got nothing to say about that. I'm no rat bastard."

Very looked at Meade. "How about you? Have you got anything you want to share?"

"Not a thing," Meade answered coldly. "I don't even know why I'm here."

"Fine, have it your way, Meade. It'll all shake out. I just hope you weren't planning a nice cushy retirement tootling around on a golf cart in Boca, because you can kiss your pension goodbye."

"Before you got back into the cab with Meade," I said to Jocko, "you showed Tommy your gun and warned him you'd be watching him. 'Say one word about this to anyone and you're a dead man,' you told him. Tommy was justifiably terrified. In fact, he was so afraid that he ended up spending one whole night on my roof in the pouring rain. Why did you threaten him that way?"

"Mel figured if we threw a scare into him he'd vanish, which would drive Sylvia even crazier."

I turned to Very. "Tell me, during the time we spent with Mel Klein, did he strike you as a fiendishly clever individual?"

"Not really. More like a small-timer who was just trying to keep his head above water. You?"

"Same." I turned back to Jocko. "You don't really think we're buying that the little guy came up with this whole scheme on his own, do you?"

Jocko glared at me before he said, "Believe what you want. I don't give a fuck."

"No, this whole scheme was someone else's idea. Someone who had a huge ax to grind." My gaze fell on Sylvia's bitter enemy, Norma Fives, the woman who'd hurled a Stanley Bostitch stapler across a conference table at her and nearly blinded her. It fell on Bart Shackleford, son of the late Gerrard Shackleford, whom Sylvia had driven to suicide. It fell on Kathleen O'Brien, Tommy's high school sweetheart and wife of more than twenty years. Kathleen, whom Tommy had dumped for the much younger, thinner Norma. Kathleen, who sat there holding hands with Richie Filosi, who'd worked with Jocko at the two-four and knew all about how the law can be bent, twisted and stretched. Finally my glance fell on Yvette, who'd started blackmailing middle-aged men way back when she was a teenaged babysitter. "It was a good scheme, too, Yvette. No *Tulsa* manuscript would certainly mess with Sylvia's head."

Yvette said nothing. Just sat there across the partners desk from Addison, calmly waiting for me to continue.

Addison peered at her, then at me. "Why would Yvette care about Sylvia's 'head,' as you so ineloquently put it?"

"Because she wanted Sylvia's backing, which she was never, ever going to get unless she had extraordinary leverage over her."

"Backing? What sort of backing?"

"Jocko was spot-on. Yvette is desperate to renegotiate that cheapskate prenup she agreed to when she married you. And she wanted Sylvia to persuade you that it would be the right thing to do."

The old man scoffed at me. "Nonsense. I don't believe a word of it."

"She also wanted to give Sylvia a taste of her own medicine. You see, Yvette happened to hate Sylvia, who treated her like nothing more than a trampy little gold digger."

"So what? Everyone hated Sylvia. She was impossible to like. That's not an easy thing for a father to say, but it's true."

"And yet Detective Sensenbrenner here says that she was very well liked in Willoughby. Isn't that right, Detective?"

Sensenbrenner sat his narrow self up a bit straighter on the sofa and cleared his throat. "Quite right. Miss James was regarded around Willoughby as a kindly and generous person. She did many, many fine things for the people in our community and asked for nothing in return. Just her peace and quiet. She was a private person. But she was respected and well liked, as Mr. Hoag says."

Addison peered across the office at him. "You must be talking about someone else."

"No, sir, I'm not."

"Well, I never knew a thing about that."

"Possibly because she didn't want you to," I suggested.

"Why would that be?"

"Because she was afraid you'd heap scorn and ridicule on her."

"Young man, did you come here tonight to berate me for my parenting skills?"

"No, I came here because Sylvia hired me to do a job, find *Tulsa*, and I intend to do it."

"Fair enough. I've always respected professionalism. But are we finished now? I'm tired and I want all of these people to leave."

"Not just yet, Mr. James," Very said.

Jocko Conlon had gotten up off the sofa, fetched a Moosehead ale from the cooler and stood at the table drinking it, his eyes flicking around the office at the pocket doors, at the door to Addison's bedroom.

Very's eyes never left him. "Who killed Tommy O'Brien, Jocko?"

Jocko took a gulp of his beer before he said, "Mel did."

"You just told us he was a wuss. You expect us to believe that?"

Jocko shrugged his meaty shoulders. "Believe what you want. It's what happened."

"And Mel's no longer around to say otherwise. I'd call that mighty convenient, wouldn't you, Hoagy?"

"Yes, I would." At my feet Lulu let out a low moan. "And I'm not the only one." I stood there for a moment, tugging at my ear. "You know, Jocko, I keep thinking about something that Tommy told me."

"Which was what?" Jocko wondered.

"That he smelled ex-cop all over you when you were threatening him on the sidewalk outside of that copier shop. Tommy was a police beat reporter for five years. Damned good one, too. You knew his byline. Every cop in the city did. You also knew that once the dust from this mess settled, he was the kind of reporter who wouldn't rest easy until he found you. He'd work his old sources and contacts for as long as it took until he was able to attach a name to your face and man boobs. Deep down inside, you knew it. And it unsettled you. It would certainly unsettle me."

"Me, too," Very agreed.

"Leave no loose ends," Addison said in a soft, hollow voice.

I turned to look at him. "What was that, sir?"

"Leave no loose ends," he repeated in that same soft, hollow voice.

"Which was exactly what Tommy was," I said, nodding. "And it started to eat at you, didn't it, Jocko? Eat at you so much that you went to Mel and said that you couldn't risk letting Tommy walk around alive. You told Mel that you wanted to take Tommy out, didn't you?"

"I'm not saying yes and I'm not saying no," Jocko answered, slowly and carefully. "I *will* say that the idea did happen to come up in conversation, and that Mel was a hundred and ten percent for it—with one major stipulation."

"Which was what?"

"That *he* wanted to be the one to take care of Tommy, not me. He saw me serving strictly as backup."

"What kind of backup?"

"He needed me to drive him into the city. He was afraid to drive in the city. The traffic terrified him. Too many crazies."

Very looked at Jocko in disbelief. "Are you trying to tell us that it was little Mel Klein, attorney at law, who brained Tommy O'Brien and shoved him off of Hoagy's roof?"

"It's the truth," Jocko insisted, gazing over at Yvette. "You've got eyes, haven't you? Look at her."

I looked at her. Yvette continued to sit there at the desk, perfectly calm and composed, the very portrait of innocence.

"I've never, ever seen a guy go so nuts over a woman. That poor little schnook was so desperate to prove his manhood to her that he would do *anything*. 'Don't you understand, Jocko?' he says to me. 'She's the one I've been waiting for my whole life.' He actually thought he had a shot at her. He had no clue that she was only interested in the dough, not him. She's damned good at working a guy, I have to give her that. Mel would have jumped off that roof himself if she'd asked him to. The little guy was a goner. Totally pussy mad."

"Would you kindly choose a different expression?" Norma Fives said with chilly disapproval. "Something less repulsive?"

"Excuse me, miss," Jocko said apologetically. "Mel was madly in love with Yvette, is what I'm trying to say. He couldn't stop talking about her. Kept telling me about how she'd promised him they were going to run off together to her house in Maui when this was all over. He said that she liked to swim nude in the pool there. That they'd swim nude in the pool together. He must have mentioned swimming nude in that damned pool to me twenty times."

"It seems to me I've heard about that particular pool myself," I said.

"Tell us your version of how it went down, Jocko," Very ordered him.

"Sure, okay. Except it's not *my* version. It's the only version. The God's honest truth." Jocko had started to sweat like crazy in the warm office. He swiped at the beads of perspiration on his forehead with a damp, meaty forearm before he said, "It was Mel who set things in motion. He called Tommy at Hoag's apartment and made an appointment to meet him there that same day at around five o'clock to discuss his contract situation with Mr. James. I drove Mel to the meeting in my Coupe de Ville. The little guy was afraid to drive in city traffic, like I said. When we got to your place, Tommy buzzed him in. I waited outside in my car. They went up onto the roof because it's like a furnace in that apartment of yours. I couldn't believe how hot it was in there when I installed the tap on your phone last week. I swear, I felt like a boiled lobster by the time I got out of there."

"I'll have you know I pay extra for that," I pointed out.

"When they got up onto the roof, Mel brained Tommy with a foot-long length of cast-iron pipe that he had tucked in his waistband, gave him a good shove, and over he went."

"I'm not buying one word of this," Very said to Jocko. "You're spinning a yarn."

"It's no yarn," Jocko insisted. "It was Yvette. She'd convinced Mel that if he took care of things, it would really happen. That they would really run off to Maui together. Swim nude in that pool. She's a cruel person, if you ask me, not that you did. It was just plain nasty the way she jerked that decent little guy around."

Yvette let out a mocking laugh. "Like you'd know from decent."

"You turned him into a crazy person," Jocko said to her accusingly.

"You're wasting your breath, Jocko," she responded coolly. "Not one person in this room believes a word you're saying."

Addison said nothing. Just sipped his champagne in sullen silence.

"And now I'm guessing you're going to tell us that Yvette talked Mel into killing Sylvia, too," Very said to Jocko.

"Absolutely. Let me tell you, just because a guy's got a law degree don't mean he can't turn out to be a complete yutz."

"I've often thought that the two go together, actually," I said.

"Mr. Hoag, I happen to resent that remark," Mark Kaplan said sharply.

"Go right ahead. I don't mind."

Yvette let out a weary sigh. "Am I allowed to speak, Lieutenant?"

"Of course," Very replied.

"Just exactly how long do I have to sit here and listen to this grossly fat boor tell one lie after another about me?"

"You'll sit here and listen just like the rest of us," Addison snarled at her.

Yvette recoiled in shock, her huge blue eyes widening.

"What was your role in Sylvia's murder?" Very asked Jocko.

"Strictly logistical. I'd been casing Sylvia's street."

"Lane," Sensenbrenner corrected him.

"Huh?"

"In Willoughby they're called lanes," I explained.

"Yeah, whatever. I tailed her home from the office on the Metro-North train. Worked out her schedule. Staked out the vicinity surrounding her house for regular dog walkers, joggers and such."

"How many days did that take?" Very asked him.

"Three."

"That's a lot of legwork. Plus it's a long drive into the city from Babylon and then out to Willoughby. Did you recruit some backup?" I asked him, glancing Richie's way. "Maybe an old running buddy who needed a few bucks?"

Kathleen glared at Richie.

"You trying to pull *him* into this?" Jocko wondered. "No way. Richie had squat to do with any of it. I worked it alone and fed my info to Mel. And it was *his* idea to head straight out there once he'd pushed Tommy off your roof. He was such a meek-looking guy no one gave him a second look when he came walking out of your building right past Tommy lying there dead on the sidewalk. But when he jumped into my car, Mel was like a man possessed. There was this, I dunno, crazed gleam in his eyes. He told me he wanted to drive right out to Willoughby and take care of Sylvia *right now*. And that *he* wanted to be the one to do it, just like with Tommy."

"And you went along with the idea," Very said disgustedly.

"You don't understand, I *had* to. He was my boss. I did what he told me to do. And you have no idea how crazed he was. If I'd tried heading back home to Babylon he would have blown a gasket, I'm telling you. Besides, it wasn't such a bad idea, to get it over with in one fell swoop, the more I thought about it. If we'd waited another day, Sylvia might have gotten spooked and asked the Willoughby PD to keep a car staked out in front of her house, which would have messed up the whole plan."

Very stared at him for a long moment before he said, "And you're sticking with the story that it was Mel who ran Sylvia down while she was out getting her mail."

Jocko nodded his head of graying red curls. "It's no story. It's the truth."

"Did you use a stolen car?"

He nodded again. "I jacked it from a ShopRite parking lot in Scarsdale on the way. It was a Ford Explorer. Green. Left my own car parked in a shopping center across the street. Mel drove the Explorer from Scarsdale to Willoughby. We idled down the street—"

"Lane," I interjected.

"*Lane* from her house, waiting for her to pull into her drive-way in that big Mercedes of hers. By then the little guy was shaking like a leaf. To calm himself down he lit up one of those dumb-ass Tiparillos of his."

"We know all about that," Sensenbrenner said. "Mr. Hoag's sidekick found the plastic tip in the gutter not far from the body."

Lulu let out a whoop of satisfaction, her tail thumping. I reached down and patted her.

"Sylvia arrived home on schedule, pulled into the driveway and opened her garage door. Got out of her car and started walking toward the mailbox. That's when he floored it. Slammed right into her and sent her flying. The mailbox, too. But he wasn't done. He ran over her body while she was lying there in the street, hit the brakes, put it in reverse, floored it and ran over her again. Then he hit the brakes, put it in drive and ran over her yet again. I said to him, 'Mel, we're done here. She's dead, for crissakes. Let's split.' But he went totally nuts, I swear. Sat there panting like he'd just run the New York Marathon. Finally he tossed his Tiparillo out the window and floored it out of there. After a few blocks I told him to pull over and let me drive. We retrieved my car in the parking lot in Scarsdale and headed on home. The little guy didn't say a single word the whole way back to Babylon. All he did was stare out the window. He'd just killed two people in the span of, what, three or four hours, and all he did was sit there. When we got back to the office I poured him a stiff bourbon from my office bottle. He drank it down, said, 'Good night, Jocko. Thank you for your help. See you in the morning.' His voice sounded weird. Kind of wooden. Then he got in his Volvo and drove home."

Everyone in the office fell into stunned silence for a moment.

"Why?" I spoke up.

"Why what, dude?" Very asked me.

"Why did Sylvia have to die?"

"What are you thinking?"

"I'm thinking that messing with Sylvia's head by stealing *Tulsa* wasn't nearly enough for Yvette. I'm thinking she wanted Sylvia *gone*."

"I don't have to sit here and listen to another word of this," Yvette fumed, getting up out of her chair.

"Yes you do," Addison said to her in a low voice. "Sit back down."

"Not a chance, Addy. I'm outta here."

Lulu let out a menacing growl to convince Yvette that she did in fact need to sit back down. Lulu has a mighty menacing growl for someone who was once beaten to a pulp in Riverside Park by a Pomeranian named Mr. Puff Ball.

"Why did Yvette want Sylvia gone?" Very asked Jocko.

Jocko let out a harsh laugh. "Why do you think? So she'd inherit everything, duh. She's one nasty little piece of work. I tried to tell Mel that. I ran a criminal background check on her. I knew all about her scuffles with the law before she married Mr. James here. She's bad to the bone and wants it all when he kicks off. No offense, Mr. James."

"None taken, sir," Addison assured him.

"But Mel was so crazy about her he wouldn't listen to me, the poor slob. See, he'd never had a shot at someone like Yvette. Not that he *did* have a shot at her. All she cares about are the crown jewels."

Mark Kaplan frowned at him. "The crown jewels?"

"Mr. James's bank accounts and stock portfolios. His royalties. Look around you at all of these books, will you? And you want my personal opinion? Being the poor white trash that she is, it's his houses that she really, really wants. She'll come into that waterfront mansion in East Hampton plus his multimillion-dollar country estates in Aspen, Jackson Hole, Montecito, Maui, and a bunch in Europe. He's got one in Tuscany, one in Provence, one in-in . . ."

"Geneva," Kaplan said crisply.

"And she wouldn't have gotten any of those if Sylvia was still around," Jocko explained.

Addison glowered across the partners desk at Yvette for a long moment with his one not-so-good eye before he let out a chuckle followed by another chuckle that exploded into a huge, roaring laugh that went on and on as he slapped the desk with the palm of his hand, tears streaming from his eye.

Everyone stared at him in disbelief. Almost everyone, that is.

"What's so damned funny?" Yvette demanded furiously.

"I believe I can answer that question for you, Mrs. James," said Kaplan, whose own face remained impassive as Addison continued to roar with laughter.

She scowled at him. "Well . . . ?"

"Mr. James instructed me to alter his will quite some time ago so that upon his death none of those properties would have passed to Sylvia. He'd made other plans for them."

Yvette gaped at Kaplan in shock. "*What* other plans?"

"He's donating all of them to the Veterans Administration to serve as rehabilitation facilities for wounded Gulf War and Vietnam veterans."

"And don't forget Korea," Addison interjected, wiping the tears of laughter from his eye. "Everyone else has, except for the poor bastards who were there."

"The funds to staff and maintain the facilities," Kaplan went on, "will come from his personal fortune as well as the continuing royalties from the sale of his books. He intends to give it all back, every penny he's earned, because it was the VA that saved him at a facility in Asheville, North Carolina, after he was wounded during the Second World War."

Yvette whirled and glared at Addison. "How could you do something like that and not tell me?"

"Because it's *my* money, not *yours*. And because . . . because . . ." Addison tried to continue but couldn't get another word out. He'd started roaring with laughter again.

"Would you stop that laughing, you crazy old bastard!" she screamed at him. "This isn't funny!"

"Oh, but it is!" he assured her. "That look on your face right now is . . . it's priceless. You did all of this for nothing!"

"Now that you mention it," I said, "this *is* what book critics mean when they label something as 'richly ironic.'"

"It's fucking hilarious, is what it is!" Addison roared, slapping the desk with the palm of his hand again.

"You evil bastard!" Yvette spat at him, her face blazing with fury. "You sick, evil fucking bastard!"

"Lastly, there's the matter of Mel's murder this afternoon," I said. "He wasn't done in by any amateur. Whoever shot him was swift, professional and armed with a .357 Magnum equipped with a silencer."

"I got nothing more to say." Jocko crossed his arms in front of his saggy chest. "Not one word. Not without a lawyer."

"Fine, then I'll say it for you. Mel panicked after the lieutenant and I visited him at his office today, didn't he? Told you that he was convinced we were onto him. You knew he'd start blabbing his head off just as soon as the men with handcuffs showed up there, isn't that right, Jocko? And that once Mel started blabbing, he'd take you down with him. So you followed him home from work, pulled into his garage after him and tapped on the window of his Volvo. As soon as he lowered it, you let him have it. You were in and out of there in thirty seconds. No one heard you. No one saw you."

Jocko continued to stand there with his arms crossed. "I told you, I got nothing more to say."

"Not a problem," I assured him. "You'll get your lawyer and stand trial for his murder. Justice will be served—in a manner of speaking."

Very frowned at me. "Meaning what, dude?"

"Meaning Jocko may have pulled the trigger on Mel, but he's not the real killer. Nor was Mel the real killer when he pushed Tommy off my roof or ran that Ford Explorer over Sylvia, again and again. No, the real killer is the person who manipulated this sorry series of events by taking advantage of that weak, lonely little guy in his dreary little office in Babylon. The real killer is *you*, Yvette."

She glared at me with those big blue eyes of hers. It was an icy, hate-filled glare. And it was my first glimpse of the real Yvette—a hardened, amoral hustler named Phyllis Yvette Rittenaur. Phyllis, whose father ran off before she was born and whose mother deserted her when she was four. Phyllis, who'd been raised by an aunt who was a hooker. "You can't prove a damned thing," she said to me dismissively. "And if it comes down to my word against Jocko's, who do you think a jury will believe—a loathsome, corrupt slob who's been kicked off two different police forces or sweet, darling little me? Wait until you see my lower lip start to quiver. I can make grown men cry."

"I have no doubt that you can. I also have no doubt that you'll get away with what you did. It's Jocko who will take the fall. But you won't get Addison's houses or his fortune. And his lawyer over there, Mark Kaplan, will make sure that your prenup is voided."

"Count on it," Kaplan said with total assurance.

"You failed, Yvette. It's like Addison said—you did all of this for nothing. Not one cent."

"Not one cent," echoed Addison, who started laughing again, roaring and roaring with laughter.

"Will you stop that damned laughing?" Yvette shrieked at him. "This *isn't* funny!"

The old man stopped laughing and inhaled several times, slowly and deeply, before he said, "You're absolutely right, it's not." Slid open his top desk drawer, swiftly removed his loaded Ruger and shot Yvette right between the eyes as she sat there across the desk from him. The shot rocked her back in her chair before she crumpled over to one side, her dead eyes open, a stunned expression on her face. Some blood trickled down her face. Not a lot. Her heart had stopped pumping blood the instant that the bullet penetrated her brain.

Norma Fives let out a horrified scream. Everyone else in the office froze.

Until Very rushed toward Addison with his own piece drawn. "Drop it, Mr. James. Put the gun down."

"Not a problem, Lieutenant Very." Addison calmly set the revolver down on the desk and sat back in his chair with his hands clasped behind his hairless pink head. "I was simply doing what Wild Bill always told us to do."

"Which was what, sir?"

"Leave no loose ends behind. They'll bite you in the ass every time."

At the sound of the gunshot, the uniformed cop out in the hall had hurried in with his own gun drawn. Very told him to send for an EMT van and more men. Then Detective Lieutenant Romaine Very of the NYPD read America's wealthiest, most famous living author his Miranda rights.

While he was doing that, I overheard Kathleen O'Brien say, "Richie, I swear to god, if you had anything to do with this we're through."

"I didn't, I swear," he insisted.

"Then where were you yesterday afternoon while I was watching *Oprah*? And why'd you ditch me in that movie today?"

"I've been making money drops for a bookie I know, okay? He gives me a thou in cash for an hour's work. I have to eat, don't I?"

"You're breaking the law, Richie."

"He runs a sports book. It's no big deal."

"It's a big deal to me. I won't associate with that kind of life."

Meanwhile, Jocko Conlon was being cuffed by one of the cops in uniform who'd been stationed downstairs. Jocko's bluster had gone out of him. I stood before him, studying him intently. My right eye had started twitching, I realized.

"What do you want now?" he asked me in a defeated voice.

"Just the answer to one more question. Where are the two copies of *Tulsa* that you snatched from Tommy O'Brien?"

"Tucked in Mel's office safe."

"Was Mel the only one who knew the combination?"

"Nah, the receptionist, Roseanne Leto, knows it."

"Good."

He gazed at me curiously. "Why are you asking me about that? What difference does it make now?"

"Tommy spent the last two years of his life on it. He was proud of it and I want to make sure it gets published, even if his name isn't on it. I owe him that much."

"I don't know what the hell you're talking about," Jocko grumbled, shaking his head.

"That's okay. I didn't expect you would."

Chapter Ten

W hen America's richest, most famous living author shoots his beautiful young wife right between the eyes in front of a roomful of people, it tends to become front-page news. So the next morning's *Times*, *Post*, and *News* were chock-full of the lurid details of Yvette James's murder, not to mention its connection to the murders of Addison James's daughter, Sylvia, his research assistant, Tommy O'Brien, and Yvette's personal attorney, Melvin Klein of Babylon, Long Island. The newspaper stories were still a bit sketchy on the details about the arrest of Jocko Conlon, a private detective formerly of the NYPD and Nassau County Sheriff's Office. Also about Nassau County Sheriff's Detective Peter Meade being placed on administrative leave pending an Internal Affairs investigation into his involvement. But by the time I was up making my morning coffee in Merilee's schmancy espresso machine, CNN was already saying that "unnamed sources close to the investigation" believed that it was Jocko and Mel together who were responsible for the deaths of Tommy and Sylvia and that Jocko had then shot Mel to death in the basement garage of his Amityville condo complex in order to silence him.

Reporters soon started to dig up story upon story about the "troubled" childhood and criminal past of Phyllis Yvette Rittenaur, aka Yvette James. Her ex-partner, Mick the Quick Rafferty, who'd gallantly taken the rap for that failed jewelry store robbery in Nyack way back when, was now serving twenty years in Rahway for a botched bank heist in Newark. He was only too happy to talk about her. He had nothing better to do.

A cool breeze had blown in during the night, bringing a hint of early fall in with it. After I'd fed Lulu and downed my orange juice and espresso I threw on an old chambray work shirt, jeans and my Chippewas. Rode the elevator down to the lobby, waved good morning to Patrick the doorman and took Lulu for a walk in Central Park, savoring deep breaths of the freshening air while she ambled alongside the path with me, sniffing here, there and everywhere. As we walked, a bicycle caught up with us from behind and eased up next to us, its rider pushing his way along with his feet on the pavement.

It was Romaine Very, his jaw working on a piece of bubble gum. He had a somber expression on his face but didn't look nearly as drained by the events of last night as I felt. Very never seems to get as disheartened as I do by the reality of what people are capable of doing to one another. I guess he can't allow himself to in his line of work. Not if he wants to keep doing it.

Lulu let out a low whoop to greet him. He whooped back at her. "Your doorman said I'd find you here."

"I sure do like the sound of those two words."

"Which two?"

"*Your doorman.* What's going on, Lieutenant?"

"Just wanted to tell you I was sorry about your friend Tommy. What with all of the bodies dropping here, there and everywhere I don't think I ever got a chance to say the words out loud."

"Thank you. I appreciate that."

"I also wanted you to know that we did find those two copies of *Tulsa* in Mel's safe. You had that figured right all along."

"Glad to hear it. Where do things stand with Jocko?"

"He's being arraigned later this morning on a charge of first-degree murder for shooting Mel, not to mention being an accessory to the murders of Tommy and Sylvia as well as a colorful array of other felonies like carjacking that Ford Explorer in Scarsdale, setting up the snatch of *Tulsa* and illegally tapping your phone. The big fat slob isn't bothering to deny a thing. Regrets nothing. Just thinks of himself as a pro doing a pro's job, and assumes his lawyer will figure out a way for him to skate."

"And what's the latest on Addison?"

"He's being held at Bellevue for psychiatric evaluation. My sense is that there isn't a huge appetite on the part of the DA to prosecute him in criminal court for shooting Yvette, considering that he's elderly and senile and happens to be a beloved American literary figure. Besides, Yvette's hands weren't exactly clean."

"Yvette's hands weren't even remotely close to clean."

"My guess? He'll live out his remaining years in a cushy mental hospital somewhere."

"As long as he can do his Royal Canadian Air Force exercises and watch reruns of *Perry Mason,* he'll be a happy camper."

A pair of slender, beautiful young blondes—fashion models, by the look of them—went jogging past us, chattering gaily. I felt a sudden pang in my chest, missing Merilee.

"Incidentally, that attorney of his, Kaplan, logged face time with the DA this morning and the old guy was speaking the real. He's leaving everything he owns to the Veterans Administration for the rehabilitation of wounded veterans. Pretty admirable thing to do. I mean, considering he's a nut job and all."

We walked along in silence for a while, Very easing his bike along next to me, Lulu continuing to sniff and snort. Quite a few people were out enjoying the fresher, cooler air in the park that morning. They were moving a bit faster than they had been in previous days, and stood a bit straighter.

"Are you going to call Norma, Lieutenant? She's perfect for you. She's brainy. Works twenty hours a day. Never sleeps. You should call her."

"Already did. We're having dinner Saturday night. Dude, can you recommend a place that a classy, literary sort of woman would like? I want it to be someplace quiet where we can hear each other talk."

"The Blue Mill on Commerce Street. Order the calves' liver."

"I hate calves' liver."

"You used to. You won't anymore. Just make sure you get both the sautéed onions *and* the bacon. And plenty of mashed potatoes."

"Will do, thanks. And thanks large for your help on this case. Couldn't have broken it without you."

Someone let out a low cough at our feet.

"Either one of you," Very hastened to add.

"It *was* Lulu who found the Tiparillo in the gutter," I pointed out. "And kept us from getting lost in Stuyvesant Town. If it weren't for her we'd still be wandering around there looking for Oval No. 11. Possibly even sitting on a bench somewhere, sobbing. She also warned us that Richie Filosi was no good and that Kathleen ought to show him the door."

"Red or white?"

"Excuse me?"

"With the calves' liver. Red or white wine?"

"Red. I'd go with a Côtes du Rhône. Any other questions?"

"Yeah. Norma's boyfriend was just murdered. How patient should I . . . ?"

"Take it slow. Very."

He frowned at me. "Yeah, dude?"

"Take it very slow."

"Gotcha."

"In that case, I think my work here is done."

AS THE NEXT few days unfolded word trickled out that Guilford House would be publishing *Tulsa* by the great Addison James on schedule next summer. Also that the president of Guilford House had decided that the late Tommy O'Brien's name would go on the cover as coauthor and that his widow, Kathleen, would receive the one-third share of the royalties that Sylvia had promised him but reneged on. The Silver Fox, who's as cynical as they come, labeled it a public relations stunt intended to blunt any ill will that readers might be harboring toward Addison for murdering his wife. Ill will that might translate into diminished book sales. She also told me that Guilford House was searching for a new editor in chief to replace Sylvia, and that the top name being bandied about town was none other than Sylvia's former assistant, Norma Fives.

Busy as she was, Norma did find time to read "The Eighty-

Yard Run" by Irwin Shaw and leave me a brief phone message at Merilee's apartment: "Hi, it's Norma, and I'm a big fat idiot."

As for me, I wasn't sleeping too well despite all of the posh comforts of life on Central Park West. In fact, I was wide-awake when the phone rang at three A.M. and it was Merilee calling from Budapest. The connection was scratchy, but I could hear her plenty fine.

"*So* sorry to call you at this ungodly hour, darling, but I just saw the story about the Addison James mess in the *International Herald Tribune* and I needed to hear your voice. Are you okay? I'll catch the first plane home if you're not."

"I'm fine, Merilee. Haven't got a scratch on me."

"That's not what I mean, and you know it."

"I'm a bit shell-shocked, but I'll be okay. Although my apartment's going to feel haunted for a while."

"Then it's a good thing that you don't have to stay there."

"A mighty good thing. We've been extremely comfortable here."

Lulu snuggled up close to the phone, whimpering. Somehow she always knows when it's her mommy on the other end of the line.

"Is that sweetness whom I hear?"

"None other."

"I miss you both terribly and . . . I've been thinking about the night I left."

"So have I," I said, remembering the way she'd unsnapped her denim shirt and flung it across the hallway floor.

"I rather enjoyed it."

"So did I."

"I wouldn't mind a repeat performance."

"Nor would I."

"Perhaps we should have a serious talk when I get back."

"Feel free to delete the word *perhaps*."

"I'll let you get back to sleep now, darling."

"I wasn't asleep."

"And do take care of yourself. I feel as if I've found you again. I don't want to lose you."

"You won't."

"Promise?"

"Boil me in oil and fry me in lye."

"Good gravy, I used to love that expression! Haven't heard it since I was a little girl. Don't be surprised if I steal it and say it in the movie."

"I won't be."

"Good night, darling." She rang off.

Lulu returned to her own acre of bed and stretched back out, grumbling and grousing. I lay there with the dead receiver in my lap for a moment before I returned it to its cradle. Then I went back to doing what I'd been doing in lieu of sleeping—spinning my wheels. I thought about Tommy, the authentic shoe-leather beat reporter from Jackson Heights who'd gotten in over his head with the wrong crowd and would never live to see his dream of becoming the next Jimmy Breslin or Pete Hamill come true. I thought about Sylvia and wondered what sort of person she'd have become if she hadn't had such a cruel bastard for a father. I thought about her cruel bastard of a father, who'd married Phyllis Yvette Rittenaur despite knowing exactly who and what she was—and when it came time to make her pay for what she'd done, how he hadn't hesitated to dispense justice himself. I thought about Mel, a lonely South Shore schnook who'd killed two people because Yvette had plopped her bare foot in his lap at the bar of the American Hotel in Sag Harbor and sent him on an all-expenses-paid trip to cuckoo town. I replayed the events of the past couple of days and nights over and over again. Kept asking myself if there was anything—any one small thing—I could have done differently that would have changed the outcome. I couldn't think of a single thing. I did try awfully hard to convince myself that justice had been served in the end, but I couldn't talk myself into believing that. Not with Tommy's death weighing on me. No, this one was never going to sit right with me and I knew that. I'd just have to deal with it.

And so as the dawn's sky over Central Park began to turn purple, I got out of bed and dealt with it the only way I knew how to. Made the espresso. Fed Lulu her morning ration of 9Lives mackerel for cats and very weird basset hounds. Carried my cup of fresh hot espresso down the hall to the office and parked myself in front of my Olympia. Rolled a fresh sheet of paper into the machine. Cranked up the Ramones on my turntable. Took a deep breath, let it out slowly and went back to work on *The Sweet Season of Madness*.

I wrote. That's how I dealt with it.

The sun came up. Lulu wandered in, climbed into the Morris chair and dozed as I wrote for hours and hours. For a reader, a novel, if it's a good one, is an absorbing and enlightening experience. For me, it's my refuge when real life becomes unbearable. I keep it together by transporting myself to a world of my own creation. A world where things turn out the way they're supposed to. Because in the real world there are times, too damned many of them, when they truly don't—no matter how hard I try to make them.

And this was one of those times.

Insights,
Interviews
& More...

About the author

About the book

Read on

Meet David Handler

D. L. Drake

DAVID HANDLER has written eleven novels about the witty and dapper celebrity ghostwriter Stewart Hoag and his faithful, neurotic basset hound, Lulu, including the Edgar and American Mystery Award–winning *The Man Who Would Be F. Scott Fitzgerald*. His other series include the Berger and Mitry franchise and two novels featuring private eye Benji Golden. David was a member of the original writing staff that created the Emmy Award–winning sitcom *Kate and Allie* and has continued to write extensively for television and films on both coasts. He lives in a two-hundred-year-old carriage house in Old Lyme, Connecticut. ᴄᴧ

The Long Arm of the Law, Gen Next

When I first came up with the idea for Stewart Hoag way back in the mid-1980s, the crime-fiction world was in the midst of a major generational change. The Rex Stout–Agatha Christie era was over and out. And while terrifically talented writers such as Donald E. Westlake, Robert B. Parker and P. D. James were keeping the genre alive and well, hardly anyone who was writing crime in those days belonged to my age group—those of us who had come of age in the tumultuous sixties listening to rock 'n' roll and smoking pot as the world around us roiled with assassinations, riots, Vietnam and Watergate.

In fact, when I attended my first mystery convention—Bouchercon in 1989—I was shocked to discover that practically everyone there was at least twenty years older than I was. I still remember wandering around the banquet halls like a lost teenage kid, even though I was in my midthirties and was there because my initial Hoagy novel, *The Man Who Died Laughing*, had been nominated for an Anthony Award.

When I created Hoagy I was determined that, while he'd give a respectful tip of his fedora to crime ▶

3

The Long Arm of the Law, Gen Next
(continued)

fiction's past, it was vital for him to speak for *me* and for my generation. New era. New hero. I quickly discovered that this would also have to be true of the homicide detectives that my ghostwriter sleuth and his faithful, neurotic basset hound, Lulu, encountered along the way. I did not want Hoagy trading barbs with rumpled, cigar-chomping, old-school flatfoots. I wanted homicide detectives who were young and, well, different.

The first such cop whom Hoagy encounters is Emil Lamp in *The Man Who Died Laughing*. Emil Lamp, the LAPD's go-to celebrity homicide ace, is a freshly scrubbed, bright-eyed, eager little guy with neat blond hair and wholesome apple cheeks who doesn't cuss, lives with his mom and bears an eerie resemblance to Howdy Doody. He has appeared in three Hoagy novels, most recently *The Girl with Kaleidoscope Eyes*, which marked Hoagy and Lulu's return in 2017 after a twenty-year hiatus.

But the cop who has made the strongest impression in the series by far is the NYPD's celebrity homicide ace, Romaine Very, who has a BA in astrophysics from Columbia. Very is a short, muscular hipster who chews gum with his mouth open and is easily mistaken for a bike messenger because he dresses like one. He is also a hyperactive bundle of neuroses who ricochets back and forth between admiring Hoagy and being driven absolutely crazy by him. I love writing the two of them. Love their rapport. One of the main reasons I set the *The Man in the White Linen Suit* in New York City was because I wanted to write Very again. This marks his fourth outing in a Hoagy novel, and the fifth novel of mine that he's appeared in. After I ended the Hoagy series in 1997, I missed writing Very so much that in 2010 I figured out a way to work him into *The Shimmering Blond Sister*, the seventh novel in my Berger and Mitry series, which takes place in the historic Connecticut shoreline village of Dorset. Very's NYPD mentor, who has retired to Dorset, is murdered. Very jumps on his motorcycle and rides out there to give Resident Trooper Des Mitry a hand—whether she wants one or not.

I can't tell you how many readers through the years have written to urge me to give Romaine Very a series of his own. I considered the idea seriously but never had a feel for how to pull it off—so I figured what the hell and just went ahead and started writing Hoagy again. It's much easier this way. Also way more fun.

David Handler
Old Lyme, Connecticut ∾

More from David Handler

THE MAN WHO COULDN'T MISS

Hollywood ghostwriter Stewart "Hoagy" Hoag has chronicled the rise, fall and triumphant return of many a celebrity. At last he's enjoying his own, very welcome second act. After hitting a creative slump following the success of his debut novel, Hoagy has found inspiration again. Ensconced with his faithful but cowardly basset hound, Lulu, on a Connecticut farm belonging to his ex-wife, Oscar-winning actress Merilee Nash, he's busy working on a new novel. He's even holding out hope that he and Merilee might get together again. Life is simple and fulfilling—which of course means it's time for complications to set in. . . .

When the police call to ask if he knows the whereabouts of a man named R.J. Romero, Hoagy learns of a dark secret from his ex-wife's past. It's already a stressful time for Merilee, who's directing a gala benefit production of *Private Lives* to rescue the famed but dilapidated Sherbourne Playhouse, where the likes of Katharine Hepburn, Marlon Brando and Merilee herself made their professional stage debuts. Her reputation, as well as the playhouse's future, is at stake. The cast features three of Merilee's equally famous Oscar-winning classmates from the Yale School of Drama. But it turns out that there's more linking them to one another—and to their fellow Yale alum, R.J.—than their alma mater. When one of the cast is found murdered, it will take Hoagy's sleuthing skills and Lulu's infallible nose to sniff out the truth . . . before someone else faces the final curtain call.

"Hoagy is a thoroughly engaging amateur sleuth, as appealing to readers as he is enraging to the authorities, who can't abide his unconventional methods. This tenth installment in the series is pure pleasure."

—*Booklist* (starred review)

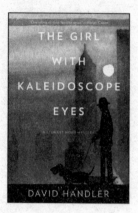

THE GIRL WITH KALEIDOSCOPE EYES

Once upon a time, Hoagy had it all: a hugely successful debut novel, a gorgeous celebrity wife, the glamorous world of New York City at his feet. These days, he scrapes by as a celebrity ghostwriter. A celebrity ghostwriter who finds himself investigating murders more often than he'd like.

And once upon a time, Richard Aintree was the most famous writer in America—high school students across the country read his one and only novel, a modern classic on par with *The Catcher in the Rye*. But after his wife's suicide, Richard went into mourning . . . and then into hiding. No one has seen him or heard from him in twenty years.

Until now. Richard Aintree—or someone pretending to be Richard Aintree—has at long last reached out to his two estranged daughters. Monette is a Martha Stewart–style lifestyle queen whose empire is crumbling; and once upon a time, Reggie, a gifted poet, was the love of Hoagy's life. Both sisters have received mysterious typewritten letters from their father.

Hoagy is already on the case, having been hired to ghostwrite a tell-all book about the troubled Aintree family. But no sooner does he set up shop in the pool house of Monette's Los

Angeles mansion than murder strikes.
With Lulu at his side—or more often
cowering in his shadow—it's up to
Hoagy to unravel the mystery, catch
the killer and pour himself that perfect
single-malt Scotch . . . before it's too late.

"*The Girl with Kaleidoscope Eyes* is
Handler at his best, drawing us close
to his hero and the hero's beloved pooch,
Lulu, while introducing us to some of
the scuzziest Hollywood characters this
side of James Ellroy."
—CTNews.com

Discover great authors,
exclusive offers, and more
at hc.com.